THE FAIRFAX INCIDENT

Terrence McCauley

THE FAIRFAX INCIDENT

Copyright © 2018 by Terrence McCauley
Cover and jacket design by 2Faced Design

ISBN 978-1-947993-05-1
ISBN 978-1-947993-33-4
Library of Congress Control Number: 2018933149

First trade paperback edition June 2018 by Polis Books, LLC
1201 Hudson Street, #211S
Hoboken, NJ 07030
www.PolisBooks.com

POLIS BOOKS

Also by Terrence McCauley

Chapter 1
NEW YORK CITY
1933

I stifled a yawn as I listened to the old lady repeat herself for the third time. Or maybe it was the fourth. I'd lost count by then.

"I don't care what you may have heard or read about my husband's death, Mr. Doherty, but I can assure you it was not a suicide. It was murder, plain and simple. And I wish to hire you to prove just that."

She wanted me to defy logic and prove the impossible. All I wanted was a cigarette, but when I'd first arrived at the Fairfax mansion, the maid warned me that Mrs. Eleanor Blythe Fairfax forbade smoking anywhere in the house.

So, I sat there and did my best to look interested while Mrs. Fairfax once more ran through the many reasons why her husband had not taken his own life, despite all the overwhelming evidence to the contrary. Homicide detectives, coroners, and plain, old- fashioned common sense be damned. Her Walter could not have possibly killed himself.

I didn't bother arguing with her because one simply did not argue with Mrs. Fairfax. One was expected to nod and give way to her every opinion. Some people might've gotten away with it, but certainly not a commoner like me.

Besides, I was already being paid to listen to everything she said and report it back to my real client, Mr. Harriman Van Dorn. He'd referred me to her because I was a private detective she could trust and knew how to handle such matters.

The truth was that he wanted to know more about such matters as soon as I did.

The setup was fine by me. Thanks to Mr. Van Dorn, I was making a damned fine living making my wealthy clients feel like I genuinely cared about their ivory-tower troubles. Empathy came easy when you made the kind of money I was pulling in, plus expenses.

Mrs. Fairfax was like a lot of my clients. Rich, well-fed, and happily isolated from the problems most people in Manhattan and the rest of the country were facing at the time. The Crash had happened a few years before, and now the Depression had everyone choking on the dust. But the Fairfax clan was one of those families that managed to remain wealthy more out of habit than anything else. They stayed in their tight-knit neighborhood that spanned "from Park to The Park," as they called it; a stretch of pricey Manhattan real estate that went from Park Avenue all the way over to where Fifth Avenue abuts Central Park.

The phrase had always grated on my nerves. I had been a private detective just long enough to know the richer they got, the worse their pet phrases tended to be.

Mrs. Fairfax was an elegant, moneyed product of good breeding who had sailed into middle age with all the dignity she could muster, and had held a steady course in the years since. Her black mourning veil was stylishly thin; her black dress had been carefully tailored to flatter her roundish frame. What little jewelry she wore was as minimal as it was expensive. She looked every bit the mourning matriarch of one of New York's finest families.

I found myself distracted by a quiet autumn rain rapping against the drawing room windows as she tried convincing me yet again, in that elegant tone of hers, that "my Walter" really hadn't killed himself.

An authoritative rumble came to her voice and caught my attention. "So, I say it now as I have said it before, and will continue to say for the rest of my days, Mr. Doherty—my husband simply wasn't capable of suicide. It had to be murder."

I knew convincing her wasn't going to be easy, so I started slow. "I was a police detective for a long time, Mrs. Fairfax, so I understand how difficult this kind of tragedy can be for those left behind. But, to be fair to my former colleagues, they officially ruled your husband's death an accidental shooting. That means—technically and legally—it wasn't a suicide."

Mrs. Fairfax waved that off with a black-gloved hand. "Everyone sees that semantic nonsense for exactly what it is: Chief Carmichael's flimsy attempt to help my family avoid scandal. And so we could collect on the insurance policies, of course. Insurance was my late husband's stock and trade. After all, he'd built a fortune from it."

I realized Mrs. Fairfax was a lot sharper than my usual well-heeled clientele. "Perhaps, but Chief Carmichael oversaw the investigation personally."

"For his own aggrandizement, I'm sure. I fully expect him to darken my door one day soon with hat in hand, seeking to be repaid for a favor I neither requested nor wanted. The chief has never extended a courtesy without being repaid for it tenfold."

I couldn't argue with her about that one. Few people knew Andrew Carmichael better than I did. He wouldn't cross the street for someone if there wasn't a buck in it for him somewhere. We had grown up together, ran the streets together, and joined the force around the same time. When the war started, I got drafted, while he got the chance to stay home and work on his career. After the war, he brought me with him as he rose through the ranks. I was his bag man for the same crooked Tammany Hall machine that got us our jobs. I also handled the occasional dirty job he needed doing. I was Chief Carmichael's Black Hand, and I'd had no complaints.

But when Roosevelt became governor on a reform ticket, Tammany's days were numbered. Carmichael hadn't gotten to be chief by being stupid, and was smart enough to jump sides to become a reformer, too. He needed a scapegoat for corruption in the department, so he stuck his best friend with a pair of goat horns and kicked him to the curb, just to prove how honest he was.

Unfortunately, that best friend was me.

And as much as I enjoyed hearing the old lady run down Carmichael, I tried to keep her focused. "I can't speak to the chief's motives, Mrs. Fairfax, but whatever he did seems to have worked. I've read every article published about your husband's death, and I've never seen suicide mentioned. It hasn't even been hinted at in the gossip columns as a blind item."

"They wouldn't dare," she said. "Neither would any of the ladies who have come here to pay their respects. They have been nothing but gracious and polite and proper, making a grand show of tripping all over themselves to line up and pat my hand; cooing and fussing about how unfortunate it was for me to lose Walter to such a terrible accident. 'Such a shame,'" she mimicked in a high-pitched voice. "'Such an awful, awful shame. Poor, dear Eleanor.'"

Her eyes narrowed as a subtle hardness crept into her voice. "But I know their game all too well, Mr. Doherty. All the time they're acting as though they're comforting me, they're really just studying me like I was something under glass; hoping to see a glimmer of the unspoken truth in my eyes. They're all so wholesome and kind while they're here visiting me, but as soon as they walk out that door and go to their lunches and cocktail parties, their fangs come out. They indulge in their acrimonious gossip, spreading venomous lies about Walter committing suicide. Speculating as to what could have possibly driven such a quiet, unassuming man to do such a thing. The cause inevitably boils down to one reason. Me." She folded her hands on her lap and looked away. "The damnable curs."

I didn't know how much of this was paranoia or anger or grief, but she wasn't rambling. I let her keep talking, and this time I didn't have to fake looking interested. I'd seen my share of families in denial when I was on the force.

Mrs. Fairfax wasn't in denial. She believed.

I watched the lines around her eyes get a little deeper. "I've never been one to abide scandal or pity, and I'm certainly not going to start at this age. Not for my sake, nor for the sake of my children and grandchildren. For more than thirty years I have protected the Fairfax name, and I refuse to allow it to be degraded by unfounded accusations."

Her sharp chin rose a little higher and pointed right at me. "That's why I want to hire you, Mr. Doherty. To put an end to all this speculation once and for all. I want you to prove my husband did not take his own life."

I didn't answer her right away. Mr. Van Dorn had already told me that I'd be taking the case, but I didn't want to lie to her, either. That could've sent her into a rage, and angry widows were bad for business. Mr. Van Dorn might be bankrolling me and feeding me clients, but it was still my name on the business card. That didn't always mean something to me, but it did now.

I said, "I did a lot of digging before I came here today, Mrs. Fairfax. Not just newspaper articles, but I've seen the evidence for myself. I've seen the crime scene photos, too, and I don't know if I can prove what you're asking me to prove."

"I hope it's not a question of money." She made a sweeping

gesture to the ornate room where we were sitting. "As you can see, that won't be a problem."

The Park Avenue crowd never failed to disappoint me. They always thought throwing enough money at a problem could do the trick, even when their wealth was often the cause of their problems. "It's not a question of money, but of facts. One of the detectives who worked the crime scene is an old partner of mine. He let me read his initial report, the one he wrote before Chief Carmichael filed his own version. I also talked to the coroner who was at the scene. Both agree that your husband walked into his office that morning, took his gun from his desk, and shot himself. There's absolutely no reason in the world for them to lie or for you to believe otherwise."

Her sharp chin rose even higher. "I believe otherwise, Mr. Doherty, because, as I have already told you, Walter was incapable of suicide. Not that he wasn't a coward, mind you, for Walter Fairfax was most certainly a cowardly man. He simply wasn't considerate enough to kill himself. For had he been a considerate man, he would have done us the favor of ending his own life long ago, freeing the children and me from decades of mediocrity and mendacity."

I admit I didn't know what mendacity meant, but judging by the tone in her voice it didn't sound good. But judging by the mansion I was sitting in and the framed paintings on the walls, mendacity seemed to pay pretty well.

But she'd given me a chance to dig a little deeper below the surface. "I take it that your marriage to Mr. Fairfax wasn't exactly a happy one?"

"Who's happy?" Mrs. Fairfax sniffed. "I surrendered any illusions of happiness or love in our marriage long ago. As far as Walter was concerned, I had served my purpose once I had given him an heir to his family's insurance business. He insisted that we name our son Walter J. Fairfax, III, as if the first two of the name had been worthy of commemoration, which I assure you they were not. Walter's father was an angry, miserable little man who crafted my Walter in his own image."

The widow's narrow shoulders sagged a little as she looked out at the rain streaking down the stained-glass windows of her study. "I had once dreamed of a large family, you know. Four children at the very least. My first child was a daughter, Evelyn. I had hoped that a girl might change Walter, warm him somehow, but I was wrong. Mercifully, my next child was Trip, so for all intents and purposes our marriage died the day my husband got his heir. His legacy secure, my husband was able to dedicate himself to his true love: that damnable company of his. The Fairfax Liability Company. That was some thirty years ago."

Then, just as quickly as her sadness had appeared, Mrs. Fairfax shook it off. The moment of weakness had passed. The armor of society and breeding was back on and she pointed that long chin at me again, offering a grim smile.

"Forgive me for going on like a silly school girl, Mr. Doherty. Rich women have no right to complain. I chose my life. My place in the Fairfax clan had been clearly explained to me by Walter's mother the morning we married. 'Raise the children, run the household, and make sure Walter has everything he needs.' Walter's purpose in life was to make The Fairfax Liability Company a success. The friends we had. The dinners we attended. Even the rare holidays we took. All of it served the solitary purpose of building upon the insurance empire his father had left him. A company I now own. Not my son, Trip. Not any of Walter's brothers. Me. I insisted upon that before we got married. I never wanted to be one of these widows forced to rely on the kindness of her in-laws for subsistence in the event of her husband's demise. His family wanted to make use of my family's name and the benefits it could offer their business, so they eagerly accepted."

Mrs. Fairfax managed a small laugh. "Business was the only thing Walter was ever good at. He got that from his father, too. The only thing that gave the Fairfax men any pleasure, any real sense of accomplishment, was that damned company. God knows they didn't derive much pleasure from their family, except as a mechanism to create more heirs to run their company."

She went on. "I'm telling you all of this, Mr. Doherty, because the Fairfax men are insurance men through and through. Even my son shows all the promise of being every bit as dull as the two Walters who preceded him, despite my best efforts to make him a better man." She looked at me. "Do you know much about insurance, Mr. Doherty?"

"Only that it's expensive."

"More expensive than you know. The lives and fortunes of insurance men are based on calculations and charts and payment schedules that were created on the off chance that something terrible might happen to a policy holder one day. Do you know that they even have charts that can determine how long a policy holder will live based on certain factors? What's even more troubling is how accurate the charts are." That grim smile again. "And that is why, Mr. Doherty, I know my husband did not take his own life."

I thought I'd missed something in her diatribe, but knew I hadn't. "I fail to see the connection, ma'am."

"Because I just told you Walter was an insurance man through and through. Insurance men are not impulsive, emotional souls. They plan everything in advance and leave very little to chance. Walter was no different. In fact, he was the most deliberate human being I have ever known. He would never just kill himself on the spur of the moment. Not without leaving instructions as to how his estate should be handled. Or his business. My God, he would have at least left a suicide note, which, as you must know, he did not."

If I hadn't known so much about her husband's death, I might've given her the benefit of the doubt. But I'd seen too much of the evidence to know she was grasping for something that just wasn't there.

I said, "Sometimes people who take their own lives leave notes behind, but sometimes they don't. I told you that I've read the police report. It contains statements from ten people who work for your husband, who say he was alone in his office with the door closed when he shot himself."

"It could've been staged to look like a suicide," she offered. "What about the windows? Someone could've been hiding in his office, shot him, and then hid in his private bathroom.

Or they could have escaped out the window. Or maybe they shot him from a rooftop across the street through an open window."

"His office is on the sixtieth floor of the Empire State Building. There's no rooftop close enough for anyone to have taken a shot at him. There are no ledges and no way out of his office other than the door, which was closed when it happened. And the only fingerprints they found on the gun belonged to your husband."

"But—"

I didn't let her finish. "I was a cop far too long to believe in absolutes, Mrs. Fairfax, but if there was ever such a thing as an open and shut case, I'm afraid this is as close to it as it gets."

"Yes." The bitterness crept back into her voice. "Chief Carmichael made that much clear when he told me how he would change the facts in the case. But it still sounds like a lot of double-talk and circumstantial evidence to me. I don't doubt that you and your friends on the force know all about crime scenes and death, but I knew Walter Fairfax. He had no reason to take his own life."

Mr. Van Dorn had already warned me that convincing her of the truth wouldn't be easy, but I kept trying. "Maybe he'd gotten some bad news about the business. You said the company meant everything to him. These are difficult times, Mrs. Fairfax. Companies fail every day."

"Impossible. Walter may not have been much of a man or a husband or father, but he was an excellent businessman. He worked day and night to ride out the Crash in 1929. His companies have not only weathered the storm, but thrived in its wake. Walter hated surprises. He could not adjust to the unknown, so he worked harder than anyone else to keep surprises to a minimum. Besides, an examination of his holdings proved his companies were doing surprisingly well considering the current economic climate."

I had another idea, but had to present it carefully. These society gals were awfully touchy about their health. "Perhaps he had a medical problem he hadn't told you about."

"Nonsense," she said. "My brother was his personal physician, and he says Walter was in perfect health. Besides, Walter was incapable of keeping secrets, least of all from me. I was his confidante in everything. Business, financial, and personal."

I caught that last part. "Forgive me, Mrs. Fairfax, but you've just spent the last half hour telling me you two weren't close. Now you're saying he always confided in you. Which is it?"

She squared her narrow shoulders and aimed all that breeding right at me. "There are degrees of closeness, Mr. Doherty, just as there are degrees of distance. Walter was not the kind of man who could maintain friendships. Most men found him dull and annoying, and chose to avoid his company whenever possible. However, as I'm sure you are aware, wealthy men hold a certain appeal to a certain kind of woman. Even men like Walter. I knew of quite a few such women over the years, as a matter of fact."

"That's rare," I said before I'd really thought it through. "Most women would have left him for that."

I didn't think she could sit any straighter in her chair, but she pulled it off. "Most women aren't married to Walter Fairfax, Junior, Mr. Doherty. I was his wife, and I'd be damned before I surrendered my marriage and my name to some harlot with designs on his fortune and the legacy of my children. Besides, Walter's indiscretions were always mercifully brief. It was never about love, because Walter simply wasn't capable of feeling love. Or receiving it. Both of us learned to find our comforts elsewhere long ago."

My respect for the old gal went up a few notches. Most people didn't like to look at things the way they were, even when everyone else could see them plain as day. Having money helped keep ugly things like the truth hidden. Mrs. Fairfax had perfect vision.

Against my better judgement, she was beginning to win me over to her side. "You're really convinced that Walter didn't kill himself, aren't you? Even in spite of everything I've just told you."

"Given the hasty manner in which he did it and the lack of a suicide note? Yes. I would not be interested in hiring you otherwise. Don't let my wealth fool you, Mr. Doherty. I am not in the practice of wasting my money on foolish notions."

If I had learned anything in the past year as a private detective, it was that rich people didn't stay rich by pissing away their money. And they didn't stay rich for long if they did.

"Then you might as well tell me where you'd like me to begin, Mrs. Fairfax."

She took a long, cream-colored envelope from behind the pillow at her side and placed it on the table between us.

I knew she expected me to take it, but I left it where it was. I wanted to hear what she had to say first.

"Inside that envelope," she told me, "you will find a list of Walter's principle associates. I would suggest you contact them in the order in which I have listed them, but I will leave that up to your professional judgment. I have taken the liberty of contacting each of them and asking them to cooperate fully in your investigation. If any of them prove uncooperative, please let me know."

Then, almost as an afterthought, she added, "I have also enclosed a personal check that should cover your retainer fee. Mr. Van Dorn advised me as to the proper amount."

But I already knew that he had.

Mrs. Fairfax stood, effectively ending our meeting. "The Van Dorns spoke very highly of you, Mr. Doherty. They are grateful to you for bringing their son home alive and catching the men who killed their daughter. They assured me that you are both thorough and discreet, which is high praise coming from them. I hope I can rely on your abilities now in uncovering the true circumstances behind my husband's death."

I shook her gloved hand, then slipped her envelope into the inside pocket of my suit jacket. "I promise I'll do everything I can, Mrs. Fairfax. I'll be in touch in a day or so to let you know what I've learned."

The butler was at my side before I knew it and guided me out to the vestibule. He handed me my hat and umbrella before quietly closing the door behind me. The rain had turned into a light mist by then, so I didn't bother with the umbrella.

Chapter 2

I pulled out my cigarette case and lit up a smoke as soon as I hit the Fifth Avenue pavement. I drew the smoke deep into my lungs and held it for a long while before letting it out again. A quick check of my pocket watch told me it was only eleven in the morning, almost an hour before my next appointment.

Right after Mr. Van Dorn told me I'd be working the Fairfax case, I asked a contact of mine at the New York Public Library to do some digging into Walter Fairfax's past. She'd already pulled all the articles on the death for me, but I knew all about Walter Fairfax the victim. I wanted to know about Walter Fairfax the man.

She told me she should have all the information I needed by the time my appointment was over, so I began the long, slow walk down Fifth Avenue toward the library. I could have taken a cab, but I wanted to use the time to clear my head.

It was a mild morning in early March, and the air smelled of the recent rain. The vague smell from the cook fires wafting out from the Hooverville in Central Park drifted across the avenue, giving a certain sweetness to the air. It wasn't entirely an unpleasant smell, so long as I didn't think of the poor, ragged bastards who were cooking around it. Or what they were cooking.

But I was in no position to pity anyone because I knew I had just taken on a case that would be nothing but trouble.

I never would've taken it if Mr. Van Dorn hadn't already ordered me to do so. Maybe "order" was too strong a word. He was always too polite to flat-out order me to do anything. He preferred to politely ask me to look into various problems that friends of his were having. And Mrs. Fairfax happened to be a very close friend of the Van Dorn family.

The previous year, I had defied Chief Carmichael's orders by working on the murder of Mr. Van Dorn's daughter, Jessica, and the kidnapping of his son, Jack. Since the chief had put me out to pasture as part of his new, clean image with Governor Roosevelt's reformers, I had originally wanted the case so I could get on Mr. Van Dorn's good side. I hoped I'd uncover something unsavory about the family that would lead to a nice chunk of hush money for yours truly.

But the case quickly became more than just a payday for me. I realized the Van Dorn family wasn't just another of those wealthy New York clans who cared more about their name than their kids. Mr. and Mrs. Van Dorn both genuinely loved their children and each other. The case stirred something in me that I thought had died with my own marriage and self-respect years before.

I killed the men who'd taken Jack and killed Jessica. The newspapers had called it the "Grand Central Massacre."

Sure, I'd brought Jack home alive, but three railroad detectives had gotten killed by the kidnappers I'd been chasing. Chief Carmichael blamed my recklessness for their deaths. The fact that I'd brought Jack home alive was forgotten by everyone except the Van Dorn family.

Carmichael cited my long ties to Tammany Hall and my "careless disregard for public safety" as reasons for kicking me off the force. He conveniently forgot to mention he was every bit as crooked as I had been. I guess the truth gets blurry when justice is involved.

But Mr. Van Dorn pulled some strings, saving my pension as thanks for saving his son's life. His gratitude went further than I had expected.

He offered me a job.

The deal: Mr. Van Dorn set me up in my own private detective practice. He paid for everything. Bills, a place to live, and a guaranteed client base among his wealthy friends. I even got to keep anything my clients paid me.

The catch: Mr. Van Dorn saw everything about every case before the client did. Photos. Records. Everything.

I figured Mr. Van Dorn had his reasons for building files on his friends, but his reasons were none of my business. I'd been a Tammany hack my whole life, so I knew how valuable leverage could be.

Most of the cases he sent my way were easy. Tracking down wayward kids on a bender with their parents' money. Divorce snoops. A few extortion cases where I convinced the blackmailer to walk away. Sometimes, the blackmailer wasn't able to walk after our discussions.

It was easy work and I had no complaints. I saw more money in one month than I had in my previous three years on the force, payola included.

This Fairfax case was the first curveball he'd thrown me, because I knew there was no question that Walter Fairfax had taken his own life. The only question was why Mr. Van Dorn wanted me to take it.

The initial report my ex-partner Floyd Loomis had shown me was solid: Fairfax got into the office at nine in the morning, took a phone call at nine fifteen, closed the door, stuck a gun in his mouth, and, at nine thirty, pulled the trigger.

Alone. No one in his private bathroom. No one hiding under his desk.

It was suicide. Plain and simple.

The papers all ran it as a tragic accident, just a brief mention in the first paragraph of a long obituary featuring Walter's many achievements and charity work. But just because it was in print didn't mean anybody actually believed it. After all, insurance executives usually didn't clean guns in their office first thing in the morning.

Everyone knew it was suicide. Why couldn't Mrs. Fairfax see that? Why couldn't a smart woman like her realize that?

That's when it hit me; I stopped walking, dead in my tracks.

Mrs. Fairfax wasn't asking the right question.

She knew he had killed himself. What she really wanted to know was why.

That was why she had given me a list of people she wanted me to interview, and in a certain order, too. A list of people who knew Walter best, people who might be able to tell me the answer to the one question that lingered.

Why?

The police hadn't bothered to investigate Fairfax's motive. Why would they? It had been officially ruled an accident, courtesy of Chief Andrew J. Carmichael's office. Case closed. My old partner Loomis saw no reason to put up a fight. He'd never been a fighter anyway. If the brass wanted to say it was an accident, then it was an accident.

Mrs. Fairfax's list started to burn a hole in my pocket, and I picked up the pace toward the library. The sooner I read through Walter's background, the better prepared I'd be to talk to the people on the list.

The late morning strollers walked past me as I dug out the envelope and opened it. Her check for the retainer was the first thing I saw.

I let out a low whistle as I saw the amount she'd written on the check. The number was larger than what I'd made in a year on the force, even when I was on the take. Christ, if I'd known there was this much money in being honest, I would've gone straight a long time ago.

A strong breeze kicked up, so I tucked the check back into my pocket for safe keeping. I opened the list of names and saw Mrs. Fairfax's handwriting was every bit as neat and legible as I'd expected it to be. The four names were:

Dr. Matthew Blythe: Personal Physician - New York Athletic Club

Mr. Jeffrey Hess, Esquire: Fairfax Liability Corporation

Mrs. Beatrice Swenson: Walter's personal secretary

Mr. Eric Frank: Captain of our yacht

Mrs. Fairfax had told me to interview each person in the order they appeared on her list. Her brother, Dr. Matthew Blythe, was first, so I'd start with him. Mr. Van Dorn had already told me that Blythe wasn't just Walter's brother-in-law, but his physician and friend. If anyone knew why Walter had taken his own life, the good doctor was a good place to start. Mrs. Fairfax's list said he was at New York Athletic Club. I'd see if I could reach him there after I spoke to my contact at the library.

I put the list and the check back into the same envelope and slid the whole thing into the inside pocket of my suit. I was feeling a bit better about where things were headed now that I'd figured out what Mrs. Fairfax was really after, even if she didn't know it herself. Maybe things weren't looking so bad after all.

The flow of traffic onto Fifth Avenue made me stop at the next corner, on 67th Street. I caught a glimpse of myself in the window of a passing car and was reminded what a difference a year could make.

I was almost tall enough not to be considered short. I was still pretty thin despite being well past forty. They'd first cropped my hair close when I'd gone into the Marines back in the war, and I'd kept it that way ever since. It had been darker back then, of course. It was salt and pepper now.

My double-breasted suit was from Brooks Brothers, and I had eight more just like it in my closet in the bedroom of the brownstone apartment Mr. Van Dorn had given to me. No seedy office with a bottle of booze in the bottom drawer for Charlie Doherty. I had money to spare and a damned cozy setup in the bargain. Yes sir, what a difference a year—and the Van Dorns' influence—could make.

Traffic turning onto Fifth eased up enough for me to cross the street and I began walking south again, looking forward to a nice, quiet stroll on my way to meet with my contact at the library.

But there's really no such thing as a nice, quiet walk in Manhattan. Trucks were always backfiring. The sound of pneumatic hammers pounding away at concrete or asphalt was never too far away. Car horns honked and people cursed. Throw in the flutter of pigeon wings for good measure and that was as tranquil as New York City got.

It's a whole lot of different sounds all mixed together in one big urban symphony, but it's usually the same sounds heard over and over.

That's why when you heard something new, you knew it.

And I'd just heard it.

A combination of sounds that caused my instincts to kick in and send me diving for the pavement.

The squeal of brakes followed by a clean, metallic clack.

The roar of a Thompson cut through the air above me just as I hit the sidewalk. Dozens of rounds slammed into the stonework of the apartment building on my left. I lay as flat as I could—maybe even flatter—as the bullets scored the façade and shattered windows. I heard women scream and dogs bark as the Tommy gun cut loose.

When the firing stopped, I heard something else. Someone running past me. Who the hell ran in the middle of gunfire, especially in Manhattan? People stayed low, they didn't get up and run. Unless they knew for certain the shooting was over.

I reached for a gun I forgot I didn't carry anymore. My Fifth Avenue clientele didn't carry guns, so why should I?

I looked up in time to see someone had run past me. A skinny little bastard in a gray overcoat. Fast, too. He hopped into a Ford that had pulled up just down the street before the car sped off down Fifth. I ran into the street to get a better look at the car, but no luck. The Ford took the next right turn into Central Park and was gone from view.

A doorman from the apartment building was just getting to his feet as I picked my hat off the sidewalk. "You all right, mister?"

I smacked at some of the scuff marks on my suit, but other than that I was fine. At least physically. No one had shot at me in a long time, and the idea took some getting used to. "Don't worry about me. What did you see?"

"Not a damned thing, mister," the doorman said. "I ducked back inside when the shooting started, mister. Had all my hero notions pounded out of me in France during the war."

I put the crease back in my hat and swiped dirt from the brim. "Yeah, me, too. What about that guy who ran past me and into the Ford? You get a look at him?"

"Not really. Gray coat, best as I could make out. Little fella. Kinda like you."

The last thing I needed was a fat doorman making wisecracks. "Thanks a lot, Slim. More alert citizens like you, we'd have every crook behind bars in a week."

I placed the hat back on my head and started walking south again. I was just about halfway down the block when the doorman called after me: "Say, you think those guys were shooting at you?"

"No," I yelled back over my shoulder.

I lied.

Chapter 3

When I got to the library, I didn't see any reason to tell Mary Pat about my run-in with the Thompson uptown. Besides, she was too taken with the pastrami sandwich I'd just brought her to care.

"Doesn't Lindy's make the best sandwiches in the whole wide world?"

The kid's sincerity almost made me forget about just getting shot at. Almost. "It's the mustard. And the bread."

But I didn't think she heard me. She was lost again in the splendor of her meal.

Mary Pat Dennehy was a sweet, lonely kid who'd started sending me fan letters during the Grand Central Massacre business. While I was getting torn apart in the papers, Mary Pat wrote me long letters, telling me how much of a hero I was for bringing the Van Dorn boy home alive. She wrote that she prayed for me every night before she went to sleep and once more when she woke up the next morning before school.

It might not sound like much now, but back when it felt like the whole world was against me, her letters helped keep me going. After a while, I responded to one of them, and we kind of became pen-pals.

Mary Pat had graduated back in June and got a job as a

clerk in the central library on 42nd Street. Now, for the price of a pastrami on rye from Lindy's and a little conversation, she'd research anything I needed. I would've felt like a heel using her like that if I didn't think she was a sweet kid.

She was a shy, heavy girl with bad skin and thick glasses. She'd gotten teased a lot in school, and even more so by her old man at home. But even though she was only nineteen years old, I could see her entire life was already planned. She'd spend her youth looking after the cantankerous old bastard who'd driven away her mother because he had no one else to wash his clothes and make him dinner. She'd continue to live at home, enduring his teasing about her weight and the quality of her cooking. She'd grin and bear it, telling herself she was saving up for the day when she could finally move out on her own. But she'd never leave him. Nineteen would become twenty-nine, and thirty-nine would follow soon after. The old bastard would have the decency to die one day, but not before he took the best part of her life from her. And if he died too soon, he'd break her heart forever.

Girls like Mary Pat were a dime a dozen in this town. No one could save them all. Hell, I couldn't even save Mary Pat. But if a pastrami sandwich from Lindy's and a little bit of conversation made her happy, it was the least I could do.

"Their pastrami sandwiches are the best," she went on, "but their roast beef sandwiches are a close second," she said. "Everything's good at Lindy's."

I actually knew a couple of delis in the area that were better than Lindy's, but I didn't tell her that. She loved Lindy's more for its history than its food. She was like millions of other girls who'd grown up reading about how Lindy's had been one of the places where dashing criminal types like Archie Doyle and Howard Rothmann ate, back when the two hoods ran New York City like their own private kingdom. To her, Lindy's was parties with Norma Shearer and Babe Ruth and Gloria Swanson.

She had grown up believing that hoods like Doyle and Rothmann lived charmed, glamorous lives of speakeasies and nightclubs, with movie stars and lots of friends and fun. She longed for a New York she was too young to know. She mourned the death of a New York that had never really existed. Because all the booze and fancy parties and actors and actresses had never just been about having fun.

Babe Ruth and Gloria Swanson and Rudolph Valentino were no different than Howard Rothmann and Archie Doyle. It was about that same, miserable common denominator of life: money. How to get it, how to spend it, and how to hold on to it once you had it.

But I didn't have the heart to tell Mary Pat any of that. It might have spoiled her lunch. I just smiled and watched her enjoy her pastrami on rye. Extra mustard.

"I almost forgot." She put down her sandwich and pushed a stack of papers a couple of inches thick at me. "Here's the information you wanted about Mr. Fairfax."

I cringed when I reached for the bundle. My right arm was starting to ache from when I hit the sidewalk. Guess private life was making me soft. I played it off by saying, "That's an awful lot of stuff for an old guy like me to read."

"You're not old," she giggled, "just lazy. That's why I wrote some notes about everything. It's on a sheet of paper at the top."

Like I said, Mary Pat was a sweet kid. While she finished her sandwich, I read her notes. She had itemized everything she had found on the recently-departed Walter Fairfax, Junior. Where he'd been born. The universities he'd studied at in Europe. His marriage and child announcements. Articles on Fairfax Liability, his charitable donations, and so on.

I folded her notes and tucked them into my inside pocket, next to Mrs. Fairfax's list. "Nice work. How about giving me a quick rundown on what you found out about him?"

"Boy, you're even lazier than I thought." She wiped her hands on the napkin as she started in. "Walter was born in 1872, right here in New York City. His father was Walter Fairfax, too, and he ran the family's insurance business, but I guess you already knew that. But here's something I'll bet you didn't know. I found the obituary for Walter's mother from when she died a few years back. She killed herself soon after Walter got married."

She was right. I hadn't known that. Interesting. "No kidding? How'd she do it?"

"Arsenic poisoning. She got hold of a bottle of it somehow and drank the whole thing right down. They think she stole it from the gardener's stash at the family greenhouse. She probably thought she'd just die right away, but arsenic doesn't work that way. It's not as romantic as the old plays and paintings make it look, you know. It takes a couple of days to die. Pretty painful, too."

I knew suicide often ran in families. I supposed Mrs. Fairfax knew that, too. That's probably why she hadn't told me about Walter's mother.

Mary Pat went on. "It's a shame, too. She was born in Prussia and belonged to the Tessmer family, which was some kind of Prussian nobility. That means she was descended from Prussian royalty, so Mr. Fairfax actually had some royal blood. Isn't that exciting?"

Titles had never impressed me. Especially Prussian titles. I'd seen my share of Prussian aristocrats in France during the war. Most of them lying dead in the mud along with the commoners. Titles and bloodlines didn't make you bulletproof. "Enough about his mother for now. What other stuff did you find out about Fairfax personally?"

"From what I found in the society pages," she went on, "he spent a lot of time in Germany with his mother's family when he was younger. All the way through college and after." I watched Mary Pat's eyes go soft and dreamy. "Doesn't that sound romantic, Charlie? Summering in Europe. Visiting beautiful ancient castles. Learning things in universities and colleges all over the world. You ever been to Europe, Charlie?"

"Uncle Sam sent me on a trip to France back in '17. All expenses paid."

She looked like she was about to apologize for not remembering the war, but I hated when she pouted so I said, "When did Fairfax come back home?"

"When he was twenty-five or so, as near as I can guess from newspaper accounts. He immediately went to work at the family's insurance company. Took full control of the company when he was forty and was there until, well, he died."

"What about Fairfax himself? He give to any charities?"

"All the usual museums and hospitals and so on. He also gave a lot of money to some German-American organizations over the past couple of years." She shrugged. "Maybe he was lonesome for his childhood or something."

That caught my interest. "What kind of German organizations?"

She handed me another sheet of paper. "The kind I know I'd never be able to pronounce, so I wrote them out for you."

I looked through Mary Pat's list for myself. Her neat handwriting read:

The Teutonia Association

Friends of New Germany

Der Stahlem

Gauleitung-USA (NSDAP)

The last two groups on the list worried me.

I'd heard of Der Stahlem before. It was an old German veteran's group whose name literally meant The Steel Helmets.

But seeing the last group on Mary Pat's list didn't make any sense to me. "NSDAP? That's the German Worker's Party, isn't it?"

"It's the American branch of the same group that made all that noise that got that Hitler guy elected in Germany a few months back." She shuddered. "Have you seen his pictures in the papers? He gives me the creeps. He's got such dead eyes. How could anyone vote for someone who looked like that?"

But I had other questions on my mind than German politics. "But the NSDAP are socialists. Why the hell would a wealthy guy like Fairfax be supporting a socialist group in his own country? Even if they are German?"

"Beats me." Mary Pat shrugged. "All I know is that the papers are filled with articles on him going to parties thrown by those kinds of German groups for the past two years. He hosted some events for them, attended ribbon-cuttings for their offices, went to their galas, stuff like that. I can pull out all the articles for you if you want, but it's kind of all the same stuff so I made the list instead."

I didn't care about stories or the parties he attended. I cared about the causes. A big-time capitalist like Fairfax giving socialists money wasn't unheard of, but it made me curious. "What about the Fairfax Liability Corporation? How's it doing?"

"It's a privately-held company, so their financial statements aren't public. But I wouldn't know what I was looking at even if I saw them. From what I've read in the business articles, it seems to be doing pretty well."

Damn. I had been hoping there might've been a financial reason why Fairfax had blown his brains out. Maybe trouble Mr. Fairfax had been able to keep from his wife. That would've wrapped this up quick. "What about bad habits? Scandals? Things like that?"

"Some pictures had him with a cigar," Mary Pat said, "but that's as scandalous as it got. Nothing in the gossip papers or anything like that, at least for the past year or so. Except for liking German socialists, Mr. Fairfax seemed pretty dull." She frowned a little. "Hope I didn't waste your time, Charlie."

I gave her a kiss on the cheek as I got up to go. "You never have and you never will. Thanks for digging this stuff up for me, especially the part about the Germans." I patted the thick pile of papers she'd bundled together. "Keep this in a safe place for me. And don't forget to keep all of this just between you and me, okay?"

She looked slightly worried. "Sure, but who cares about a boring old guy like Fairfax anyway?"

"Hopefully no one, but let's play it safe." I looked down at the sandwich. "Don't let the rest of the pastrami go to waste."

She giggled as I threw her a wink before closing the door behind me.

Chapter 4

I felt better now that I had knew more about Walter Fairfax as a man, not just the victim in a police file. I hoped Mary Pat's research had given me enough pieces to figure out why Fairfax had killed himself. Making those pieces fit together would be the hard part. I decided the best way to start was by working the list Mrs. Fairfax had given me.

I used one of the pay phones in the lobby near the main entrance to the library and called the first name on the list.

Dr. Matthew Blythe – New York Athletic Club.

I called the NYAC and asked to speak to him. About a minute later, a man came on the line. "May I inquire as to who wishes to speak to Dr. Blythe and why?"

The formality almost made me laugh. The AC was a jumped-up gymnasium with better furniture, but I didn't let the high-hat routine bother me. "This is Charles Doherty," I said, using my full name for the first time since grade school. "I have been told he's expecting my call."

"Hold the line, please."

I heard him put the phone down. I checked the library lobby while I waited for him to come back on the line. I was still more than a little shaky after my run-in with the Thompson. I wanted to see if anyone in particular was watching me, especially a blond kid in a gray overcoat.

Fortunately, I didn't see anyone who fit the bill.

I heard someone pick up the other end of the line again. "Dr. Blythe would prefer to see you rather than speak on the telephone. He is most anxious to see you. Would you be available to come here to meet him this afternoon?"

I checked my pocket watch. It was one thirty. "I'm available now if that's okay with him. Say half an hour?"

"The doctor will be expecting you at two o'clock. Please stop by the front desk, where you'll be escorted up to the lounge."

As I put the earpiece back in the cradle, I couldn't believe my luck. Matthew Blythe was Fairfax's doctor, friend, and brother-in-law. He might be able to tell me something Mrs. Fairfax didn't know. Hell, depending on what Blythe told me I might even have this whole thing wrapped up by dinner time.

I'd almost forgotten that I was never that lucky, but I was reminded soon enough.

***

Now that I had an appointment at the New York Athletic Club, I decided to buy a couple of good cigars for the occasion. I'd always been more of a cigarette man, but I appreciated a good cigar now and then. After all, it wasn't every day a guy like me got to go to such a swanky place.

I walked down the steps of the library, keeping an eye out for the bastards who'd taken a shot at me uptown. I didn't know what the shooters looked like, but the punk who had run past me was my size in a cheap gray overcoat. In a city full of skinny guys in cheap gray overcoats it wasn't much to go on, but it was something.

I watched for slow-moving cars with open windows as I walked to 38th and Broadway to Nat Sherman's Cigar Store.

The counterman who greeted me was a bald, fat little man who looked like he'd been born with a cigar in the corner of his mouth. "What can I get for you, mister?"

"How about a cigar? On second thought, make that two cigars."

"Big spender." Though the guy didn't look impressed. "What kind?"

I thought about it for a second. I was actually proud of myself when I said, "Something mild, but good."

The look he gave me sent my pride down the tubes. "We only sell good cigars, mister." His cigar shifted from one side of his mouth to the other. "I'll go back and pick out a couple of winners for you."

The counterman went about his business and I caught my reflection in the large mirror behind the counter. I noticed a small spot of dirt I'd missed on the top corner of my hat.

I took off my hat and tried swiping off the dirt, but my right hand was shaking. Badly.

I balled up my fist and told myself it was just because of the ache in my arm. A mild sprain, nothing more. It wasn't nerves. It couldn't be. I had been shot at dozens of times when I was on the force, and a hell of a lot more than that over in France. People had been trying to kill me for most of my life. Nothing rattled me anymore.

But as good as I was at lying to other people, I had never

been good at lying to myself.

The shaking was from nerves. I just wasn't used to getting shot at anymore. Things were different a year ago, back when I was in the Life. Hell, I was different. The well-dressed reflection in the mirror proved it.

Maybe I really had lost something working as Van Dorn's personal detective after all. But whatever I had lost, it was nothing I'd miss. Because if having the shakes after getting shot at was the price I had to pay for the life I had now, I'd gladly pay it. I'd grown up poor, then had plenty of money on the force, then flat broke again after they kicked me out. Now I had more money than I could spend. Having money was a hell of a lot more fun.

I opened my fist and my hand wasn't shaking anymore. I swiped off the remaining dirt from my hat and put it back on my head. I checked my reflection in the mirror behind the counter and set it to the proper angle. I wanted to make a good impression on Dr. Blythe.

I watched the mirror while I waited for the counterman to return, enjoying Broadway in all its grimy, bustling glory. Street cars and people and taxi cabs and trucks of all shapes and sizes zipping uptown and downtown; east side to west side and back again.

I saw something else, too.

A skinny blond man eyeballing me from a doorway of an office building across the street.

About my size.

Maybe twenty years old, in a cheap gray overcoat that was too big for him.

Even though he was across the street I could see he had wide, serious eyes that were staring right at the cigar shop's front door, like it was the most important thing in the world to him.

He could've been the same son of a bitch who'd been with the men who shot at me that morning.

He also could've been just a kid in a gray coat killing time, waiting for his girlfriend to meet him for lunch. The fact that he fit the description of the man who'd run past me could've just been a coincidence.

But I'd been a cop far too long to believe in coincidences.

It had to be the same punk from earlier that morning, only now he was tailing me. I'd pegged him for an amateur because a pro would have been much tougher to spot. His wide-eyed glare told me he was timid, but eager. He thought I couldn't spot him from a doorway across the street. He was wrong.

The counterman brought me a couple of light brown cigars and showed them to me. I barely glanced at them as I paid for them and pocketed them. I kept my eye on Blondie's reflection in the mirror instead.

I exited Nat's and started walking up Broadway, toward the New York Athletic Club on 59th Street and 6th Avenue, just south of Central Park. The street was jammed with cars and the sidewalks packed with people. Considering the amount of traffic, I figured the Ford wouldn't be able to roll up and take another shot at me. Too many witnesses and too much traffic to make a quick getaway, either behind the wheel or on foot.

That meant if trouble came, it would come on foot from Blondie, which was just fine by me. I may have lost a step or two in the past year, but I was still good enough to get the jump on a punk like him.

I walked up Broadway at a normal pace, hoping that would make it easier for Blondie to trail me. With this many people on the street, chances were that someone would scream or yell if he pulled a gun. I was ready to hit the deck again if I had to.

I stopped short in the middle of the sidewalk and lit a cigarette, turning sideways as if I was shielding the flame from the wind. I caught a lot of dirty looks and curses from the people behind me for the sudden stop. More importantly, I caught a glimpse of Blondie ducking into a store about a quarter of a block behind me. Too close, little man, even in the crowded environs of Times Square. Definitely an amateur.

But I didn't relax any. Amateurs got lucky, too.

I smoked my cigarette as I headed uptown again. I wanted Blondie to relax. Let him think this was going to be a lot easier than his buddies in the Ford had probably told him it would be. I kept the same pace for a few blocks until I got to 44th Street, where foot traffic was knotted by a group of people stopped dead on the corner, gaping up at the signs and buildings along the Great White Way.

I took my chance and ducked through the crowd and quickly doubled back, pressing myself flat against the building at the corner.

I figured Blondie would panic; he didn't let me down.

The crowd had thinned out a bit and I saw people's heads being jostled from one side to another as he knocked them out of the way, trying to see where I'd gone.

When the crowd thinned out enough, I pushed off the building and nailed him with a sucker punch left hook square on the jaw. I'd put enough into the punch to stagger him, but not enough to knock him out. I grabbed him by the coat collar and tried to keep him on his feet.

The punk surprised me by slipping out of the coat and darting up Broadway, all in one fluid motion. Horns blared and people cursed as he sprinted between the cars and the crowd and disappeared in the sea of people.

I hardly even noticed how much my left hand hurt. I'd chased a good number of punks in my day and I knew how to put a man down with one punch. But I'd never seen anyone move with that kind of speed and power outside of a football field. Hell, I'd never seen anyone move like that on a football field, either.

Blondie had disappeared in no time flat and left me standing alone on the corner with a dumb look on my face, a cheap coat in my hand, and a whole lot of questions on my mind.

I patted down the coat, but the pockets were empty. No tags inside it to tell me where it had come from or who it belonged to. I balled it up and tucked it under my arm as I started walking up Broadway again.

I kept wondering:

Who was trying to kill me?

Why had they sent a rank amateur to tail me?

And what was a kid who could run like that doing with a bunch of killers?

I couldn't think of anyone, but I had a feeling I'd find out soon enough.

Chapter 5

I stashed Blondie's coat with the New York Athletic Club's coatroom before they had someone take me upstairs. I figured it might come in handy at some point down the line. Their coatroom was just as good as my place, maybe even better.

The lounge of the NYAC looked like a lot of the places where I met my clients these days. Dim lighting. Heavy drapes. Lots of dark wood. Plenty of thick leather lounge chairs and couches where white-haired men nodded off. The men who weren't dozing were either having hushed conversations over cigars or were reading the newspaper.

It wasn't as lively as The Longford Lounge on New Year's Eve, but it beat the hell out of raiding a whorehouse on Canal Street.

Dr. Matthew Blythe looked like someone I'd expect to see in such surroundings. He was tucked into a plush leather chair next to the fireplace, glasses perched on the end of his nose as he read through the latest edition of The New York Evening Journal. He was a round, fleshy man; mostly bald except for a crown of white hair swept back behind his ears. A large cigar burning away in the standing ashtray at his elbow.

There were also two coffee cups at his elbow on the

table, saucer and all. But judging from the doctor's ruddy complexion and the slight whiff of gin I caught as I got closer, I figured those cups weren't just for coffee. The doctor had that paunchy, bloated look rummies tended to get when they bent the elbow too much.

The porter who had escorted me up to the lounge cleared his throat to draw Dr. Blythe's attention away from the newspaper. The doctor quickly got to his feet, palmed the porter some cash, and eagerly shook my hand.

"An honor to meet you, Detective Doherty." He motioned to the chair opposite him. "Why don't you sit down and make yourself comfortable?"

"I'm afraid it's just plain old Charlie or Doherty these days, Doctor." I sank into one of the leather chairs opposite him. And I wasn't ashamed to admit it was damned comfortable. I might nod off myself if I wasn't careful. "I'm not with the police department anymore, so rank doesn't apply."

"Nonsense. I believe rank, once earned, can only be rescinded through an official process, and even then it's debatable. I know how poorly they treated you at the end of your tenure at the police department. Why, they should have given you a medal for bringing the Van Dorn boy home alive the way you did." He leaned in closer and lowered his voice. "And they should have given you another medal for killing the bastards who took him and killed poor Jessica, too. You saved the taxpayers the great expense and anguish of a trial, sir, and for that I'm grateful."

Whenever anyone brought up the Van Dorn case, they

either talked about the shootout or how I'd brought Jack home alive. Dr. Blythe was one of the few who mentioned Jessica's death. That was human nature, I guess. Focus on the shiny objects, not the commonplace.

Talking about it made me feel uncomfortable, so I tried to get to the point. "I wish you and I were meeting under better circumstances."

"As do I, young man, as do I." He produced a large, dark medicine bottle from the floor next to his chair and poured some clear liquid into both coffee cups on the table at his elbow. "Here's something that should take the sting out of our conversation."

I caught the smell right away and knew I'd been right about the doctor's favorite drink: gin. He probably figured gin was a safer drink because it wasn't supposed to smell. The only people who really believed that were gin drinkers.

And judging by how the cup rattled in its saucer as he handed it to me, Dr. Blythe had the shakes. Not from nerves, but from need. Blythe was a drunk.

"You don't look well, my boy," he said from over his glasses. "I suggest you try some of this fine elixir sent to me by my colleagues from across the pond." He dropped his voice to a stage whisper. "Some Beefeater gin sent by friends over in London. The club doesn't mind us nipping now and then so long as we don't get too soused. But the bastards refuse to provide ice so I've grown accustomed to sipping it warm. It's an acquired taste, but well worth the effort, I assure you. Goddamned Puritans and their Prohibition! They've made our minor vices turn us all into bunch of common criminals."

He poured more into his own cup before setting the medicine bottle back on the floor next to his chair. He cleared his throat as he toasted me with his coffee cup. "To repeal, sir."

I took a swig to be polite, but left most of it in the cup. Gin and I had never gotten along.

Blythe licked his lips after a healthy swallow. "I find that a couple of tablespoons a day tends to take the edge off a bit."

I knew he didn't have the shakes that bad from a couple of tablespoons, but I let it go. "Nothing wrong with that. I've always been more of rum man myself."

"To each his own tastes, I suppose. I acquired a preference for gin back when I served with the British during the last unpleasantness."

That explained the earlier comment about rank. "You were in the war, sir?"

"Indeed, but strictly in a supervisory capacity. I never saw any action firsthand, only its aftermath. I served on the Armed Forces Medical Board in London. America was neutral at that point in the war, but as I was the only son in the family and my father insisted I find a way to help the war effort. He was a doctor, too, and, given my medical background, the medical board seemed like a good fit. We tried to provide the boys in the field with the best care we could manage, but always came up short. I suppose most efforts like that always fall short during war, despite the best intentions."

The doctor looked at me again over the glasses at the end of his nose. "I'd wager you saw plenty of action, didn't you?" He took a closer look at me, like he was examining a wound. "Yes, you have that look one can always see when one knows what to look for."

I knew then that Blythe wasn't the toddling old rummy he probably let people think he was. "You're very perceptive, sir. I was in the Third Battalion, Fifth Marines."

His white eyebrows flicked upward. "You were at Belleau Wood, then."

I didn't like talking about Jessica Van Dorn's death. I liked talking about Belleau Wood even less. "Along with a lot of other guys, sir."

Neither of us had to say how many guys hadn't come back. Human nature again.

The doctor sipped from his cup. "And I'm sure your experiences in France and your years as a policeman taught you a thing or two about perseverance. You'll certainly need it in dealing with my sister. For some strange reason, Eleanor has gotten some damned fool notion into her head that Walter didn't take his own life. What do you think of her hypothesis, Detective Doherty?"

He held up a hand before I could answer. "And I don't take you for a delicate man, sir, so please don't disappoint me by being polite just because we're talking about my family."

I kept it as direct as I could. "I've spoken to the lead detective in the case, the coroner, and I've read the police report. Walter Fairfax went to his office that morning and shot himself in the head. There's just no other way to see it."

"No question in your mind? No room for doubt?"

"None, sir."

Dr. Blythe frowned like a man used to smiling. "I was afraid of that. I also happen to agree with you, which makes me wonder why we're having this discussion at all. Or why you took this case in the first place." His eyes narrowed. "I should hope you're not the type of man who would take advantage of my sister's wealth in her time of mourning."

"Mr. Van Dorn can confirm that I have no intention of taking advantage of anyone," I said. "But I do think your sister is asking the wrong question, even though she doesn't realize it yet. She knows Walter killed himself, but what she really wants to know is why."

"I'd like to know that, too, Detective. Because, for all of his many faults, Walter Fairfax was my oldest and dearest friend. His loss has affected me far greater than I could have imagined."

Blythe placed his cup back on the saucer on the table at his elbow. "I keep hoping the gin will help make his passing easier to take, but it doesn't seem to be working."

"In my experience, it usually just makes things worse, sir."

The doctor's lower lip began to quiver. "He called me that morning, you know. Right before he killed himself."

I felt myself move toward the edge of my seat. "No, I didn't know that. I know he received a call at nine fifteen, but there's nothing in the police report about him making one."

I felt the room begin to spin and it wasn't from Blythe's

gin. Loomis's reports were meticulous. He usually put too much in them, not too little. How could he have missed an important detail like Fairfax making a phone call? "May I ask what you talked about?"

Blythe's eyes glazed over with a faraway look of remembrance. "The police told my sister that Walter shot himself at nine thirty in the morning. Is that accurate?"

"As far as I know. That's what the initial report said based on witness statements."

The doctor closed his eyes. "That's what I was afraid of. Walter called my office just after nine fifteen. Unfortunately, I happened to be indisposed at the time and was unable to take his call." He offered a quick smile. "Indisposed is a polite way of saying I was still drunk, Detective. But when one comes from a wealthy, respected family such as mine, one can never admit to such failings, so they say one is indisposed." The smile became a grimace. "And I was quite indisposed that morning. On the one morning when my friend needed me most."

I knew nothing I could say to make him feel any better, so I didn't say anything. I just sat there and made damned sure I heard everything the good doctor said.

Because, from the look on his face, he wanted to say quite a bit.

"I suppose I wasn't technically drunk," Dr. Blythe went on, "just hungover in epic fashion. I'm a fairly predictable man when it comes to my drinking, Detective. I prefer gin during the daytime hours and progress gradually to scotch in the afternoon and evening hours. You could say my liquor gets darker as night approaches. I'd had far more to drink than usual the night before Walter killed himself."

"Any particular reason why?"

"Just a miscalculation of indulgence," the doctor admitted. "I woke the next morning in a terrible state, too sick to answer the phone. I was curled up in bed, shivering like a sick dog while my best friend called, begging me for help. I didn't even hear the damned phone ring, and wouldn't have been able to answer even if I had. My maid answered the phone for me."

He surprised me with a short, sharp laugh. "As drunk as I was the night before, I'd apparently been sober enough to leave a note for my maid telling her not to disturb me under any circumstances."

Blythe's voice cracked. "He even told her it was vital that he speak to me, but she told him I was...indisposed."

The doctor shut his eyes again and tears ran down his cheeks. "God, I didn't even know Walter was dead until hours later, when I was finally sober enough to comprehend it."

I could see Blythe's guilt was doing a number on him, so trying to console him would just be a waste of time. His gin and his guilt were all the consolation he wanted right now. But since he was in a talking mood, I wanted to keep him that way. I liked Dr. Blythe. I even felt a little sorry for him, but I was still working for his sister. I had a job to do. "Why do you think Walter killed himself, Doctor?"

Blythe wiped his tears away with the palm of his hand. "Have you had much experience in working with insurance men, Detective?"

"No, but your sister gave me a quick lesson about them this morning."

"Yes, I suppose spending over thirty years with Walter has made Eleanor something of an expert on insurance men. I could never understand how anyone could simply boil down the factors that make up a human life into cold numbers on a chart. But Walter Fairfax could. He and his family had built a sizable fortune doing that very thing."

He picked up his medicine bottle from the floor and refilled his cup. "Then again, I suppose I've had a different exposure to the intricacies of the human condition than Walter did."

"What about the intricacies of Walter's condition, sir? I mean, how was his health?"

"He had fewer vices than any man his age had any right to have. He hardly ever smoked, save for the occasional cigar, and he drank even less. He suffered from ulcers and other stomach troubles, but he wasn't overweight. His blood pressure was a little high, but that's to be expected of a man who runs a company the size of Fairfax Liability."

"But no illnesses or disease?"

"Just terminal gloominess. In fact, when I examined him a month ago, Walter was the picture of health."

"What about his mental state? Do you know of anything that might've been troubling him?"

"Something was always troubling Walter, Detective. No matter how much money he made, it was never enough. It was almost as though he had a fear of settling."

I tried to think of a more delicate way to say what I wanted to say next, but decided just to come out with it. "I understand Walter's mother killed herself—arsenic poisoning. I know depression runs in families and wondered if that might be the case here."

Blythe didn't let my question hang for long. "My compliments, Detective. I know my sister didn't tell you that, so you must have done your research. Walter's mother was a beautiful woman who suffered from a persistent case of melancholy. She was Prussian, you know, descended from a minor noble family. Her family's fortune was just about played out when she married Walter's father. He was a rather melancholy bastard himself, and being married to him only made her dark tendencies even darker. She tried to kill herself a couple of times over the years. Cut her wrists, that sort of thing, but suicide can be a rather difficult undertaking if you try to be subtle about it. Those actions were more cries for help than any serious attempt of suicide. Walter tried to get her help, but his father wouldn't risk the scandal of admitting to having a wife given to depression."

Dr. Blythe went on. "Walter did his best to help her, but with a young family to raise and a business to learn, he simply didn't have the time. She ultimately gave herself a healthy dose of arsenic one morning with her tea. She'd been under the unfortunate misconception that arsenic was a romantic, painless death. That she'd just go to sleep and never wake up. That's possible if you get the dosage right. Unfortunately, Walter's mother didn't get the dosage right."

Dr. Blythe got that far-off look again. "I was a young

physician at the time and helped my father tend to her. It took her almost two days to die, and she screamed for almost every minute of it. Walter was never the same after that."

"That kind of thing is never easy to take."

"You would have thought his experience with his mother would cure him of his attraction to women of Teutonic extraction." The doctor frowned. "I suppose that's why I was surprised when he took up with that Austrian whore last year."

There it was.

I'd known all along that there had to be more to Walter. No one that rich was that clean. Now we were getting somewhere. "Mrs. Fairfax told me she was aware of other women in his life. I didn't know you were aware of them, too."

"I certainly didn't approve of it," Blythe said. "Eleanor might not be the most pleasant woman in the world, but she's still my sister. But if she tolerated Walter's indiscretions, who was I to object?"

I didn't care about his objections. I cared about the woman. "Tell me more about this Austrian whore you just mentioned."

"Well, she isn't actually a whore, I suppose," Blythe admitted. "It's not called prostitution when one plies their trade under the pretext of aristocracy, even though the motives and the practice are the same. She even has a title, too, just like Walter's dear departed mother." He cleared his throat and said, "The Countess Alexandra von Holstein, to be precise." He reached for the medicine bottle and poured himself more gin. "On the lam, as they say, just like all the other Bosch blue bloods sent scurrying after the Treaty of Versailles. No room for aristocracy in the new Germany these days, and good riddance, too. But now the bastards are scattered all over the globe like locusts. Why, you can't spit anywhere in Europe these days without hitting someone of peerage."

Blythe took a healthy swig from his cup. "Unfortunately, the Countess von Holstein got bored with Europe and decided to ply her trade here in Manhattan."

I'd already pulled out my pad and started writing things down. "When?"

"About a year ago. Americans are suckers for people with old world titles, especially when they happen to be beautiful women—and Alexandra is most certainly beautiful." That sneer again. "It didn't take long for the Kraut bitch to set her sights on poor old Walter."

"How'd she hook him?"

Dr. Blythe smiled. "An apt turn of phrase, Detective, for hook him she did. Like some kind of flounder or carp. It wasn't difficult, given Walter's love for all things Germanic. He had spent most of his life dreaming of the forgotten grandeur of a dying empire held together more out of habit than practicality. It had always been his dream to sell all his possessions here one day and move back to his mother's homeland."

The doctor wagged a shaky finger at me. "And that's the hook the countess used to reel him in. It didn't matter to him that Alexandra's title was purely ceremonial by then. Reparations for the war took her family's land, fortunes, everything. That's why she and all the others of her ilk came scurrying across the Atlantic as poor as church mice, finding fertile ground here in the bosom of wealthy people like Walter who admired them for what they used to be."

"Did Mrs. Fairfax know about the countess?"

"I never discussed Walter's indiscretions with my sister. They were always benign, temporary things. But Countess Alexandra was different. I'd never seen him so smitten before. I'd never thought he was capable of such emotion, and I've known the man my entire life."

I'd already figured out the answer to my next question, but asked it anyway. "He give her any money?"

"Of course. Women of the countess' breeding have standards that must be maintained. Walter set her up in an apartment, paid for the lifestyle she desired. Supported all of those lunatic causes of hers."

I stopped writing, remembering the list Mary Pat had given me. If they matched with whatever Blythe told me, I'd be on to something. "What lunatic causes?"

"Esoteric nonsense like heightened awareness and streams of consciousness. Mysticism based on ancient Germanic pagan practices. I can't tell you much about them for I never paid much attention to any of it, though it seemed to have struck a chord in Walter."

I made a note of that, too. The more I heard about Countess Alexandra, the more I wanted to speak to her next. "Did a lot of people know about her and Walter?"

Blythe shook his head. "Just about the only thing she didn't take from Walter was his discretion. She got him to pull away from his business, his family, his friends." A wince. "Even me. He'd devoted a good portion of the past year to Alexandra's oddball assortment of friends. Deposed aristocrats like her. The royal refuse of Europe."

I wrote all that down. "Your sister said he was still committed to his insurance business."

"Yes, but he gradually let his son, Trip, handle most of the daily affairs. I tried talking some sense into Walter, of course. I wanted him to see how Alexandra was slowly destroying his life with her Friends of New Germany and all that rabble. But by then he had stopped coming to see me for his usual examinations."

My rush over getting a match on one of the groups on Mary Pat's list was short- lived. "But earlier, you just told me you examined him a month ago."

"It was my first examination of him in almost a year," Blythe explained. "He preferred the countess' idea of herbs and potions, or whatever botanical nonsense she fed him, over my prescriptions of modern medicine. I know Walter wasn't feeling well, but wouldn't tell me why. He complained about feeling different somehow, more sluggish. He blamed the whole thing on age catching up with him, but I wasn't so cavalier about it. His color was off. His balance, too, and his stomach was giving him problems again. I offered him something that might give his system a boost, but he ultimately refused my help and swore me to secrecy. I didn't have any grounds to force the issue, and had no choice but to allow him to leave without helping him." Blythe's hand quivered as he reached for his cup. "Now he's dead."

I could see the gin was already beginning to affect him. A few more sips and all I'd get from him then was guilt and regret.

I forgot about the other names on the list Mrs. Fairfax had given me. The countess had just gone to the top of my list. "Any idea on how I can find Alexandra?"

"No." He took another sip of gin. "I know Walter set her up in an apartment, but I don't know where. I don't enjoy her company, and the feeling was more than mutual. Perhaps Walter's secretary, Mrs. Swenson, could help you."

I got nervous when the old man stopped talking. His face was flushed and I thought he might keel over. But he surprised me when he said, "Wait a moment. The Stuyvesant Society is having their annual gala tomorrow night at the new Waldorf-Astoria on Park Avenue. All the best families in the city will be there, and I'm sure Alexandra will somehow find a way to weasel her way in. She wouldn't miss an event like that for the world, especially now that she's lost Walter. Parasites like her always need new hosts to feed on. I should get you a ticket so you can meet her for yourself. See what you can deduce firsthand."

It sounded like a good idea to me, but there was only one problem. "If the event's tomorrow night, do you think I could get in?"

"I don't see why not, seeing as how I sit on the board," he said. "I'll make the arrangements as soon as possible. You do have evening attire, of course."

Thanks to Mrs. Van Dorn helping me pick out my wardrobe, I could say, "Of course."

"Splendid." Dr. Blythe was smiling again, the kind of face that made me want to smile, too. "Seven o'clock sharp, tomorrow night." He took a final swig out of his cup and stood up, full of resolve. His sister had ended our meeting the same way. I guessed standing up must've been the way the Blythe family liked to end meetings. "I'll make all the necessary arrangements. How might I get a hold of you?"

I dug out a calling card from my inside pocket and handed it to him. "All my information is right there. You can call me when it's all arranged."

I didn't know why I added the next part. Maybe it was all the talk earlier about the war and Germany. Maybe it was the doctor's guilt about losing someone he cared about that got to me. Anyway, I said, "Feel free to call me anytime you want. Even if it's just to talk. I know a thing or two about regrets. I've got a few myself."

Blythe didn't look up from my card.

I added, "You might not have picked up the phone when Walter called, but you didn't pull the trigger. Walter did." I looked down at his empty cup. "If you leave that elixir alone long enough, you'll realize I'm right."

The doctor tucked my card away. "Reminds me of an old saying: 'Physician, heal thyself.'"

"Or another old saying: 'Quit kicking yourself in the ass.'"

Blythe laughed. "Serves me right for asking you not to be delicate."

Chapter 6

It was just past three thirty when I pushed through the revolving doors of the New York Athletic Club.

I stood in the alcove entrance and checked the street for any sign of Blondie or his friends in the Ford. No one paid me any mind. Just the regular flow of people and cars heading across town along Central Park South on a mild March afternoon.

The coatroom attendant hadn't seen me leave and I hadn't looked for him, either. I decided I'd leave Blondie's coat where it was. It might come in handy later, and the staff at the club would keep a better eye on it than I would.

A good breeze kicked up and I moved behind the alcove to fire up one of the cigars I had bought at Nat's. I might not have had the chance to smoke it with Blythe, but there was no reason I couldn't enjoy it now. I took a good pull and let the smoke drift out nice and slow through my nose. Nothing like fine tobacco to get the brain in working order. At least my brain, anyway.

Because my brain had plenty to work on.

I had no place where I had to be in a hurry, so I pulled out my notebook and wrote down the new timeline while it was still fresh in my mind.

9:00 a.m. – Walter Fairfax arrives at the office.

9:15 a.m. – Walter takes a private call and closes the door.

9:20 a.m. (approximately) – Walter calls Dr. Blythe—urgent—no record of the call.

9:30 a.m. – Walter puts gun in mouth and squeezes trigger.

The time between the phone calls was everything. Something happened to make Fairfax call Blythe before he killed himself. I knew that first phone call had to be the reason. I needed to find out where that call had come from.

I also needed to find out why that second phone call to Dr. Blythe wasn't in the police file.

And even though I didn't have the slightest bit of proof to back it up, I knew it had something to do with Countess Alexandra von Holstein. I wrote her name in my notebook and underlined it twice. She was a wild card. If she wasn't the key to all of this, she could help me fill in a lot of blanks.

I'd seen this scenario hundreds of times before. Lady friends tended to be expensive. Lady friends with pedigrees even more so. The countess wasn't some shop girl Walter had stashed away in a joy pad on 52nd Street. She wasn't one of those meek, thankful girls who spent their days thumbing through magazines and listening to the radio until her rich lover dropped by for a poke in the whiskers and left a couple of twenties on the nightstand.

The countess would have standards. She'd want good clothes and fine wine and the best cuisine. She'd require an apartment suitable for a woman of her standing. According to Blythe, she loved the nightlife, which only would have added to Fairfax's bill. She'd also want money of her own and access to it on her terms. That meant a lease for an apartment and a bank account somewhere.

Although Fairfax could afford all that and more, those things left a paper trail I could follow once I had a place to start. Not to mention all the money she had Walter donate to all those "oddball causes" Blythe had mentioned and Mary Pat had listed.

I had no idea what Countess Alexandra looked like, but I knew she had a special hold on Walter. Because keeping a high-end girlfriend from his wife broke the insurance man's pattern, and Walter Fairfax was a man who lived by patterns.

The countess was growing more interesting by the minute.

I knew I'd be seeing her at the Stuyvesant Society gala the next night, but seeing her wouldn't be enough. Even if I did have the chance to meet her, an interrogation was out of the question. She was probably skilled enough to dodge my questions, especially in a social setting. I'd need facts before I faced her, and plenty of them. That paper trail connecting her to Walter would help.

I puffed on my cigar as I thought about where I should start. Where would a careful, methodical man keep his mistress' leases and bank records? At his mansion? No, his wife might find out. A safe deposit box at the bank? Possibly, but what if the bank was closed when he needed access to the papers? A well-connected man like Walter could always call the manager to come down and let him in whatever the day or hour, but that would cause suspicion. Walter was a planner and far too careful for that.

No, Walter would keep those kinds of documents close at hand, at the one place where he spent most of his time. His office.

I smiled. The cigar had done the trick after all.

***

The Fairfax Liability Company had leased several floors in The Empire State Building right after the dump first opened a couple of years before.

It might have been the tallest building in the world, but they'd built the damned thing in the middle of nowhere, a dead spot on the city map. It wasn't near any subways. Penn Station was several blocks away and Grand Central was even further. Throw in the fact that you could actually feel the building sway on windy days, and let's just say companies weren't exactly lining up, begging for space. With the Depression on, there weren't that many companies left.

When I got off the elevator on the seventy-fifth floor, the receptionist in the Fairfax Liability lobby insisted on calling Walter's secretary, Mrs. Swenson, to escort me back to the main offices. I remembered Swenson's name from Mrs. Fairfax's list.

I didn't have to wait long. A prim, dark-haired woman with thick glasses ran out to greet me about a minute or two later. Her clothes were a few seasons out of fashion and too matronly for her age, which I pegged at around thirty. I'd expected the executive secretary of a big wig like Fairfax to dress better than that.

She was too flustered to bother with shaking hands or

other pleasantries. "I do wish you would have called first to make a proper appointment, Mr. Doherty. I'm afraid you have come at a most inopportune time. I had no choice but to inform Mr. Fairfax that you were here, and he made it perfectly clear that he doesn't want you in his father's office."

I didn't let the stiff-arm treatment throw me off. "Then I guess it's a good thing that I don't work for Mr. Fairfax. Or do you call him Trip? Anyway, I work for his mother, the new owner of the company. She's already given me permission to see her husband's office."

"But—"

I picked up the earpiece from the receptionist's phone and held it out to Mrs. Swenson. "Call her if you don't believe me."

She pulled away from the device like I was waving a snake at her. "No?" I set the earpiece back in the cradle. "Then either step aside or point me in the right direction, and I'll be out of your way."

Mrs. Swenson bit her lip and fidgeted with her hands. She seemed to like doing that. "Do you have some identification to prove who you are? I can't let just anyone back there who claims they're working for the family."

I fished out my private cop license and showed her. She leaned in and studied it closely, like she'd know a fake if she saw it. I doubted she would. "Seems real enough. Do you carry a gun, too?"

"Only when I deal with difficult secretaries. Now, if I could see the office?"

Reluctantly, she held the door open for me and led me

into the inner sanctum of The Fairfax Liability Company.

The space was nothing fancy. Office doors ran along the sides, with columns of desks lining the middle of the floor. Even though all the women at the desks seemed to either be on the phone or banging away at typewriters, we drew stares from every one of them as we passed by. A few heads poked out of offices like groundhogs sniffing out spring, only to duck back inside. I'd never been good at multiplication, but there had to be about forty or so desks crammed into the space. The uniformity of the scene made me almost feel sorry for them.

Mrs. Swenson spoke to me over her shoulder as she led the way. "Mrs. Fairfax has already told us to cooperate fully with your investigation, Mr. Doherty. I hope you understand I wasn't trying to be difficult, but Mr. Fairfax isn't adjusting well to his father's passing. None of us are, considering the manner in which Mr. Fairfax died. It's already been a month, but it feels like only yesterday. Such a terrible accident."

Something in the way she'd made a point of adding the part about the suicide being an accident made me think she didn't believe it. I figured she was holding the company line for the benefit of the employees who were listening as we walked by them. I decided to find out.

"Death is never easy, Mrs. Swenson. Especially when it happens in such a sudden way. According the police report, you were the first person in the office after the shot."

Mrs. Swenson's step faltered and I almost bumped into her. "You read the report?" She kept her voice low as she resumed her stride. "But that's impossible. I was told the report was supposed to have been sealed. No one is supposed to see it."

"I used to be a policeman. I have ways of getting my hands on things like that." I lowered my voice. "Don't worry. The family secret is safe with me. We're all on the same team, remember?"

That seemed to calm her down a bit, but only a bit. "Yes, I suppose we are." She picked up the pace a bit. "And to answer your question, you're right. I was the first person to find him. I don't think I'll forget that sight for as long as I live."

I had seen the crime scene photos, and knew it hadn't been pretty. Since making her queasy wouldn't help me, I decided to change the subject. "How long did you work for Mr. Fairfax?"

"Five years. And he was a good and generous man, Mr. Doherty."

I figured that was more of the company line. Of all the things I had heard about Walter that day, good and generous just didn't fit.

We reached her desk at an inner office at the far end of the floor. The door to Mr. Fairfax's office was closed. Now that we were out of earshot of everyone, I could see she was relaxing a bit.

I eased into the questioning. "Did you notice anything different about Mr. Fairfax on the day it happened? Was he troubled? Annoyed? Nervous?"

She appeared to give it some thought, maybe a little too much. "Since you've read the report, you already know what

I said."

Defensive. Why? "Refresh my memory."

"He came into the office a bit before nine, which was later than normal, but not late enough for me to think anything of it. I remember noticing he was perspiring despite it being a cool morning. I went in to give him his messages and other relevant correspondence, just like every other morning, when he told me that his stomach was bothering him. I knew he had suffered from ulcers in the past, so that wasn't unusual, either."

I'd already known about the ulcers from Dr. Blythe, but the police report hadn't mentioned anything about Fairfax feeling ill. I began to wonder what else, besides the second phone call, was missing from the report. "Go on."

"I offered to get him some boric acid. That usually made him feel better, but he refused. He told me he wanted to be left alone for a bit and to hold all of his calls. That's why I was surprised that he overheard me answer the phone and demanded that I put it through."

Now we were getting somewhere. "Do you remember who called him?"

Mrs. Swenson opened a notebook on her desk. "Mr. Fairfax had me keep a detailed log of all of his calls." She flipped to the last page. "A woman calling herself Miss Schmidt called at seven minutes past nine that morning. She insisted Mr. Fairfax was expecting her call. I usually never put someone through to him once he asked me to hold his calls. When Mr. Fairfax overheard me repeat her name as I wrote it down, he called out for me to put it through and shut the door."

I pulled out my notebook and wrote down Miss Schmidt's name. I played a hunch. "Do you remember if she had an accent?"

Mrs. Swenson thought about it. "Yes. Not British, though. Similar, but harsher. German maybe?"

German. And I bet Miss Schmidt was actually Countess Alexandra von Holstein. "Do you remember this Miss Schmidt ever calling here before?"

"Never," she said. "I would've remembered the accent. And even if I didn't remember it, I would have logged it. I already checked; she never called here before."

An urgent call from a strange woman with a German accent just before Fairfax killed himself. Things were getting interesting, especially because none of this was in the report, not even in Loomis's preliminary report. That didn't fit.

"How long did the call last?"

"I haven't the slightest idea." She nodded at Fairfax's door. "The door remained closed until I heard...the shot."

But that didn't fit my new timeline. "What about the call you placed for Mr. Fairfax to Dr. Blythe?"

Mrs. Swenson didn't look happy that I'd doubted her memory. "I didn't place any call for him that morning. If he made one, he must have used his private line after ending his call with Miss Schmidt. I always thought she had been the last person who'd spoken to him."

A private line in his office made sense, but the lack of detail about the caller in Loomis's report didn't. "Did you tell the detectives who were here about that phone call from this Miss Schmidt?"

"I tried." She went back to her notebook. "I was being interviewed by a Detective Loomis when men from Chief Carmichael's office arrived and told him to leave. A Detective Hauser took over the investigation and interviewed me. I had the feeling that he wasn't all that interested in anything I had to say, not like Detective Loomis. But I noted that he made several phone calls of his own while he was here." She blushed a little as she said, "I didn't mean to eavesdrop, but I couldn't help but overhear that he seemed to be speaking to Chief Carmichael directly."

Now the blank spots in the report were beginning to make sense. Detective Steve Hauser was my replacement as Carmichael's latest errand boy. Hauser was the perfect man for the job. He was smart enough to know how dumb he should be.

Hauser's involvement explained why details about the last phone call had been kept out of Loomis's version of the report. Loomis probably hadn't been given a chance to stick around long enough to ask Mrs. Swenson about it. I could understand why Hauser decided to leave it out. Why complicate a perfectly good false accident report by adding a lot of facts?

I decided it was finally time to take a look at Fairfax's office for myself. I knew I'd made some progress with Mrs. Swenson, and wanted to stay in her good graces. She'd been Fairfax's secretary for a long time, and might have some more information that could come in handy later on.

"If you have no objections, I'd like to take a look at his

office now, Mrs. Swenson. I'll be respectful, I promise."

Her right eyebrow rose, and I suddenly found myself wondering what she looked like without those thick glasses. "You already have Mrs. Fairfax's permission, Mr. Doherty, so we both know you don't need my permission to do anything."

"I know, but I'd like to have it anyway. You worked for him for a long time and deserve that kind of respect."

The charm worked. Any ice that had formed between us melted right away. She even walked me to the door. "By all means, Mr. Doherty. But I'm afraid you won't find much inside. We cleared out the office out some weeks ago. All that's left is furniture."

"That's fine. I won't be long." I turned the knob and pushed the door in. There was still plenty of daylight coming through the windows, but I turned on the light switch anyway. Thanks to the crime scene photos in Loomis's file, I had already seen the office from several different angles, but nothing beat seeing something with my own two eyes.

On the left: A set of empty bookshelves against the far wall. A small bathroom next to them. The door was open.

In the center: Walter's desk and chair, facing the door. A wall of clean windows behind them faced north. The view was seventy-five stories above Manhattan, and I could see they were putting the finishing touches on one of the new Rockefeller buildings several blocks away. It was the kind of view I could look at all day and all night if I had the chance, but I wasn't there for sightseeing.

On the right: Another empty bookcase against the wall.

Cabinets on the bottom. All doors closed.

I picked up on an odor that didn't belong and quickly knew what it was. Smells of new carpet and new paint that had been trapped, then dulled by the closed door and windows. There was no sign of the blood splatter I'd seen on the windows in the crime scene photos. And the top pane that had been shattered by the bullet exiting the top of Walter's head had since been replaced.

The whole office looked brand new, like nothing had ever happened here. Like a man hadn't decided to end his life here. I guessed that was the point.

I didn't have to look behind me to know Mrs. Swenson was standing just outside the office. Lurking, even though she didn't mean to.

I decided to push whatever good will I might've built up with her and take a risk. "Why do you think he did it?"

Mrs. Swenson shook her head. "I've asked myself thousands of times, and I don't have the slightest idea. I wish I did. I wish there was something I could've done to keep him from doing something so drastic. I've often wanted to ask Trip about what his father had written in the note, but I've never had the courage."

"Note?" I didn't mean to snap at her, but I had. "What note? There was no mention of a suicide note in the police report."

"Well, there should've been." She pointed at the desk. "It was in an envelope right there when we found him. It was addressed to Trip in Mr. Fairfax's own handwriting. Trip was in his office downstairs when it happened. He was the first one who dared to go inside while I called the police. Trip took the note with him before the police arrived."

I took off my hat and ran my fingers across my scalp.

A suicide note. Jesus. That hadn't been in the report, either, but in Hauser's defense, the son might not have told them about it. "Did you tell Detective Hauser or Loomis about the note?"

"No, because he didn't seem very interested in anything anyone had to say. As I've already told you, he was on the phone much of the time he was here."

That fit Hauser's style. He hadn't been sent here to investigate anything. He'd been sent to report what he saw to Carmichael and wait for instructions. I knew the drill. I'd run it plenty of times myself over the years.

But if he knew about a suicide note, it should've at least been in the initial report. Loomis had been on the scene first, before Hauser. He would've written it up, just like he would have written up the phone call to Blythe if he'd known about it.

I wondered if I should give Hauser a pass on the suicide note. I wondered if Trip had told them about it in the first place.

The answer to that question could be as important as the contents of the note itself.

I said to Mrs. Swenson, "Please call Trip and tell him I'd like to speak to him, but don't mention anything about the suicide note. I'd like to ask him about that personally."

She fidgeted some more with her hands. "He won't be happy. He's already on the phone with his lawyer to see if he can fire you without his mother's permission."

I didn't know Trip, but I'd met his mother. I didn't think he'd have much luck on that front. "Call him anyway. I'll just take a quick look around in here while I wait."

I quietly closed the door behind her as she went to her desk to place the call. I leaned against it and looked around the office, absorbing the quiet.

I spoke to the empty room. "Come on, Walter. Show me something."

I decided the desk would be the best place to start. I checked all the drawers. All of them had been cleaned and emptied. Not even a scrap of paper or a pencil left behind. Whoever had cleaned it out had been very thorough.

I checked the bathroom next, and my conclusions from the crime scene photos were right. It was too small for anyone to hide in after the shooting. In fact, there was barely enough room for a toilet, a sink, and a small shower.

It was the small shower that bothered me. The wall was much deeper than the rest of the small bathroom. Deeper than it needed to be.

My ex-brother-in-law was a plumber. I had worked a few jobs with him from time to time when I'd first gotten married and money had been tight. I knew you needed some clearance in the wall for pipes and drains and things like that, but this was way too much space.

Something more than pipes was in that wall. I knocked on the tiles and all of them seemed solid. Whatever might be behind that wall couldn't be accessed from the shower.

I went back into the office and checked the bookshelves

against that same wall. Every shelf was empty. Not a speck of dust. I knocked on the wall behind them.

The back of one sounded different than the others. Not as hollow. I knocked on it again, only harder. The entire section of the bookcase, about one foot high by about a foot and a half wide popped open on a hinge. Framed by shelves above and below it, the door was almost impossible to see. With books on the shelves, it would've been completely hidden.

Walter Fairfax had been a very careful man indeed.

I pulled the small door all the way open. A gunmetal-colored safe door was right behind it, built into the wall. A dial for the combination lock, but no key.

I tugged on the handle, but it didn't budge. Locked. There'd been no mention of the safe in the police report, either, but I couldn't blame Hauser for this one. The cause of death was clear. Hauser had no reason to poke around looking for anything, much less a safe.

But I wondered if Mrs. Swenson knew about the safe. Or Trip. I wondered what might be in there, or if it had been cleaned out yet. Did it contain the bank accounts and leases I was looking for? Did it contain something else that tied Fairfax to Countess Alexandra? Or was it empty?

There was only one way to find out for certain. I had to find a way to open the damned thing.

I opened the office door just as Mrs. Swenson was just hanging up the phone. "Mr. Fairfax said he's on his way, Detective."

But I had other things on my mind. "Do you know the

combination to this safe?"

"What safe?" Her expression was genuine.

"The safe that's in the wall in bookshelf next to the bathroom."

She got up from her desk and went into the office to see for herself. I could tell she had never laid eyes on it before. She moved the wall panel back and forth on its hinge. "I had no idea this was even here."

"So you don't know the combination."

She looked at me like it was the dumbest question she'd ever heard. Maybe it was. "You really are a detective after all, aren't you?"

That made me smile. "I have my moments." I turned my attention back to the safe. "We've got to try to get this thing open. I need you to write down the month, day, and year of Mrs. Fairfax's birthday, his children's birthdays, and his anniversary for me while you're at it. Mr. Fairfax's birthday, too. He might've used them as the combination. Birthdays and anniversaries are the easiest to remember."

"You're the first man I've ever met who said that," she said. "I'll start making a list now. But if none of those combinations work, what then?"

"I've got some ideas," I admitted, "but it'll be a whole lot easier if one of those dates work."

A younger, sterner version of the picture I'd seen of Walter almost knocked Mrs. Swenson over as he barreled into the office. Trip had his father's flat face and dead eyes. Lucky for him, he had his mother's sharp features, which keep him just north of being ugly.

"How dare you come barging into my father's office like this?" Walter Fairfax, III yelled. "Get out of here right now before I throw you out!"

Mrs. Swenson quietly shut the door behind her as she made a tactical retreat.

I'd come up against his type before. All Ivy League swagger and no common sense. He'd probably been a tough guy back at Harvard or Princeton, but that had been more than a decade ago. Now he was just another doughy brat with a bank account and a snappy last name in a town lousy with doughy brats with snappy last names.

Now that it was just the two of us, I saw no reason to be polite for the sake of Mrs. Swenson. I crossed my arms across my chest and leaned against the bookcase. "The only one who barged in here was you. Your mother gave me permission to be here when she hired me this morning."

"I know all that!" He didn't look too happy about it, either. "I had tried talking her out of it, but Mother can be stubborn once she gets an idea in her head."

"I noticed that," I said. "Like the crazy idea she has about how your father couldn't have committed suicide because he didn't leave a note behind." I smiled. "But you and I both know he did, don't we, Trip?"

The younger Fairfax checked to make the door was closed and lowered his voice. "Who told you about that?"

I wouldn't let Mrs. Swenson take the blame. "It was mentioned in the draft police report that I got from an old friend of mine on the force. The same report that was written before Chief Carmichael wrote that beautiful piece of fiction calling your father's death an accident."

That took some of the fire out of him. "The family never asked him to do that."

"Well, he did it anyway," I said, "and now you owe him whether you like it or not. You'll have to deal with him eventually, but for now we've got bigger things to worry about, like that suicide note. Where is it?" I inclined my head toward the safe. "You tuck it in there for safe keeping?"

I could tell by the look on his face that it wasn't good news. "Is that a safe? I've never seen that before. My father never said anything about a safe. We don't even have one in the mansion."

That meant I'd have to handle the safe on my own. But for now, I cared more about the note. "Then give me the note."

It was Trip's turn to fold his arms. "Give me one good reason why I should tell you anything."

"Because I'll tell your mother that you've been hiding the note from her for the past month. And then I'll call Chief Carmichael and tell him you have it. Your mother will want to read it, and Carmichael will be furious you've got evidence he covered up a suicide. Both of them will keep tearing pieces out of you until you hand it over. It's even money on who wins, but I think your mother will win out." I smiled. "So just save yourself a lot of trouble and give me the goddamned note."

I stayed quiet while I watched him run through his options. He didn't have many, so I didn't have to wait long. When he looked away, I knew it wasn't good news. "I don't have it."

I pushed off the bookcase and took a step toward him. "Don't lie to me."

Trip took a step back. "I'm not lying. I told Chief Carmichael's man about the note when he got here. He took it with him when he left. A Detective Houseman, I think it was."

"Hauser." Of course. The son of a bitch.

"He said it was important evidence in the case and demanded that I hand it over immediately. Neither he nor Chief Carmichael ever brought it up again, so if you want to read it, you're going to have to ask them."

Of course Carmichael had the note. It proved his accident ruling was a lie. It gave him leverage to make sure the Fairfax family paid up when he told them to or else the world would get proof that Walter had killed himself. Sure, Carmichael would look bad if the note got out. But people would quickly forget about a botched police investigation. The stench of suicide would hang around the Fairfax family for a generation.

The suicide note had been a good lead while it lasted. I could've used it as leverage against Carmichael for years. But since he already had it, there was no way I'd ever see it. "Did you read the note before you gave it to Hauser?"

"Of course I read it," he said. "It was the last thing my father wrote. I could barely make out what it said because his hand must have been shaking badly when he wrote it. He normally had such beautiful penmanship."

I didn't want to lose my patience, but it was getting

tougher by the second. "What did it say?"

"It said, 'I'm sorry I had to do this. I had no choice.' That was all."

"I had no choice," I repeated. That phrase was important. It spoke to a distressed state of mind. But it didn't explain why Walter had decided to kill himself so suddenly. That last phone call from Miss Schmidt must have pushed him over the edge. It obviously caused him to call Dr. Blythe. Those two lines told me a little, but not enough. "I know it's painful, but do you have any idea what he was talking about?"

"How the hell should I know?" Trip's voice finally broke and his eyes watered over. "It was a suicide note, for God's sake, not his autobiography."

Trip's tears came on full force, washing away every trace of rage and anger he'd brought with him when he'd first barged into his father's old office. And that's when I remembered this was the very same place where his father had taken his own life.

Trip was a spoiled brat and a grown man, but he was also a son who had seen his father's corpse in the same space we were in now. He'd seen the terrible things left behind after someone sticks a gun in their mouth and pulls the trigger.

No child would ever be old enough to see their parent in that condition.

I might've had Mrs. Fairfax's permission to be there, but suddenly I felt like I was trespassing. But as much as I wanted to leave him alone with his grief, I still had one last question for him. "How about telling me what you found in the safe?"

Trip shook off his tears. "I didn't even know that safe existed until you showed it to me. My father treated this office like his private sanctuary. He didn't even like having meetings in here if he could avoid it, even with me. Mrs. Swenson probably knows about it. Why don't we ask her?"

A light knock came on the door as Mrs. Swenson eased the door open. She looked at Trip when she said, "Mrs. Fairfax is on the phone and would like to speak to Mr. Fairfax if it's convenient."

"Go talk to your mother if you want to," I said, "and ask her if she knows the combination to the safe if you get the chance. I'll ask the chief's office if we can have the note back. I know it means a lot to you and your family."

The natural punk in him returned. "Don't do me any favors, Doherty. Just remember that I have no intention of allowing my mother to be taken advantage of by some cheap gumshoe."

I let him have the last word. He'd earned it.

Now that it was just the two of us again, I asked Mrs. Swenson, "He always that cheerful?"

"He's under a terrible strain," she said. "He's normally—"

"Don't tell me," I said. "A kind and generous man. I know the drill. Any luck on getting those dates I asked for?"

She handed me a piece of paper and stood there while I worked the dial for the right combination. I tried all the dates. His wife's birthday. His daughter's birthday. His son's birthday. I even tried Walter's birthday.

None of them opened the safe.

"Can you think of any other numbers I should try?"

"No, but I can ask Mr. Fairfax if his mother might've had any suggestions."

"You do that," I said as I picked up the telephone on Mr. Fairfax's desk. The private line he must've used to call Dr. Blythe. It was one of those fancy new devices that had the ear- and mouthpieces connected to each other. "What time is it now and what time do you usually go home?"

She looked outside and checked the clock on her desk. "It's half past four now. I usually stay in the office until six or so. Why do you ask?"

The operator came on the line and I gave her the number I was looking for. I pressed the mouthpiece against my chest. "Because I'll be back here in about an hour with a guy who'll know how to get that safe open. I'd appreciate it if you were still here."

Chapter 7

It was going on five o'clock by the time I walked into The Stage Left Bar. Most people called the place Lefty's, back from when it had been one of the most popular speakeasies in town.

Before the Crash, you couldn't get near the place when a new show or play opened. Prohibition may have been the law of the land, but Manhattan considered itself an island and hadn't paid it much attention. Places like Lefty's only thrived in the years after the do-gooders outlawed booze.

Back then, Lefty's had been a sea of tuxedoes and top hats, minks and pearls, the place where the swells liked to slum before and after taking in a show. Cocktails and champagne flowed. Volstead could drop dead.

But a lot of things in this town had dried up since the Crash, and Lefty's had been one of them. These days, the place saw more roaches and rodents than black ties and feathered boas. It was just another worn-out gin mill huddled deep in an alley off West 45th Street where the glow of the bright lights of Broadway just didn't reach anymore.

Times were tough, and people had to worry about putting food on the table. They didn't have money to waste on things like plays and musicals anymore.

Some people had run out of things to care about. Those were the people who came to Lefty's now. It was more soup kitchen than hot spot; an old bus depot at the end of a long, dull ride. Prohibition was still the law, but Treasury agents didn't even raid the place anymore because it wasn't worth the trouble.

The bar drew a regular crowd of old stagehands and rope rats waiting for word about a new show that might open. Any show would do. They had been waiting a long time and would be waiting longer still. Superstition prevented the men from standing too close to each other. They kept enough distance between themselves for Lady Luck to stroll in and take her place at their side. It might sound silly to some, but superstition was all these men had since no one was making dreams like they used to anymore.

At the tables, a scattering of broken-down character actors with familiar faces and little else going for them pored over industry rags for anything that might resemble a job. Possibilities got circled with a stubby pencil.

The sorriest of the bunch were the press agents who nursed warm beers while eying the bank of phonebooths in the back, praying for that one call from the right client that would change everything. A call they knew would never come, but hope sprang eternal at Lefty's.

Add a few petty criminals and other undesirables into the mix, and you'd have a pretty good idea of what the dump was like when I got there that night.

I had no trouble spotting the man I'd come to see. Wendell Bixby was in his usual spot at the rear table by the phonebooth. He always sat facing the door.

People who didn't know any better might have figured Bixby for another red-nosed press agent who liked Lefty's for the cheap booze and charming company. Few people knew he actually owned the dump. The poor bastard had signed the papers the month before the market crashed in 1929. Now he was every bit as tied to the place as the people who crawled in for a drink every evening and crawled out of there at night with nowhere else to go. I was one of the few who knew he slept on a cot in the storeroom.

Bixby didn't bother looking up from his typewriter as I slid into the booth across the table from him. He was too busy typing out another column for the New York Journal. Bixby's Box was still the most influential gossip column in the city. Just because people couldn't afford to go out anymore didn't mean they didn't like to read about those who could.

No one in the city was beyond Bixby's reach, especially a city on its heels. He still found a way to scrape up enough money to pay the most for the best dirt on all the finest people. Socialites, captains of industry, actors, actresses, and politicians all fell under his scope. One mention in Bixby's Box could either start a career or stall it, depending on what nouns, verbs, and adjectives he stirred into the mix. A reference in a blind item at the end of his column was even better. Vagueness could be its own reward, and kept Bixby from being sued for libel.

Just about the only thing worse than being mentioned in his column was not being mentioned at all.

I couldn't remember the last time I'd seen Bixby anywhere other than Lefty's, even before he'd bought the place. That's because the information he put in his column always came to him here, either by one of the phones in the back or in person. A river of scandal and shortcomings flowed right past Bixby's dark perch in the back booth.

"Look at what the cat dragged in." Bixby's fingers flew across the typewriter keys. "Haven't seen you since New Year's."

I dug out a cigarette from my case and lit it. "Christmas. You were already shitfaced by the time I got here on New Year's."

"That's what you think, kid." Bixby winked. "I'm never as drunk as I'm supposed to be. What brings you down here with us common folk? Want to sell some dirt on your Park Avenue pals? Don't insult me by telling me you're not the kind who tells because I know better, remember?"

He certainly did. I used to feed him Carmichael-approved dirt back when I was on the force. Dirt that always served the chief's purposes in one way or the other.

Bixby had returned the favor by being one of the few scribes who'd stuck up for me during the whole Grand Central Massacre fiasco. The support had caused him a hell of a lot of trouble with his bosses at the paper, but he did it anyway. They didn't want to end up as a blind item in one of his columns, either. They never would've let him print it, of course, but they would have known he had something on them and the threat of exposure would be enough.

For a man who didn't have many good qualities, Wendell

Bixby had more than most.

I knew telling him anything about the Fairfax incident would be in the morning's paper, so I kept my mouth shut. But Countess Alexandra was a different matter entirely. "Suppose I asked you about a woman who goes by the name Countess Alexandra von Holstein."

Bixby made a show of yawning while he typed. "I'd have to put toothpicks under my eyes to keep them open. She's white toast, kid. No butter, no crust. She's one of those society gals who hobnobs with the kinds of people you work for these days. As dull as she is beautiful, and she's pretty goddamned dull." He quickly looked at me before going back to the keys. "Nice suit, by the way. Bonds?"

"Brooks Brothers."

He shook his right hand like he'd burned it. "Fancy. Anyway, I wouldn't pay for any dirt on the countess alone. Throw in something with her and a male friend of hers, preferably a married, wealthy male friend, and maybe I'd bite. Not too hard, mind you, but I'd throw a couple of bucks your way."

"What kind of men does she like, anyway?"

"The same kind women like her always like. The kind that have a bunch of zeroes after their last name. Word is she's from some hellhole in Europe, who came over here when her family lost the farm after the war. Got off the boat a year ago, poorer than my Aunt Ethel, and now she's got herself a nice place to hang her hat on Central Park West. Like the lady in the harbor says, 'Give me your tired, your huddled masses who used to have stables of polo ponies and servants and estates, yearning to be free.' Must've gotten herself a rich boyfriend or three to make the leap from refugee back to countess again. I'm not surprised, though. She's beautiful so I'm not surprised she's popular. Most of those leggy European types usually have a couple of studs in their stable, and your countess is leggier than most. Ever seen her?"

I shook my head as I took a drag.

"Then you're missing out on a complete life." Bixby sighed dramatically and went back to his typing. "Whoever she hooked must have deep pockets because, from what I've heard, she's one of the few people in town who isn't shy about shelling out the ducats."

"You said she's on Central Park West," I said. "I need an address."

Bixby laughed as he typed. "And I need my place at The Dakota back, along with all the money I lost on the market. I don't know where she lives." He stopped typing and looked at me. "But I can find out easy enough if you tell me why you want to know."

I let smoke escape my nose. "No way. I'll pay if you want, but nothing in the papers. Not yet, anyway."

Bixby frowned. "Information's the coin of my realm, kid. My readership is falling and my editors are thinking of cutting my column in half or, worse, they want me to go back to covering sports." He exaggerated a shiver. "I've seen Babe Ruth naked enough for one lifetime. No, thanks. Besides, I need the meager pittance the paper pays me in order to keep this dump open. You don't think these deadbeats pay their way, do you?"

I knew they didn't, but I also knew people still paid Bixby plenty to stay out of their columns, or to be placed in them. But there was no reason to make him angry. He was a friend and I needed him.

"Then what'll it take to make you interested enough to look for the countess?"

"Don't give me that hangdog look." He waved a crooked finger at me. A typist's finger. "The last time you came in here looking for dope on someone, it led to the Grand Central Massacre and one of the biggest scoops of my career. You only come to see your Uncle Wendell if it's something big, and I can sense whatever this is must be pretty damned big, so spill. You want an address, I want to know why you're interested in a broke aristocrat who runs around with a bunch of German intellectual types."

He smiled as soon as he said it. "See what I did there, you Irish bastard? I fed you something you didn't already know. I can tell by the look in your eyes." He pointed to his temple and went back to typing. "Uncle Wendell is always right. Tell me why you need to know where the countess hangs her tiara, or that's all you get from me."

I laughed at him as much as at myself. If anyone else had called me an Irish bastard, I would've kicked their teeth down their throat. But Bixby had a way of making even the worst insults sound like a compliment.

It was still too early to trade information for the countess, so I stalled. "Maybe I'll have something for you by tomorrow." I looked back at the crowd that had grown at the bar since I'd walked in. "In the meantime, let's get to the real reason why I'm here. Any of your distinguished customers any good with a safe?"

Chapter 8

I watched Billy Donohue squint as he placed his ear against the door of Walter Fairfax's wall safe. He was prison-pale and skinny, thanks to the slop they hash out in stir. He was ten days out of Sing Sing on a four-year bounce for possession of stolen property. The fact that he hadn't been put away for safecracking had left a deep scar on his professional pride.

"A guy like me with the skills I got, goin' away for somethin' as stupid as possession." His long fingers adjusted the dial as if he was adjusting a radio knob. "It ain't hardly fair, Charlie. It wasn't even my score. My brother, see? He—"

"Stow the tale of woe and work the safe." From her spot in the office doorway I could see Mrs. Swenson was getting nervous, and I couldn't blame her. Billy was the type of guy who made you want to take a shower. Fortunately, the rest of the office workers and staff on the floor had already gone home, otherwise Billy would've been the source of office gossip for days. At least Trip wasn't around, so that was one less headache for yours truly. "Can you open the goddamned thing or not?"

"Of course I can open it." He took a stethoscope from his tool bag, stuck the earpieces in his ears, and placed the bell against the safe. "Damned thing should be called an un-safe. Might as well have stuck whatever's in here in a shoebox and hid it in the closet. A blind newsy could crack it just by listening to the tumblers." He looked at Mrs. Swenson while his fingers worked the dial. "Bet whoever put this in here for you charged you plenty for it, too."

She was going to answer, but I motioned for her to ignore it. It just would've launched him into another defense of his professional pride.

Donohue went back to fiddling with the dial. "That's the problem with people in this business today. No one's got any professionalism anymore. No decency."

"A convicted safe cracker talking about decency," I said. "What's the world coming to?"

Donohue turned the tumbler for a third time, then grabbed the handle. "I went up for stolen property, remember?" He turned the handle down and the safe's door opened. "Never got pinched for safe crackin', Charlie."

I put my hand on the door to keep him from opening it all the way. I didn't know what was inside and I'd be damned if I'd let Donohue know, either. Everyone in Lefty's would know what he'd found within five minutes. Bixby would know even before that. What he didn't see couldn't hurt me or the Fairfax family.

I palmed him the money I'd promised him and nodded toward the office door. "There's what I owe you, plus a little extra to help you remember to forget how you earned it. Understand?"

"Come on, Charlie. If I was a talker, I would've ratted

out my cousin about all that stolen silverware he stashed at my place."

A minute ago, it was his brother. Now it was his cousin. That's why the safe door would stay shut until Donohue was gone. I looked back at Mrs. Swenson. "Please show Mr. Donohue to the elevators."

She didn't seem in a hurry to go. "Why don't you do it? He's your friend."

She'd changed in the hour or so since I'd gone to Lefty's. She was a little less flustered and showed a little more backbone. I wondered why. "Because I was hired to examine the contents of the safe, not you. Please show Mr. Donohue out."

She didn't seem to like that idea. "Whatever's in there is likely company property, which means—"

I gestured to Donohue behind his back. "Not in front of the baby, Mrs. Swenson. Get our guest on an elevator, make sure you ride all the way down with him, and come back. We'll examine the contents of the safe together."

"Of course." And that's when something came to me. It might not have been important, but I had to ask. "Say, Bill. You don't happen to remember the combination to the safe, do you?"

"Sure do," Donohue said. "I just done it, didn't I?" He cleared his throat like he was about to recite Shakespeare. "Four, twenty, eighty-nine."

I pulled out my notebook and wrote the numbers down before I forgot them. Looking at them didn't make them mean anything to me. It wasn't Fairfax's address. It didn't match any of his family's birthdays, either. Maybe it was the countess' birthday. Maybe it didn't mean anything, but I'd keep it in the back of my mind just in case.

I signaled Mrs. Swenson to take Donohue to the elevator. As much as I didn't want Donohue seeing what was inside, I didn't want Mrs. Swenson seeing it either. I didn't have any reason not to trust her, but I didn't have a reason to, either.

The second she was out of sight, I opened the door.

Inside, I found a thick pile of books and papers, all neatly stacked in size-order like a pyramid, tied together by an old string. It looked like Walter kept everything in order, even his secrets.

I pulled the bundle out of the safe and brought it over to the desk. I undid the string and quickly went through the stack. It was everything I had expected to find in an insurance man's safe. A ledger. Bank statements. Stock certificates. Receipts. Deeds to various properties listing Mr. Walter Fairfax, Jr. as the owner. I bet some of the things he'd given Countess Alexandra were in there. I had hit the jackpot. I would've immediately begun examining everything if it hadn't been for something else that didn't belong.

It was a worn leather notebook, bulging with papers, secured by rubber bands wrapped around it.

I'd just started to undo the rubber bands when I noticed Mrs. Swenson was already back at the doorway. She didn't look happy.

"I thought we agreed you'd wait."

"And I thought we'd agree you'd ride down to the lobby

with Billy to make sure he left. If he got off on another floor and starts ripping tenants off, that's on you."

"You don't give a damn about that." She folded her arms across her chest. "You just wanted me out of the way so you could look over what you found in that safe. Well, what was in there?"

I wasn't sure what I had, but I knew I wanted to review it alone before Mrs. Swenson or anyone else could see it. I put the notebook on top of the pile. "Your guess is as good as mine. I'm going to need a bag to carry all of this stuff in."

"No," she said. "We can take all the time we need to examine everything right here. I'm in no hurry at all. When we're done, we can put everything right back in the safe."

I sat back in the chair and looked at her, really looked at her for the very first time since I'd met her that afternoon. There really was something different about her; a confidence and strength that hadn't been there before. I wasn't sure I liked what I saw. Not because I liked my women weak, but because the change was pretty sudden. "You mean put it back in the safe you now know the combination to? Sorry. No dice. A bag, please."

"Stop being so dramatic." She folded her arms and leaned against the doorframe, showing more curves than I knew she'd had. She even threw in a smile. "We're all on the same side, aren't we, Mr. Doherty?"

But I wasn't so sure anymore. Something had changed. "Are we, Mrs. Swenson?"

"It's not Mrs. Swenson," she said. "It's Miss Swenson. Sarah Swenson. Mr. Fairfax thought his wife would be jealous if she knew a single woman was working for her husband, so he thought calling me Mrs. Swenson would be better for all concerned."

Given what I knew about Fairfax's history, I couldn't blame her. "In that case, my name's Charlie, not Mr. Doherty. And I'm still going to need that valise, Sarah, because no one's seeing anything in this pile until I've had a chance to review it."

She opened her mouth to say something, but the lights went out.

***

It was after six o'clock and just past dusk. Some natural light still filtered through the windows there in Walter's office, but the rest of the floor was pitch-black. All the doors to the exterior offices were closed and all the secretaries had gone home.

"That damned fuse again," Sarah said. "Goes out all the time."

But I wasn't so sure. Everything had gone dark at a damned convenient time; too convenient for it to be an accident. I quickly gathered the ledgers and statements back into one pile and tied them up again with the string. I picked up the phone on the desk, but couldn't get an outside line. We were trapped.

"We've got to get the hell out of here. Get me something to put these in and do it fast."

She was as calm as I was anxious. "I'm sure there's nothing to be concerned about. It's just a fuse. Happens all the time. I'll just go check the fuse box myself. It's up by the elevators on the left. I know my way around here in the dark like I know the back of my own hand. It won't take more than—"

"Damn it, do you have a bag or don't you?"

She took a step back toward the door. "No, I don't. But if you're concerned, put the documents back in the safe."

Since that's what she wanted me to do, that would be the last thing I would do. "If a hack like Billy could get it open, whoever pulled that fuse might be able to open it, too. Now start looking for a—"

I shut up quick when I heard something get knocked over somewhere in the pitch darkness of the office. Something small, like a picture frame off a desk, but loud enough for us to hear it.

Now I was sure someone had killed those lights on purpose.

I gathered up the bundle and shut the office door. I tried to lock it but, just my luck, no lock on this side. Whoever was out there had just been plunged into total darkness. At least we were all on a level playing field.

I kept my voice low as I took Sarah's arm and whispered. "We've got to get out of here as fast and quiet as possible. You said you know your way around the office in the dark. Is that true?"

She nodded quickly.

"When I open this door, we're going to go outside and I'm going to shut it quickly behind us. We'll be in the dark, too, but so will they. You're our advantage. You're going to lead us to a stairway door and we're going to head down several floors and grab the elevator there. Not the elevator on this floor, do you understand? Not the elevator. That'll give away our position. Understand?"

She whispered that she did. I pushed the awkward bundle higher into my armpit and grabbed the doorknob. "My hand will be on your shoulder the entire time. Let's go."

***

I opened the door just wide enough for us to slip through, then shut it behind us. I knew we weren't fooling anyone. Since I didn't have a gun, we only had one play to make and that was to make a run for it. I just hoped she knew her way as well as she said she did.

I placed my hand on Sarah's shoulder and nudged her forward. I didn't like keeping her out front like that, but she was the only one who knew how to get us to safety. With my left hand on her shoulder, I used my right to cradle the bundle under my left. It was bound tight enough to use as a weapon if I needed to. It should be enough to knock someone off their feet, especially in the darkness.

I heard something brush against the wall to the left. Whoever was in here with us was using the wall as a guide, while we moved between the rows of desks. I couldn't tell how far we had moved but we hadn't knocked anything over or run into anyone else, so all was good for now.

Then I heard something move directly in front of us. A snap of cartilage or bone popping. An innocent enough sound in daily life, but deadly in the dark.

I moved Miss Swenson behind me as I lifted the bundle above my head and brought it down blind, as hard as I could.

It felt like it connected with a shoulder, not a head. It was hard enough, though, to send whomever I'd hit tumbling backwards, knocking over desk phones and lamps and papers.

I tucked the bundle back under my arm and pushed Miss Swenson in front of me, my hand on her shoulder, hoping she'd stay calm and lead us out of there as quietly as possible.

She took a hard left and I could sense we were in a clear part of the office. She opened a stairwell door, temporarily blinding us with the light.

I shut the door behind me as I heard more sounds of things being knocked over in the darkness. They knew where we were and headed our way. It would only be a matter of time before they followed us. I couldn't keep the door shut forever, especially if they had guns.

Sarah was already halfway down to the next landing, beckoning me to follow her. "Hurry! We don't have time."

My eyes had adjusted to the light by then and I saw the one thing that could buy us some time.

I tossed the bundle down to her and she surprised me by catching it. "What are you doing?" she yelled. "Let's go!"

I pulled a length of firehose coiled in the stairwell and drew it across the landing, wrapping it low around the newel post just above the first step of the landing. It wasn't tight but the canvas hose was just heavy enough to make someone trip, especially if they were running from darkness into the light.

I hopped over the hose and ran down the steps to grab Miss Swenson before she got too far. I took the bundle back from her. "I'll stay here. You keep going down until you find an elevator. Get downstairs and have them call the cops."

"Why are you staying here? This is crazy."

"Because I need to know who—"

The stairway door burst open and one of the men bolted into the stairwell. A bald, square-faced man in a gray overcoat. He squinted into the light, just as I had done, but was running. He tripped over the hose, falling face first like a log on the landing before crumpling over onto his back. The dumb bastard was out cold.

A second man came through the door and followed suit, this time tumbling as he hit each of the steps until he fell into his friend.

It was Blondie, the same punk who'd gotten away from me twice that day.

Sarah shrieked as I bounded back up the stairs and kicked Blondie in the gut as he tried to get to his feet. "Who sent you?"

He muttered something familiar that I couldn't understand. I couldn't hear what it was. I grabbed his neck with my free hand and slammed his head against the stair. "Who sent you, goddamn it?"

"Nein," came the response.

A gunshot boomed from the stairwell door above me, a blind shot fired by a blind man who knew his friends were in trouble but couldn't see. The bullet hit the wall feet above me, but since I didn't have a gun, I did the only thing I could do. I grabbed Miss Swenson and down we ran.

Five floors down we found an open door that led us to a

common lobby, where we caught the elevator down to the ground floor.

I told the men in the lobby what had happened upstairs and waited while they called the police.

When the boys in blue got there, I showed them my retiree badge, which cut down on the hassle. They searched the building but came up empty.

But the cops had Miss Swenson and me. And they wanted us to make a statement.

So much for a quiet evening at home.

Chapter 9

I had been in the midtown station house more times than I could count. I'd once been assigned there when Chief Carmichael put me out to pasture, shagging fly balls on the graveyard shift, praying I'd have enough pride to quit. I was too proud to give him the satisfaction.

The station house had been a miserable building since my first days on the force, and the years had not been kind. It was always damp and humid, even in the dead of winter. Someone always had a fan going, even on Christmas Eve. The paint that hadn't peeled had faded, pipes leaked, the walls were moldy, and the only thing bigger than the rats were the cockroaches, which seemed to be the only creatures that thrived in the environment.

In fairness, my ex-partner Loomis gave the roaches a run for their money when it came to attachment to the place. He rarely went home, often coming in earlier and leaving later than he had to. The job was his life.

He was busy questioning Sarah in another part of the station house while he let me write out my statement at his desk. I guessed it was professional courtesy, seeing as we had been partners not too long ago. I knew it would take a while for Sarah to calm down enough to make any sense, much less for Loomis to get a statement out of her.

After writing up my statement, I used his phone to make a call that was suddenly long overdue.

I called Mr. Van Dorn at the Washington, D.C. number he had given me. I didn't know why he was in Washington, just that he spent a lot of time down there, especially after Roosevelt had become president. They'd gone to Groton together and had remained close ever since, so I figured that might be the reason. But Mr. Van Dorn didn't give me any details, and it was none of my business anyway.

"Charlie," he boomed when he came on the line. "Your timing couldn't be better. How did everything go with Mrs. Fairfax?"

I gave him a rundown on everything that had happened that day. The list Mrs. Fairfax had given to me. The two attempts on my life. The kid I had found following me in Times Square. My conversation with Dr. Blythe. The news about Countess Alexandra von Holstein. The contents of Walter's safe. The people who'd attacked me in Fairfax's office, Blondie being among them.

I got the feeling he was taking notes the whole time, but I couldn't be sure.

Mr. Van Dorn didn't say a word until I was done. That's the way he worked. He never asked questions until it was all out in the open. When he figured I was done, he asked his questions in his own way. And he never forgot anything I told him, either, even when I thought he had.

"Sounds like we've gotten someone's attention. I had heard about the shooting on the news, but I didn't know you were involved. You may have wanted to let me know about that earlier."

That was as close to yelling as Mr. Van Dorn ever got. He never said I was wrong or raised his voice, only that he wished I'd considered another way to do something. "I know, sir, but things were happening pretty fast and, seeing as no harm was done, I figured I should go about my business. Next time, I'll call right away."

"I think that's best, considering everything that's happening. This seems to be a far more complicated matter than we originally thought. They must have followed you to the mansion and for some time afterward in order to catch up with you twice. That shows some level of organization on their part."

I put my feet up on Loomis's desk. "That's what bothers me, sir. I don't know if I was lucky or these clowns are lousy at this kind of thing."

"I'm afraid I don't follow you, Charlie."

"Take the shooting on the street this morning," I explained. "Those guys didn't just have a guy with a Tommy gun in the Ford. They had Blondie as a backup on the street, too. He could've shot me dead when the Tommy gun missed. But he just ran past me when he saw I was alive, and got in the car. Why was he even there in the first place? And tonight, in the office, at least one of them had a gun. They didn't have to kill the lights. They could've rushed the office and shot me if they'd wanted to. But why would they have wanted to? Why were they there at all? If they wanted me dead, they could've taken another run at me on the street, but they risked coming into the building instead. And killing the lights like they did. There's just something off about the whole damned thing."

"Yes," Mr. Van Dorn agreed. "I see your point now."

"And here's the topper. I grabbed one of the guys who came after me at the office. Blondie again. I think he was speaking German."

Mr. Van Dorn was silent a beat longer than normal. "German. You're sure?"

"He'd busted his head when he fell and was spouting a lot of gibberish, so the only word I heard clearly was nein. But the rest of it sounded close enough to German to me. I heard enough of it in France to know."

I heard his tone change. "I take it you didn't have your gun with you today."

"No. I didn't want to bring it to the old lady's house, and I hadn't gotten back to my place all day. But that's going to change as soon as I get back home."

"A wise policy. They've learned as much about us as we've learned about them today. They won't be as reckless next time, and you'll need to be prepared. Tell me what you found in Walter's safe."

I pulled the bundle over to me and began sorting through it. "Some receipts from private jewelers for pieces he had made over the past couple of months. Bank statements for a couple of accounts that he set up with Countess Alexandra's name on them. Judging by the size of the deposits and withdrawals on the account, looks like it takes a lot to make that woman happy."

"Prussian countesses aren't known for frugality, Charlie, especially the poor ones. How much did he give her?"

"Based on what I've read in the ledger I found, it looks like he gave her a million dollars in 1932 and a million and a half so far this year, sir."

I heard Mr. Van Dorn stop writing. "Two and a half million dollars in less than a year? That buys an awful lot of happiness."

I went through my pile again. "I've got a lease here in Walter's name for an apartment on Central Park West, dating back to nine months ago. He seems to have signed it over to her on the same day. I've also got bank statements that show a lot of charges from furriers, hat makers, and it looks like she spends more money on clothes than the army spends on bullets."

I heard Mr. Van Dorn resume writing. "Looks like Walter got himself quite an expensive pet."

"Doesn't seem to be shy about throwing it around, either. It looks like Walter has donated about a million to one group in particular. The Friends of New Germany. There are also deeds for properties he's bought in Sussex, New Jersey, and places I've never heard of here in New York. Probably upstate."

"What's the name?"

I fumbled as I tried as best as I could with the pronunciation. "Yaphank."

"That's not upstate," Mr. Van Dorn explained. "That's Long Island. What kind of properties has he bought?"

I read through the documents. "Seems just to be vacant

land according to what I can see."

I heard Mr. Van Dorn write that down, too. "Interesting. We'll see if we can find a way to get you to meet Alexandra at the Stuyvesant Society gala tomorrow night. I checked, and it seems she'll be there tomorrow night. Bought her own ticket, too. By the way, I understand Dr. Blythe had already arranged for you to attend."

He remembered. "Good, because there something else I found in the safe that he might be able to help me with."

"Tell me."

I opened the last part of the bundle. "It's a leather notebook, pretty beat up. The spine's half worn out and the whole thing is held together with rubber bands. I tried to make sense of it, but it seems to be written in a couple of different languages."

"What languages?"

"Looks like German. Walter knew German, so it probably is, but the handwriting is so elaborate it's tough to say for sure. There are also several pages with strange symbols that I can't figure out."

"Symbols? What do they look like?"

"Like letters. Maybe Greek, but crooked. There's also some writing in some of the margins that's tough to make out as well. Damned thing gives me the creeps."

"Yes." I heard Mr. Van Dorn tapping his pencil on the other end of the phone. He sounded distant, almost distracted. "Yes, this is good work, Charlie. Very good work; better than I expected." He quickly added, "No insult to your abilities as an investigator, of course. I just didn't expect to find so much in one place."

"I guess insurance guys like to keep things orderly." I closed the notebook and slipped the rubber bands back around it. "Too bad none of this junk explains why Walter killed himself."

"Don't be so sure." Before I could ask him what he meant by that, he said, "Lock these documents in the safe we installed in your office tonight. I'll send someone around to collect them in the morning so they can be brought down here to me in Washington, but I want you to keep the notebook."

I caught that. "Someone? Who?"

"Someone who also works for me from time to time. He'll introduce himself as a Mr. Wallace. Give him everything else, but keep the notebook."

I thought he would've wanted me to hunt down where Countess Alexandra was staying, not the notebook. "Are you sure, sir?"

"I can examine the financial materials and leases on my own," he said, "but we need to know the significance of the notebook you found. There's an old friend of mine who might be able to make sense of it. He's a Jesuit up at Fordham University, named Father Mullins. He's something of a genius when it comes to languages. I'll call and tell him you'll be by to see him tomorrow. Shall I say nine o'clock in the morning?"

"Sure, but—"

"Consider it scheduled. In the meantime, see if you can't pull some strings and have a policeman take you and

Miss Swenson home. With our German friends running around, I'd like to make sure you and the materials are safe. And don't forget your gun tomorrow, even when you go to meet Father Mullins. You'll find he's no stranger to firearms himself. He's led quite an interesting life. Good night, Charlie, and don't forget to call in tomorrow after you meet with Father Mullins. I'll be most interested in hearing what he has to say."

The line went dead just as a couple dozen questions came to me. I supposed that was by design. Mr. Van Dorn rarely did anything by accident. He'd given me my orders and that's all there was to it.

I drummed my fingers on the bundle as I thought over what Mr. Van Dorn had said. Who was this other guy working for Mr. Van Dorn? I wasn't the jealous type, but I liked to know who was on the team. What the hell was so important about an old notebook, and what would an old priest know about it? This whole thing was complicated enough without getting the Church involved.

"Get your goddamn feet off my desk."

Floyd Loomis's deadpan voice shook me out of my thoughts. He was a gaunt, lanky guy who always looked like he needed a bath and a shower, but rarely took either. He was a damned good detective, though, who paid attention to detail. I'd asked him to join me when I went private, but he turned me down flat. He didn't say much and missed even less. That's why I wanted to talk to him about why his report on the Fairfax case was so incomplete.

But first things first. "How's Miss Swenson?"

"She's fine." He motioned for me to sit up so he could get his suit jacket from the back of his chair. "Come on. I'm giving both of you a ride home."

I'd been preparing myself for a long night under the lights in an interrogation room, so I wasn't complaining. I retied my bundle instead. "I thought you'd want to take my statement."

He looked at what I had written down. "You signed it. That's good enough for me. I'll type it up later and sign your name to it." He shrugged into his jacket and didn't bother to flatten his collar. "Besides, I got enough from your lady friend to fill the phone book. Sounds like a hell of an ordeal, Charlie. What the hell were you two doing up in Fairfax's office of all places?"

I saw no reason to lie, especially to Floyd. "I had a friend open a safe. We didn't expect a couple of goons to try to rob the place. At least, that's my theory."

"Not much of a theory. All we found was a bullet hole in the stairwell and some blood on the treads. Whoever was there did a good job of making themselves scarce before we got there."

That didn't make sense. "No one saw them leave?"

"That's what they tell me. Even checked with the freight operator to see if he saw anyone escaping, and he said he didn't. Fat bastard's asleep half the time, so if you're looking for a way they got out, that'd be my bet." Loomis frowned. "Say, what the hell are you digging around this Fairfax business anyway?"

"His wife hired me to look into why her husband died."

"That one's easy. A bullet to the brain does the trick every time."

"She wants to know why, Floyd, not what."

He looked at me while he dug a cigarette from the pack in his coat pocket. "You're not taking advantage of her, are you, Charlie? I don't think much of you, but I'd think even less of you if you stooped that low."

That's what I loved about Loomis. No punches pulled. "Don't worry. She knows my opinion of the case. Even used your file as evidence, not that dime store version Carmichael created."

Loomis looked around while he brought a bony finger to his lips. "Pipe down, stupid. The chief's got eyes and ears everywhere these days."

"The hell do I care? He can't touch me now."

"Yeah, but he can do plenty to me just for talking to you. And if he ever found out I fed you that file, he'd have me in front of a judge in a heartbeat."

I hadn't thought about that. "Sorry, Floyd."

"You're a walking apology," he said as he beckoned me to follow him down the hall. "Come on. I've got the Swenson woman in Room B down the hall. We'll pick her up and I'll run you both home." He thumbed a match alive and grinned as he brought it to his cigarette. "You might get lucky tonight. She says she's too afraid to go home alone after all that's happened. Said she wants to see if she can stay with you. Asked me to see if you'd mind, seeing as how we're old partners and all."

"My place?" I said as I tucked the bundle back under my

113

arm.

He looked at me over his shoulder as we walked. "Don't look so disappointed. She's not bad looking. Seems harmless enough."

That was my problem, I thought. The most dangerous ones always did. "I found out a few things that weren't in your initial report. Like how Fairfax had a wall safe and that he had a private phone line in his office. Made a call to his doctor right before he did the deed."

Loomis shrugged. "Didn't know about the phone call or the safe because I didn't have a reason to look. Didn't have time, either. I'd just gotten there on my way home from the night shift, when Hauser showed up and told me to go home. I wrote what I saw in the file and gave it to the captain. He said Carmichael's office had come to a different conclusion and told me to back off, so I backed off. They ruled it an accident. Shot himself while cleaning his gun. How the barrel accidentally wound up in his mouth or how the trigger got accidentally pulled is beyond me, but that's the way the chief saw it and that's good enough for me."

I felt a spark of anger. "You saw your duty and you did it, right?"

Loomis stopped walking. "This coming from a guy who spent his career as a bag man for the boys downtown."

"This is different. I'm different. You know that."

"All I know is that not everyone can be a crusader like you, Charlie. Not everybody's got the same pile of dirt you've built up on half the department, either. I know it was a straight-up suicide. I also know I probably wouldn't have looked for an extra phone line or a wall safe even if Hauser hadn't pulled me off the case. Why? Because Fairfax blew his brains out. If he'd been any other schnook on the street, no one would ask twice, but he's got money and a name so Carmichael did his family a favor. Now, they're trying to make it into a mystery. Best to leave well enough alone if you ask me, especially with Carmichael involved. He likes gratitude, not questions."

I knew all that. It's what I didn't know that bothered me. "Doesn't explain why Fairfax did it, though."

"People off themselves all the time, Charlie. Christ, you know that."

We started walking again. "I thought so, too, until people started trying to kill me today." I forgot I hadn't told him about the shooting on Fifth Avenue, but since he seemed to think I was only talking about what happened in the Fairfax offices I skipped it. "There's something about this mess that someone doesn't want me to find out, but I don't know what."

"Smart thing to do would be to tell the old lady to concentrate on mourning her husband. Best for her." He poked me in the chest. "Best for you, too. Because when Carmichael finds out you're involved in one of his pet cases, he's not going to be happy. He's expecting a nice payday from the family for the favor he did them. You do anything to queer that, he'll make you pay. He hates you, Charlie. He came out looking bad after that Grand Central Massacre business turned on him, and he'd love nothing more than to hang you for something. Be smart and walk away."

I smiled. "Too bad I ain't smart."

"Can't say I didn't warn you." He stopped outside Room B and rapped on the door. "At least you'll have someone to keep you warm tonight while you think it over."

The bundle under my arm felt a little heavier as my mind began to make a lot of connections I didn't like. "Yeah. Lucky me."

Chapter 10

No one had trailed us as Loomis dropped us off at the brownstone the Van Dorn family let me live in.

It was a ground floor apartment with a nice garden in the back that I normally enjoyed, but given the day I'd been having, it was something of a liability. The glass doors made it easy for some of my new friends to take a potshot at me. So while Miss Swenson took a shower, I made sure the doors were locked and the curtains drawn.

I'd outfitted the place with two safes. The one in the wall next to my bookshelf was for show. My clients liked to see their most sensitive information was secure.

The safe I used for the important stuff had been laid into the floor under the rug beneath my desk. I'd gotten the idea from an ex-enforcer for the Doyle mob who had a similar setup in his place at The Longford Lounge. That's where I placed the bundle I'd taken from Fairfax's office.

That nagging feeling I'd gotten outside of Room B back at the station house hadn't left me, so I decided to give something a try.

I unlocked my desk and pulled out my ledger and some bank statements of my own. I even added an old case notebook to the bundle and tied it together with string. I left it in the center of my desk so Sarah could see it. Maybe my nagging feeling was just nerves, but it didn't hurt to be sure.

I pulled out my old service revolver, too, and began cleaning it. The long-barrel .38 revolver wasn't the most powerful handgun out there, but it was what I'd been using for years. A .45 had too much kick for me, and the damned things tended to jam. I was a damned good shot with a .38, so I stuck with what I knew.

I was still cleaning the pistol when I heard my bedroom door open. Miss Swenson stepped out wearing one of my shirts, showing surprisingly long, white legs that were just this side of pale. Her hair was down and her glasses were gone. She looked closer to thirty now, or even late twenties. The eyes I'd thought to be brown behind her glasses were actually a rich amber. She didn't look particularly fetching or shy, but had an open expression like she was ready to take a letter for me.

I didn't mind her borrowing my shirt without asking. I minded the view even less, but I couldn't help thinking of a term baseball announcers used on the radio during a game.

Here's the wind up…

"I hope you don't mind me borrowing your shirt," she said. "I couldn't bear to put my things back on. Not after everything that happened. Not just yet."

I set the unloaded gun aside and closed the cylinder. "Think nothing of it. How are you feeling?"

"Better. The shower helped." Her eyes flicked to the bundle on my desk, then back to me. "Thank you again for letting me stay with you tonight. I didn't want to be alone.

I'll admit the whole thing made me more than just a little scared."

And here's the pitch.

"It's not everyday people try to kill you." I decided to try something. "You take the bed; I'll stand watch out here in case our friends take another run at us."

She brought her hand to her chest, showing an outline of her bosom I hadn't seen before. "You don't think we were followed, do you? Detective Loomis said he was careful."

"And he was. But I didn't know they'd followed me before, so they may have followed me now. He's arranged for a car to swing by every thirty minutes to check things over, just to be safe."

She let out the breath she'd been holding. "That's a relief. He's a good man, Detective Loomis."

"Yes, he is. Better than most. Why don't you try to get some sleep? I can put new sheets on the bed if you want."

She looked into the bedroom, then back at me. "Well, if we're reasonably safe, I don't see why you should give up your bed. I'm already putting you out by staying here. I can sleep on the couch out here. It looks very comfortable."

It actually was. The leather couch was one of the few concessions Mrs. Van Dorn allowed me to have when I moved into the place. The rest of the furnishings had all been her doing. It was a bit too fancy for my taste, but I didn't complain.

I made a point of setting my gun on top of the bundle and came out from behind the desk. "Okay, if you insist. I'll just get some sheets from the bathroom and—"

She popped up on her toes and kissed me on the lips. I kissed her back.

She gently slipped her hands around my head as if to keep me there, but I had no intention of moving away. As we kissed she took one step back into the bedroom, and so did I.

Strike three on the outside corner. Doherty caught looking.

Maybe, but it was just the first inning and I still had more at bats coming. And it had just gotten a whole lot more interesting.

Chapter 11

She groaned as she dug her nails into my shoulders, grinding herself down against me. Shuddering. The blue veins in her long, white neck pulsed as she threw her head back, moaning deeper and deeper until she climaxed again. She held herself like that, frozen above me in a moment of ecstasy, before gently collapsing onto my chest, panting.

Her damp skin felt good against mine as a cool breeze seeped through the window. Moonlight cast jagged shadows from the blinds across the bedclothes and along her naked back. Her breathing slowed to a quiet contentment, matching the rhythm of my own. My bedroom was post-sex quiet, that gentle twilight time when there's nothing more to say or do but lie there because it's all been said and done.

Sex can stir up a lot of emotion in two people. It can also bring a certain clarity with it, too. And at that moment I was thinking clearer than I had all day.

I wished the fog had stayed for a little while longer.

She moaned as she slowly slid off me to my left, her body still flat against me. She gently trailed her nails across my chest as I reached for my cigarette box on the nightstand. I lit one and gave it to her, then one for myself. I put the ashtray on my belly. I hated ashes in bed.

She ran her tongue along my neck before taking a drag. "My God, Charlie. That was wonderful."

She felt soft and warm against me. Soft and warm enough for me to wish all of this was more than what it really was.

I flicked my ash into the ashtray on my stomach. "I probably shouldn't have taken advantage of you like that. People's emotions are usually all over the place after they go through what we did tonight."

She nipped at my neck. "Well, if you'll remember correctly, I'm the one who took advantage of you that last time."

I put my arm around her shoulders and she let me pull her closer to me. Her hair was soft and smelled like rose water. "Yes, you did. And I didn't mind one bit."

She wrapped her free arm around me just as tight and whispered, "That makes me happy."

I took another drag on my cigarette. "Know what would make me happy?"

She laughed. "I think I have a pretty good idea, though I don't think you're quite ready yet."

I laughed, too. "I was thinking of something else. Like you telling me why you set me up back at the office."

She was quicker than I'd expected her to be. She slid right across me and bolted from the bedroom, stark naked. At least I managed not to spill my ashtray.

I stubbed out my cigarette and swung my legs out of bed. I pulled my bathrobe off the back of the bedroom door and wrapped it tight. I figured at least one of us should be dressed for the occasion.

I walked into the living room and flicked on the light. She already had the bundle in her left hand and my .38 in her right. She looked something close to beautiful in the dim light, even while aiming my own gun at me. "You take one step closer, I'll kill you."

I leaned against the doorframe. "Just like you killed Fairfax?"

"I didn't kill him. He did that himself. The rest of this doesn't concern you. Now, go back inside and throw me my clothes. If you come out with anything more than my clothes, you're a dead man."

She tracked me with my pistol as I took a cigarette out of the box on the table and lit it. "I guess I should've lit one for you, too, but we're past romance now, aren't we?"

She raised the gun so it was pointed at my head. "Just because I didn't shoot Fairfax doesn't mean I won't shoot you. Get my clothes."

I sat on the couch instead. "You're not going to shoot anyone. It's not loaded. Squeeze the trigger if you don't believe me."

The bitch actually did just that, and was surprised when it clicked. She squeezed it five more times just to prove it was empty.

I blew smoke in her direction. "You can put the bundle back on the desk, too. If you look closely, you'll see it's my stuff, not Fairfax's."

She threw the gun at me, but luckily it hit the couch and not one of the expensive knickknacks Mrs. Van Dorn had placed around the office.

Sarah looked at the bundle and slammed it down on the desk. "Damn you!"

"Why? For figuring you were up to something? That's just common sense, but I'll give you high marks for effort."

She dropped into my desk chair and covered herself with her arms. "If you touch me, I'll scream."

I laughed for the first time since I could remember. "Go ahead. Somebody might hear you. Hell, they might even call the cops. I'll have a hell of a story to tell them once they get here."

She must've realized I was right, and sank further into the chair. "I didn't kill Mr. Fairfax."

"I didn't think you did. But you're wrapped up in this somehow and I want to know how. Don't bother lying to me, either, or I'll call Loomis. And I promise he won't be as gentle as he was before. You're in a hell of a lot of trouble, Miss Swenson."

"How dare you call me that," she snapped. "Not after what we just did."

"After you just fired an empty gun at me, let's stick to formality. Now, start talking. And don't bother lying, because we're way beyond that."

She looked around like she was trying to find a way out. If she got off the chair, I would've stopped her, but she was smart enough to stay where she was. Realizing she was stuck, she said, "You need to know that what happened between us wasn't part of it. You have to believe me. I really was terrified. I still am. That's how this all started in the first place."

I wasn't sure I believed her, but I didn't need to. "Go on."

"I…I've got a kid."

"So what?"

"So, I had him young. Too young to be married and too young to take care of him on my own. Get the picture?"

It was a picture I'd seen many times before. "Go on."

"I put him in boarding school, and worked my fingers to the bone to keep him there. Became a damned good secretary, and got a good job working for Mr. Fairfax."

It was all coming into focus. "Was that your cover story to get close to Fairfax?"

"It's not a cover story, damn it. It's the truth, and I'd been working for him for years before all of this happened."

"Tell me. And don't lie or I'll know it, and I won't be happy."

"A year ago, I got a letter in the mail with a picture of my boy at school. It was a picture of him sleeping, Charlie, in his bedroom that he shares with three other boys. I don't know how they got it, but they did. The letter was blank but there was a note on the back photo, with a phone number. That's all. It didn't have to say anything more than that. I understood what I had to do."

Smart girl. "What then?"

"I called the number, and the guy on the other end told me as long as I did what they said, my boy wouldn't be hurt. He said they'd already gotten into his room once and would do it again, only this time they'd hurt him."

A single tear ran down her right cheek, but she wasn't weeping. "That kid's my whole life, Charlie. He's about the only good thing I've ever done. I wasn't going to let anything happen to him."

I flicked my ash and took another drag. So far, I believed her. The story was just bland enough to be possible. "Let me guess. They wanted you to spy on Fairfax."

She nodded quickly. "They wanted me to report on everything he did. Who called him, who he called, who he met, where he went, who wrote to him, and who he sent letters to. They wanted information on the company, on his finances, pretty much anything I could get my hands on. Since he had everything sent to the office, even his personal matters, I had a lot to give them. They knew about it, too."

"How did you give them what they wanted?"

"They gave me a post office box where I mailed everything. I never met anyone or spoke to anyone on the phone again."

Whoever was playing her was smart. She couldn't identify them if she'd never met them. "This has been going on for a year?"

She nodded. "A few months later, he started in with this new woman he was seeing. He always had a girlfriend and never brought them around the office, but I always knew what he was doing based on his financial statements. I handled his personal bills, too."

I'd heard this kind of thing before. Somebody finds a weakness, in Sarah's case it was her kid, uses it to get information, and uses said information against a target. Usually it was part of a con job, but this was much more than a simple confidence game. "I guess you kept doing this right up until the day he shot himself."

"And after. They sent me another letter, telling me they

still wanted to know what was going on in the company. I still worked in the chairman's office, so I still had access to a lot of information. I wrote a letter in one of my reports, begging them to let me stop and keep me and my son out of it. They sent a letter back with one word on it. 'No.'"

Interesting. "What about the day he killed himself? Did you lie about that to the police? To me?"

"No. It all happened exactly as I told you and told Loomis and that other detective, Hauser. I haven't lied about any of that, I swear. They didn't tell me to, either."

Again, I believed her. "The German lady who called Fairfax that morning wasn't the same voice on the phone?"

Her expression softened a bit. "That was a man. He had a similar accent, but I didn't think anything of it until you mentioned it just now." She looked at me. "You think they're in on this together?"

"Skip it. Tell me about what happened today. You did hear from them, didn't you?"

She looked down into her lap. "They called the office this morning. It was the same voice I'd heard on the phone before. Male and German. He said Mrs. Fairfax may be sending someone by the office. They gave me a number to call when you got there. When you left to get Donohue, I called them back and told them you had found a safe and were going to open it tonight. They said they'd be there when you opened it, and I should stay out of the way if I didn't want to get hurt."

"That's why you were so anxious to get out of the office." I stubbed out my cigarette in the ash tray. "Guess you also mentioned that I wasn't carrying a gun. That's why they were so brazen about barging in there."

She shut her eyes. She didn't say anything. She didn't have to.

"Thanks for the warning."

"These bastards have my son, damn it. What was I supposed to do?"

I didn't have an answer for her, so I stuck to what had brought us here. "So when they missed getting the bundle, you figured you'd try to get it from me somehow." I inclined my head back toward the bedroom. "Maybe wait until I fell asleep after our romantic interlude so you could sneak out and grab the bundle. How were you going to get it to them?"

"I don't know." She dropped her head into her hands. "Call the number they gave me today, maybe. If they didn't pick up, mail it to the address I have. I don't know. I wasn't thinking that far ahead."

When she looked up at me, her eyes were red. "Don't let the early motherhood bit fool you, Charlie. I'm really not a bad girl. I'm not good at this stuff, and I don't know what the hell I'm doing. I also don't know who they are or if they think I'm helping you right now or if they're going to hurt my son." She dropped her head into her hands. "I don't know anything anymore."

I'd seen a lot of crocodile tears in my time. I wasn't seeing them now. "When was the last time you spoke to your son?"

"Tonight at the police station," she said. "Detective Loomis let me use the phone. He was fine, but I don't know."

I didn't need her spinning off into another panic, so I

kept her grounded. "Here's what's going to happen next. You're going to go back inside and get dressed. Then we're going to your apartment and getting the picture of your son with the phone number on the back. We're going to get the address you mail things to also."

"We can't go there at this time of night," she said. "I have a roommate and she'll worry if—"

I looked at her until she realized I didn't care.

I pointed at a pad on the desk. "Write down the name and address of your boy's school. While you're getting dressed, I'll make some phone calls and make sure he's safe."

She looked at me like she was seeing me for the first time. "You'd do that for him? For me? After everything I just told you? After everything I've done?"

"I've got two kids myself. It's not their fault their parents are rotten. Now write it down before I change my mind."

*   *   *   *   *

While Sarah got dressed, I called Mr. Van Dorn. If he was annoyed that I'd called him in the wee hours of the morning, he didn't sound it.

I told him everything Sarah had just told me, including how she'd tried to steal the documents from my desk. I didn't get into all the particulars about what we'd done before that. He was a man of the world. Some things were better left unsaid.

After I was finished, he said, "Seems Mr. Fairfax isn't the only one who leads a complicated life, Charlie." He cleared his throat. "I hope you didn't hurt her."

"Just her pride. The trouble is, I believe her, sir. I've got every reason in the world to think she's lying, but her story sounds legit."

"I can't say that I trust her motives, but I trust your judgement. Have you told anyone else about this? Called any of your friends on the force to help guard your apartment?"

"My ex-partner Loomis took the report about what happened back at the Fairfax office, but that's all he knows. He's having a patrol car swing by the place every half hour or so."

"And where is Miss Swenson now?"

"She's getting ready to go home now. I'll make sure she gets in safe."

"No. You've had enough people gunning for you for one day. Stay where you are. I'll send some men to your place to collect her and the material, save for the notebook you'll take to Father Mullins later. You'll find him alone on a bench in the center of the campus."

When we'd talked back at the station, he said he'd be sending one man along. Now, he was talking about more than that. "What men, sir?"

"Men who will be equipped to make sure Miss Swenson and the material arrive where they need to go. I'll fill you in later as events transpire."

He kept talking before I could ask him what he meant. "Make sure you don't mention any of this to anyone else but Father Mullins, at least not without discussing it with me first. If word about any of this gets out, it will only complicate matters. You and I will talk in greater detail at the gala tonight. The men I mentioned will be at your apartment within the hour. They'll both be wearing dark suits and will ask for a Mr. Dean. That will be the signal that they're with me. Shoot through the door if anyone else approaches. Is that clear?"

I loaded the last bullet into my .38 and snapped the cylinder shut. "This is starting to sound very complicated, sir."

"It's been complicated for some time, Charlie. I'll fill you in on the rest as soon as I can. And don't worry about reporting to Mrs. Fairfax. I'll handle her until further notice. See you tonight."

With that, the line went dead.

Sarah knocked quietly on the doorframe of my bedroom. I was sorry and relieved she was fully dressed. "Can we go now, Charlie?"

"Change of plans, Miss Swenson. My boss is sending men over to make sure you get home safe."

"Men? What men?"

I didn't answer because I didn't know what to tell her. I shrugged into my shoulder holster and slid the gun home. It was the first time in a year that I'd put it on, but it felt like I'd never taken it off.

I didn't like the tone in Mr. Van Dorn's voice at the end of our call. And I didn't like that feeling that was starting up in my stomach. It was the same feeling I'd had back in the war, right before the shells started landing. Or on the force, just before a perp reached into his pocket.

It was the feeling I usually got just before all hell broke loose.

Chapter 12

The bells from the Fordham chapel chimed eight times as I walked through a light mist to meet Father John Mullins.

I was an hour early for our meeting, but I didn't care. I wanted to be anywhere but my apartment, and the fresh air felt good. Too much had gone on at my place too quickly, and my mind was still spinning. And the idea of sleeping with a woman who had just set me up for a beating or worse still took some getting used to. All the signs had been there, but I hadn't seen them until it was too late. I was really beginning to believe I might not be cut out for this kind of work anymore.

But I couldn't afford to think that way. Not with so many facts coming together. Not with people coming after me with Tommy guns.

I figured it was probably against a dozen or so church laws to visit a priest the morning after you'd slept with a woman who wasn't your wife, but since that woman had almost gotten me killed, I hoped God might give me a pass.

Given my track record with getting favors from the Almighty, I doubted He would. Just another item in St. Peter's ledger to answer for whenever I reached the Pearly Gates. It was a conversation I hoped wouldn't happen for a while.

I was surprised to see Father Mullins was early, too. Or, at least I thought he was Father Mullins. He was exactly where Mr. Van Dorn had told me he'd be: sitting on a bench at the edge of the circular lawn in the middle of the campus. A new building was being built on the opposite side of the green from where the Jesuit was sitting.

Father Mullins's long legs were stretched out before him, crossed at the ankles as he puffed away at a pipe. He had a thick shock of gray hair ruled more by the wind than a comb. His face was deeply lined, and his skin was almost as gray as his hair.

I found myself walking slower the closer I got to him. I felt like I was intruding somehow, like I was walking in on the middle of a conversation, even though he was alone.

He didn't look at me, but he must have sensed I was there because he pointed the stem of his pipe at the building being built across the green. "Tell me, young man. What do you make of it?"

I hadn't been called a young man in a long time, but since no one else was around, I figured he was talking to me. I looked at the building: a large, half-built stone structure that reminded me of a castle I'd seen once in Europe. Workmen were laying down what appeared to be steps on a hill leading up to it. "Pretty impressive, Father."

"Pretty imposing is more like it. Looks more like an armory than a place of learning, if you want my opinion, which, I might add, no one seems to want these days. They're saying it'll be the centerpiece of the university, as if the centerpiece of a university can be limited to stone and mortar. Or should."

He smiled a warm smile that seemed more for himself than for me. "But you didn't come all this way to hear a contrary old man's views on architecture, now did you, Charles?"

I hadn't been called Charles this often in a very long time, either. "Feel free to call me Charlie, Father. Everyone does."

"But I'm not everyone." Using his pipe like a wand, he pointed at the open space next to him on the bench. "Come join me as we watch the future being built before our very eyes."

When I sat, Father Mullins finally took a look at me. "You're not at all what I expected. I thought you'd be some greasy little man in a trench coat, skulking along through the mist."

I smiled. "I'm afraid my trench coat is at the cleaner's."

His own smile widened in a way that made me feel his opinion of me had just gone up a notch. "Harry speaks very highly of you, which is rare considering Harriman Van Dorn doesn't give praise lightly."

"The feeling is mutual. He stuck by me when no one else would. Helped me get my business started. Get a new life." I felt like I was rambling, and stopped. "Sorry, Father. Didn't mean to waste time talking about myself."

"Nonsense." The Jesuit pointed the pipe stem at his white Roman collar. "Confessions come with the job. And talking about oneself is never a waste of time, as long as we're honest with ourselves about who we are and what we are. In that regard, Harry tells me you're a very honest man. He likes and trusts you. And not just because you freed his son and brought his daughter's killers to justice."

I winced at the memory. "I didn't bring anyone to justice, Father. I just killed the men responsible."

"We get the justice we deserve based on the path we choose for ourselves. Those men chose crime over work. They chose their path just as you and I have chosen ours. Fortunately, our paths have crossed at this particular point in time." He tucked the pipe into the corner of his mouth, struck a match, and lit the bowl. "Speaking of which, Harry said you had an enigmatic notebook to show me."

I didn't know what enigmatic meant, but I dug the notebook out of my overcoat and handed it over. "Mr. Van Dorn said you spent a lot of time studying old cultures and languages. Stuff like that."

"Yes." His eyes brightened. "Stuff like that. I'm sure you were surprised that a priest studied such things. Well, I learned long ago that one can never tell what will pique the interest of the Church of Rome. She has a surprisingly curious and agile mind. And it's a good thing for you she has, or else I'd be of little use to you today."

He puffed away at his pipe as he began to remove the rubber bands from the notebook. "Now, let us see what secrets you have brought me."

That made me remember what Mr. Van Dorn said about secrecy. "I hope Mr. Van Dorn told you he'd like to keep this just between the three of us for now." Then I remembered I was talking to a priest. "I guess you guys are pretty good at keeping secrets."

The Jesuit laughed as he removed the last rubber band. "You have no idea. Tell me where you found this again. Harry was appropriately vague when he phoned me. And don't be shy with details. I have been fully briefed about the Fairfax incident."

I thought a priest using a word like "briefed" sounded a little official, but I let it go. "It was in Walter Fairfax's safe, along with a lot of other things. Ledgers, bank accounts, deeds on property he'd bought. Things like that. Everything was in English, except that book. I think it's German, but the handwriting's tough to make out."

I watched Father Mullins carefully leaf through the notebook, slowly turning each page has his eyes moved over the words. "Your Mr. Fairfax has some rather unique interests, Charles. These are prayers, but not the kinds of prayers you and I are used to saying."

He flipped through some more pages, stopping on the circle of symbols I'd mentioned to Mr. Van Dorn. "Take this, for example. These symbols are Armanen runes, devised some thirty years ago by a German mystic called Guido von List."

"A German named Guido?"

"Our Teutonic brethren have always been an eclectic people," Father Mullins said. "Runes are like an alphabet, except they represent ideas rather than mere letters. Von List claimed these symbols came to him in a vision back in 1902, and that they represent ancient wisdoms of the religion of the original Germanic tribes."

"Jesus," I said before I could catch myself.

"I'm afraid Jesus has nothing to do with it, Charles, which was List's point. He said these runes represented an ancient wisdom so powerful that the Catholic Church had kept it hidden from the Germanic people as a way to enslave them." Another laugh. "As if anyone has ever been able to get a German to do anything against his will. Your last name is Doherty. I take it you were raised Catholic?"

"I was, but I'll admit I haven't kept up for a while."

"That's a topic for another discussion," Father Mullins said. "You and I were raised to believe in the power of prayer. Asking God's grace before meals or during a trying time. Guido Von List believed in a different kind of prayer, almost like a conjuring or a spell. He believed these runes had magical powers all their own. And, unlike our prayers, not just anyone could use them. He believed Germans had descended from a pure and gifted race, while all non-Germans were impure and irrelevant. He had a special hatred for all things related to Jews. Since Christianity is based on the belief of a Jewish Messiah, he said Christianity was an invalid religion as well."

All of this was beginning to get too complicated for me, so I stayed focused on my original question. "So this notebook is a prayer book?"

"Yes," Father Mullins said. "Probably written in Mr. Fairfax's own hand as a way to learn and remember them, much the way children today write the Our Father and Hail Mary." He looked at the handwriting again. "This doesn't seem to be written in a child's hand, so I'd say he wrote them much later than that. That means he must have subscribed to List's teachings recently, and therefore believed these symbols were an actual source of active power."

I had heard everything he said, but none of it really made much sense. "People these days really believe that stuff?"

"You'd be surprised," Father Mullins said. "I actually saw List speak once in Vienna, back in 1903. The man was obviously a lunatic, but he managed to convince an impressive array of German leaders to buy into his philosophy before the Great War. Industrialists, bankers, philosophers, newspaper owners. A great many members of the aristocracy as well. Some argue his teachings played a role in giving Germany their feeling of invincibility and entitlement that caused them to force the war in the first place."

"But the war's been over for a long time."

"List's teachings were largely forgotten following the war," Father Mullins explained. "Nationalistic movements like his always go into retreat after a bitter defeat like Germany suffered. But some of his followers in the upper classes kept the faith, finding particular comfort in List's prophecy that a German messiah would one day make Germany the dominant nation it was destined to be. Unfortunately, List's teachings have enjoyed something of a resurgence in popularity as of late."

"Why?"

"Because of the recent elevation of a man who some believe to be that Germanic messiah List had predicted,"

Father Mullins said. "Adolph Hitler."

"But he's a politician, not a priest."

"From what I've read of Hitler's rhetoric, he has melded religion with his political beliefs to give him an air of validity amongst some of German's leading families. And since Mr. Fairfax has a prayer book recently written in his own hand, citing List's runes and prayers, we must assume that he subscribes to at least some of Mr. Hitler's beliefs."

Even though Father Mullins had been talking for a while, it hadn't hit me until that moment. A possible explanation for everything that had happened to me the day before. "That fits, Father. See, there's a woman—"

"There often is where men like Fairfax are involved. I take it you're referring to Countess Alexandra von Holstein. Yes, Harry told me about her. I know nothing about her, but given what Harry said you found in Fairfax's safe, and the recent nature of the writings here in this notebook, it's quite possible she introduced Walter to the mysteries of Aryan philosophy."

Although everything Father Mullins had told me was interesting as hell, it didn't tell me what I really wanted to know. "Too bad there's nothing in that notebook that explains why he shot himself."

The Jesuit flipped through more pages. "Perhaps it does."

I couldn't remember the last time I'd talked to someone who made me feel so dumb without even trying. "How, Father?"

"Think it through, Charles. The people who attacked you on the street and in the office are most likely the same people. They wanted to stop you for some reason. The contents of that safe and this notebook are most likely that reason. These are arcane beliefs. Most people have the same reaction to them as you did when I told you about them. Yet, some very powerful people hold these beliefs dear and want to keep them from the general public so they can introduce them in more acceptable, subtle ways. Ways, I fear, Mr. Hitler and his ilk are employing in Germany today. I would be surprised if this Countess Alexandra isn't involved in Fairfax's adoption of these beliefs. I'm sure she wishes to keep evidence of her influence on him from being known, since it may have played a role in his suicide."

"I haven't heard of too many countesses getting involved in rough stuff, Father."

"Assuming she's really a countess at all. I think you've already learned far more about this woman than she wanted anyone to know. And you may learn even more in the days ahead. If she is involved in the attacks on you, I doubt she'll stop now."

"Don't worry about me, Father." I patted my gun beneath my coat. "I can handle myself."

"Don't be too sure." He wrapped the rubber bands back around the notebook and handed it back to me. "I doubt you've ever encountered people like this before, Charles, at least knowingly. They are dabbling in dark things they don't truly understand, which makes them incredibly dangerous." He handed me his business card. "I want you to call me should you ever feel the need. Day or night, no matter the hour. Call Harry, of course, but if you think I can be of use to you, please don't hesitate."

I didn't see why I'd need to speak to the priest again, especially now that he'd explained the notebook. But I pocketed the card anyway as I stood up. "Thanks for all of the information, Father, but all I'm trying to do is figure out why a man killed himself."

His smile was a little different this time. "For your sake I hope it's that simple, but I fear it isn't."

Chapter 13

As soon as I got back to my place, I began writing down everything Father Mullins had just told me. I wanted to get it all down on paper while it was still fresh in my head.

The Kraut named Guido. Runes. Spells. Ancient knowledge. Pagan bullshit. None of it made much sense. Trying to figure out why Fairfax had killed himself was bad enough. Dumping a new religion into the mix just made the whole goddamned thing even more complicated than it already was.

But the more complicated things got, the more important Countess Alexandra von Holstein became. The documents in the safe proved she had her hooks pretty deep into Fairfax. And if she'd pulled him into this religion Father Mullins was talking about, then she had a stronger hold on him than even Dr. Blythe thought.

Although there was a good chance I'd be seeing her at the Stuyvesant Society Gala, I was anxious to see what Mr. Van Dorn had found out from the papers I had given his men earlier that morning. I was about to give him a call when the phone rang.

"Imagine that," said the familiar voice on the other end of the line. "A big shot like you answering his own phone.

I'm impressed as hell, Doherty. I figured you'd just let the maid get it. Or the butler."

It was Detective Stephen Hauser, Chief Carmichael's current Black Hand. I'd been so used to being polite to my clients all the time, I had to remember how to be glib. Luckily, Hauser brought out the worst in me.

"It's the maid's day off. Besides, not everybody's as lucky as Carmichael to have a flunky to do their dirty work for them. What do you want, Hauser? I've got a polo match in Central Park in twenty minutes."

"No kidding?" It sounded like he was flipping pages back and forth. "Funny, I thought you'd be getting your hair done in time for that big shindig at the Waldorf tonight."

I didn't like what he'd said or the way he'd said it. "How do you know about that?"

"Contrary to popular belief, I read pretty good," Hauser said. "I'm reading all about it right here in Dr. Blythe's calendar for this evening."

I got that rotten feeling again. "How the hell did you get a hold of his calendar?"

"Because I'm calling you from his den right now. Your new pal is dead, Doherty. Looks like he's been that way for a few hours, too."

I grabbed a pen and paper on my desk. "What's the address? I'm coming over."

"Damn," he said. "And here I was, hoping you'd refuse so I could come drag you over here by your hair."

"Goddamn it, Hauser. What's the address?"

"The El Dorado. Three hundred Central Park West. Oh,

and the chief wanted me to mention that he'd like—"

I didn't give a damn what the chief liked. I hung up the phone and headed for the door.

*   *   *   *   *

The crime scene photographer was already taking pictures of Dr. Blythe's body when I got there. A kid who looked like he'd just gotten his detective badge was chewing gum like a cow chewed cud while he scribbled something in a notebook.

I might not have been a cop anymore, but I still had cop instincts. I took in the scene in sections, just like I'd been taught.

The heavy dark drapes that hung in front of the study's windows were closed. The only light in the room came from a chandelier and from the photographer's flash.

Dr. Blythe's body was slumped back in a chair behind the desk. His head was lolled off to the right, mouth slack. His dead eyes were half closed, staring into the great beyond. The tufts of hair that had been neatly combed when I'd met him at his club were now a puffy mess, sticking up at odd angles. He was wearing a smoking jacket and pajamas. The jacket was open.

The glass tumbler of cut crystal on the blotter was either half empty or half full, depending on how you looked at it. But either way you looked at it, Dr. Blythe was dead.

I stood in the doorway of the study, careful to keep out of the way of the crime scene shots. But even from that distance, I could see the liquid in the glass was clear. The stench in the room confirmed it was gin.

I had only met Dr. Blythe the day before, but there was something about the man that I had liked. Maybe understood was more like it. He was a haunted man, filled with regret over things he'd done and hadn't done. I could tell he was well on his way to realizing that no amount of booze could take away his pain or guilt. I already knew those things never faded, like scars on the soul.

All that guilt and regret over Fairfax's death had plagued him, and now he was dead, too. Just another corpse to tag and bag and file away.

At least that's what someone was banking on.

Because even though I'd just gotten there, I could see one thing plain as day:

Dr. Matthew Blythe had been murdered.

I damn near jumped when I felt a large presence near me. I was glad it was only Hank Kronauer, the city's deputy chief medical examiner.

"Mornin', Charlie," the fat man muttered as he passed me. His ancient black medical bag looked small in his fleshy hand. "They pull you out of mothballs for this one? Hope they didn't put you through too much trouble. Heart attack, plain and simple. Plain as day. Seen it a thousand times."

I hadn't seen Kronauer in the year since I'd been forced into retirement, but he hadn't changed a bit since the day I first met him twenty years before. He'd been over three hundred pounds then and he hadn't lost an ounce since. His suspenders strained to contain his girth as he leaned over to get a closer look at the corpse. The photographer was annoyed Kronauer had ruined his shot, but was smart enough to keep his mouth shut. When Kronauer arrived at a crime scene, it was his. Everyone else be damned.

His double chin swayed as his beady eyes moved over the body. He could see more in a glance than some examiners could see even after an autopsy. "Yep, coronary's my bet. No overt signs of foul play. No apparent wounds or abrasions or anything of that nature. No blood or weapon in sight."

He sniffed the air near the corpse's mouth and quickly pulled back. "Heavy presence of alcohol. Gin, I believe." Another sniff, then something of a smile. "Expensive gin at that. I'd say he'd been tipping it back pretty good when it happened, judging by the strong aroma. Probably the reason for the coronary in the first place. Silly old bastard. Can't drink like you're twenty forever, you know?"

I waited for the mope from homicide to say something, but he just stood there taking notes. So I asked Kronauer, "Ballpark on time of death?"

That got the mope's attention. "Nobody said you can ask questions, Doherty. You're here as an observer. Just stand there and keep quiet until Hauser comes for you."

He'd tried to sound tough, but came off sounding like a kid. I ignored Junior and waited for Kronauer's answer. "How about it, Hank?"

The coroner put the back of his thick hand to Dr. Blythe's forehead. "It's eleven thirty now. The maid found him at half past seven this morning and called it in." He squeezed Blythe's lifeless hand. "Rigor's come and gone already. I'd say he passed sometime around three this morning, give or take. But I'll know more when I get him on the table."

Kronauer stood up to his full height and hitched his pants up over his impressive gut. "It's got to be his ticker. Overweight male in his late fifties and, from the looks and smell of it, a heavy drinker."

He was speaking louder than normal, like he wanted to make sure for someone to overhear him. I watched him quickly glance behind me, like someone was standing just outside the room. I didn't bother to look. I knew it had to be Hauser.

Kronauer took a cigar from the inside of his jacket and popped it into his mouth. "Probably a heavy smoker, I'd wager. All in all, a prime candidate for a coronary. No doubt about it."

In all the years I'd known him, I'd never known Kronauer to be so flippant about a body. He wasn't conducting an investigation. He was putting on a performance for Hauser's benefit.

I'd heard enough. "Sounds like you're trying to talk yourself into something, Hank."

"No need to convince myself of something I already know. Overweight, heavy drinker? Coronary. Case closed."

"Christ, Kronauer. Sounds like you're looking into a mirror."

"With one key difference, Charlie." He struck a match off the side of Dr. Blythe's desk and lit his cigar. "I'm still alive."

Detective Steven Hauser walked into the study from behind me. "Well, look who showed up and decided to play detective. How's every little thing, Charlie?"

Hauser was a bit taller than me and about five years

younger. He was broader and more muscular than me, too. By a lot. He had thick, dirty-blond hair and dead blue eyes that scared the hell out of suspects, but never had that effect on me.

I kept looking at Dr. Blythe's corpse. "It was shaping up to be a pretty good day until I heard from you."

Hauser grinned. "Glad to see the high life hasn't cost you your sense of humor. Let's keep the laughs going by you telling me how you came to know the deceased."

I knew Mr. Van Dorn would want me to keep the details to a minimum, especially from Hauser. Everything he heard would go right back to Chief Carmichael. The less that bastard knew, the better.

I told him the bare minimum. "I met him for the first time yesterday afternoon."

"Where?"

"At the New York Athletic Club."

Hauser looked over at Junior. "You hear that, Bill? Be sure to write that down and underline it. The New York Athletic Club. Fancy, ain't it?"

Bill nodded. "Fancier than I could ever afford if I saved up for a year."

I smiled. "Well, when your balls finally drop, sonny, give me a call. I'll take you there to celebrate the occasion."

Junior pushed off the wall, but Hauser shook him off before looking back at me. "Still got the mouth, don't you, Charlie?"

"Wine and smartasses only get better with age." I finally looked at Hauser. "Too bad you'll only find out about the aging part."

Hauser let the insult pass. "The New York Athletic Club's an awfully tony place. What'd you two swells talk about?"

"Oh, the usual." I made a show of fishing a cigarette from my gold case and lighting it. "Half-witted cops on the take. Errand boys who wait for orders all day long." I blew the smoke through my nostrils. "Your name came up."

Hauser wasn't grinning anymore. "I'm going to ask nicely one last time. What did you two talk about?"

I knew what he wanted, but I wouldn't let him have it easily. "We talked about the weather. Polo matches. Types of caviar we like. Where we like to go on vacation. Nothing you'd understand."

Hauser took a couple of steps closer to me but I didn't budge. I knew he had a temper and liked to use his fists. I also knew how to get under his skin. Normally, annoying him would've been the highlight of my day. But the sight of a sad old man I liked sitting dead ten feet away kind of ruined it for me.

Hauser's jaw tightened. "What's your name doing in Dr. Blythe's book for seven o'clock tonight?"

"Why didn't you ask me that before? He invited me to go to the Stuyvesant Society gala down at the Waldorf. Said he wanted to introduce me to some people."

"No kidding? What people?"

"If I knew that, I wouldn't need to be introduced to them, now would I?" I shook my head. "You used to be a better detective than that."

His face was beginning to turn just a bit redder. "Don't

make this any harder on yourself than it has to be. There's only one reason why a guy like that would talk to a bum like you, and that's because you're working on a case. Maybe a case involving his dead brother-in-law. A case that's already been settled and put away."

"Or maybe he just wanted someone to talk to at the gala."

"If he did, he wouldn't choose you. I've got a feeling he either hired you to look into Fairfax's death or you were pumping him for information. I don't care which, I just want to know what."

"And I don't care what you want because I'm afraid that's none of your goddamned business."

"Sure it is." Hauser took another step closer and spoke right into my ear. "Because based on what we know right now, you're the last person who saw Dr. Blythe alive."

"That's where you're wrong, Steve," I said. "The last person who saw him alive is whoever killed him."

Kronauer's cigar damned near fell out of his mouth. "Murder? Christ, Charlie, who said anything about murder? I just told you it was a coronary."

"That's what Carmichael's office told you to say. You know better than that."

Kronauer looked away. "Goddamn it, Charlie. Leave it alone. What do you care anyway? You're not even a cop anymore."

"I care because a good man's been murdered, and for some reason, no one around here seems to give a damn."

Hauser let out a big laugh and looked at his young partner in the corner. "You know, Billy, just before the chief bounced this clown off the force he was just another Tammany hack running out his string until retirement. Tagging and bagging dead dopers and whores on the graveyard shift. A year out on his own and all of a sudden he thinks he's Philo Vance."

"Running down dead whores beat the hell out of being Carmichael's cabin boy." I winked. "But you seem to love the job, don't you, Steve?"

Hauser wasn't laughing anymore. I half expected him to hit me. I half hoped he would. He may have had five years and sixty pounds of muscle on me, but no one had ever called me a pushover. I'd always wondered which one of us would walk away. I knew he thought he would. I was never that sure.

But now wasn't the time to find out.

"Unless you've skimmed enough graft to keep you afloat for a while, step back. Because if you hit me, you'll be off the force before the end of shift."

Hauser surprised me by, indeed, stepping back. "The deputy chief coroner of the City of New York just said this looks like a coronary, pending further investigation. What makes you say different?"

Since it had nothing to do with the Fairfax case, I decided to tell him. "Because when I met Dr. Blythe yesterday at the club, he told me his drinks get darker as the day goes on. Said he starts off with gin during the day, but likes to cap off every night with a good scotch. And even the deputy chief coroner for the City of New York just said he reeks of gin. Expensive gin, I think were his exact words."

Hauser looked at Kronauer, who shrugged. "Sure, it's

gin. But that doesn't mean it's not a coronary. Maybe he just got sick of scotch last night and decided to switch to gin instead."

"And spill it all over himself?" I asked. "I can smell it from here. He reeks of it, way too much even if he'd been drinking all day and all night."

"So what?" Hauser said. "Maybe he spilled some of it while he was staggering around. You worked vice, Charlie. I don't have to tell you what drunks are like when they're on a tear."

I looked around the neatness of the study. "Does this look like a place where a drunk went on a bender? There's not a pillow out of place. Hell, the gin decanter is on the bar where it belongs. It's even got the top on it. If he was on a toot, he's the neatest drunk I've ever seen."

I could tell Hauser was getting the point, but didn't want to admit it. He said, "Maybe the maid cleaned up a bit before we got here. Didn't want us to see the place as a mess. To protect the good doctor's reputation."

"Let's say she did. What about the drapes and the lights?"

Hauser looked around the room. "What about them?"

I looked at the crime scene photographer. "Did you close those drapes to get a better shot of the body?"

He looked nervous, and quickly shook his head. "No. I didn't touch anything. Everything was like this when I got here."

I looked back at Hauser. "What about the maid? Did she close them?"

"No." Hauser didn't sound happy about it. "And she

152

didn't clean up, either. She got here at seven thirty, saw the body, and ran out again. She called it in from a neighbor's apartment down the hall. She was so scared, she didn't even close the door behind her."

I looked up at the chandelier. "She turn on that light?"

Junior said, "That was me. The whole place was dark when we got here, except for the light in the hallway. The maid turned that one on when she came in."

"You write that down in your notebook?"

The look on Junior's face told me he hadn't.

I tapped my temple. "Smart, kid. Great police work. Keep that up and you'll be chief of police in no time."

"What were we supposed to do, stupid?" Hauser yelled at me. "Look around in the dark?"

"No. You were supposed to ask why it was dark in the first place."

Kronauer took a step back and swore to himself.

But Hauser and Junior still didn't see my point. "So it was dark," Junior said. "So what?"

I decided to lay it out for them. "You got here at nine in the morning when the sun was up, right? But the apartment was still dark because the drapes were drawn." I pointed at the coroner. "Kronauer placed the time of death sometime in the middle of the night, right?"

"I still do," Kronauer said.

I looked at Hauser. "So, by your theory, a very drunken Dr. Blythe staggers out of his bedroom, walks down the hall, comes in here, pours himself a drink, puts the bottle back where it belongs, sits down at his desk, has a heart attack, and dies."

Hauser threw out his hands. "What's wrong with that?"

Kronauer answered for me. "Because with the drapes drawn and no lights on, it would have been pitch-black in here. He wouldn't have done all that in the dark. Hell, he didn't even turn on his desk lamp."

"He could've turned off the light just before he had the heart attack," Hauser offered.

Kronauer shut his eyes. "Highly unlikely."

"Not to mention," I added, "he wasn't wearing his glasses."

Kronauer took a closer look at Blythe's face and frowned. "He's right. There are indentations alongside the bridge of his nose, showing the deceased wore glasses. And there's no sign of them in the immediate area." He swore again as he backed away.

Junior and the photographer rushed past me and headed down the hall. I figured that's where Blythe's bedroom was. "You'll probably find his glasses still on his nightstand," I said. "Right where he left them when whoever killed him dragged him out here. And turned out the light when they left. At least they're polite killers."

Hauser stormed passed me, hot on Junior's heels.

Kronauer flattened down what little hair he still had. Now that it was just the two of us, he said, "You can never keep your damned mouth shut, can you?"

"Like the way you kept it shut about the Fairfax suicide being an accident? What the hell is going on around here anyway?"

"I do what I'm told, Charlie. Not all of us have Harriman Van Dorn's phone number in our wallets."

I realized arguing with Kronauer was pointless. He lived for the dead, for the job. He'd been offered the head coroner's post dozens of times over the years but had turned it down every single time. He never had the stomach for the politics then; I couldn't expect him to handle it now. "Hauser tell you to write this off as a coronary?"

"Hauser strongly suggested I consider it," Kronauer admitted. "Whether or not that comes straight from the chief's office is anyone's guess, but I'm not going to find out."

There was no need to gloat. I'd always liked Kronauer. Besides, I owed him one for talking to me about the Fairfax case a few days before. "The gin tipped me off. The rest of it fell into place after that. I had the jump on you because Dr. Blythe told me about his habits yesterday. You would've figured it out eventually."

"For all the good it'll do me. What do you think the cause of death was?"

I remembered something he'd said to me on a crime scene a long time ago and decided to use it against him. "How the hell should I know? You're the coroner."

Kronauer rolled the cigar from one corner of his mouth to the other. "I'll have the place dusted for prints, but I don't think we'll find anything."

"Me either, but do it anyway." I ditched my cigarette in a potted plant by the doorway as I turned to leave. "Let me know what you find out after the autopsy. And I want the truth, Hank, not whatever fable Carmichael tells you to invent. It'll be our secret, scout's honor."

"I should have something by tonight, tomorrow at the latest." Kronauer shut his eyes. "Christ, Charlie. What good does the truth ever do anyone anyway?"

I wished I had an answer for him, but I didn't.

Chapter 14

I'd already seen all I could see at the apartment, so I headed back to my place. Even though I had people gunning for me, I decided to skip the taxi and take my chances with the good citizens of the shantytown that had sprung up in Central Park since the Crash. Most of the poor bastards didn't have enough money to buy food, much less submachine guns.

Taking a cab would've been smarter but I needed air, and even the smell from the smoldering cook fires of Hooverville helped clear my mind.

It helped keep my anger in check.

Because I was damned angry.

Angry because I hated seeing Dr. Blythe lying dead like that. I hated thinking of the way he'd probably died, too. Dragged from his bed in the middle of the night, brought into the study he loved, and probably tortured before he'd died. Maybe it had been a coronary after all, but it wouldn't have been peaceful.

I didn't have a shred of evidence to go on, but I figured the same people who'd killed Blythe were probably the same sons of bitches who had tried to kill me in the Fairfax offices. After they'd missed me, they probably made a beeline for the doctor, hoping he would tell them what Fairfax kept in his safe. That meant they must've known we'd talked, but

I didn't know how they could've known that. I was pretty good at spotting a tail, at least when I knew I was being followed, and I was sure no one had followed me to the club. Blondie had run off into the crowd, but he was lousy at following people. If he, or anyone else, had been watching me, I would've known, wouldn't I?

Wouldn't I?

That question nagged at me as I walked through the park. Had I missed a tail, just like I hadn't realized I was being followed until someone took a shot at me? Until I spotted Blondie outside Nat's? Had I been so soft that I'd led the man's killers right to his doorstep?

No, I hadn't. I may have lost a step or two in private service, but I hadn't slipped up that much. And we had met at Blythe's club, not his apartment. Hell, I didn't even know where he lived until Hauser gave me the address.

That meant someone else had done their homework on Blythe. They knew where he lived, and went to his place to get the truth out of him. But I doubted the doctor had even known about the safe. If he'd known about it, he would've told me.

Miss Swenson was already feeding them all the information they needed, and hadn't told them about the safe until that day. Thinking Blythe might be able to tell them about its contents had been a desperate move. An amateur move, but a deadly one just the same.

Until now, I figured they'd played some kind of role in getting Fairfax to kill himself. But Blythe's death changed all that. Trying to shoot me on the street and killing Blythe showed me these people weren't afraid to kill. They just weren't particularly good at it. They had covered their tracks at the doctor's apartment just well enough to show me they weren't stupid, just ruthless.

I'd seen a lot of ruthless amateurs get a lot of good people killed over the years. In France, some of them were wearing uniforms with gold braids and a chest full of medals. Now, they'd killed someone I'd liked.

The Fairfax case had just gotten even more personal for me. And the information Miss Swenson had about her blackmailers was more important now than ever. I just hoped Mr. Van Dorn's people—whoever the hell they were—already had it and were running it down. If they didn't, I would.

Before the doctor's murder, I had a feeling Countess Alexandra was central to all of this. After everything that had happened that day, I was absolutely sure of it.

I'd make a point of bringing it up to her when I saw her at the gala later that night.

*   *   *   *   *

That night was a set of firsts for me. My first time in a tuxedo. My first time at a fancy gala. And my first time hunting for royalty.

I didn't know much about what The Stuyvesant Society actually did, just that it held its annual gala in the Grand Ballroom of the Waldorf-Astoria. I always got a kick out of the Waldorf. It reminded me of some of the big, old-style places I'd seen in France back during the war. Lots of marble, lots of brass, lots of old-world everything with a modern flair. I liked the place. It felt like New York, or at least what New York wished it was.

Mrs. Van Dorn insisted that my tuxedo be tailor-made for me from scratch, but I still felt uncomfortable in the damned thing. I'd also never developed the knack for tying a bow tie, which made me feel even more ridiculous than I already did.

When I saw the get-up on the rest of the men who were milling around the street and in the lobby, I knew my knot was too small, and crooked to boot. I didn't want to embarrass Mr. Van Dorn by looking like a slob, so I quickly ducked into the one of the men's rooms off the lobby to take another shot at tying it.

As I stood in front of the mirror, another guy in a tux came out of one of the stalls and washed his hands. He gave me a sympathetic smile as he washed up. He was drying his hands when he said, "I could never get the damned thing right either. My wife does mine for me."

I didn't bother telling him my wife took my kids and was living with another man up in Poughkeepsie. I just smiled back and kept working on the knot.

He finished washing up and left. I thought I'd heard the men's lounge door lock behind him, which didn't make sense. But when I looked over at the door, it made all the sense in the world.

Andrew J. Carmichael, Chief of the New York City Police Department, was blocking the door, all six feet three inches, two hundred and twenty pounds of him.

I'd known him too well for too long to really admire

him, even before he put me out to pasture and kicked me off the force, but I had to admit he always looked like a million bucks. His blue tunic had been perfectly pressed. His brass buttons gleamed, even in the dim light of the bathroom. His badge and medals bore a perfect shine that would've made a French general jealous.

His square jaw, broad build, and clear blue eyes made him look like he'd just stepped off a recruitment poster. For the better part of the past twenty years, scores of gangsters and criminals had come and gone in New York City, but Chief Carmichael remained. Mostly because the other gangsters and criminals who took their place paid him off to stay in business.

I also knew he was every bit as tough as he looked, maybe even tougher. And being locked in the shithouse with him wasn't exactly the way I'd planned on starting my night.

Carmichael gave me that cruel, crooked smile he usually got when he was in a playful mood.

I knew he fed off intimidating people, so I wouldn't give the bastard the satisfaction. "Evening, Andy. I thought you gave up prowling men's toilets years ago."

But Carmichael ignored the insult. "Look at you. Little Charlie Doherty all dressed up for a night on the town. The very picture of elegance. And we know what happens to pictures, don't we, Charlie?"

"Sure." I went back to fiddling with my tie. It kept my hands from shaking. "Same thing we do to tyrants and crooked police chiefs. We hang them."

He forced a laugh as he made a show of looking me up

and down. "I've got to hand it to you, though. You're the epitome of prosperity. Reminds me of something my dear, departed mother used to say: 'Put a beggar on horseback and he'll ride to hell.'"

The knot was coming along okay. "No horseback for me these days, Andy. If I ride to hell, it'll be behind the wheel of a brand new Cadillac. The whole damned way. If I have to go, then I'm going in style."

Carmichael's smile faded. "You're as smug as ever, eh, little man?"

"Smugger, if that's a word," I said. "Comes with the wardrobe. And the address." I winked at him in the mirror. "Sixty-Third and Madison is a hell of a lot better than a third-floor walk-up in the Bronx."

Carmichael started walking toward me. "It's a shame what's happened to you, Charlie. You used to be a good cop. A good man. A man of principle."

Now it was my turn to laugh. "Come on, Andy. It's just us girls in here. Save the good cop bullshit for the well-heeled dopes on the other side of the door, will you?"

"Fair enough," he said. "I suppose I meant you used to be a wiser man. Wise enough to know you should never cross me."

I pulled the ends of the tie out and was satisfied by the way it looked. "Is this a one-sided conversation, or are you going to tell me what you're talking about?"

"The Fairfax case," he said. "And don't bother denying it, either. I know the widow hired you, and you were seen leaving her residence yesterday morning. You were later spotted talking to Dr. Matthew Blythe at the New York Athletic Club later that afternoon. And you were at the crime scene today."

Not only did I have gunmen trailing me, but Carmichael's shadows, too. That led my mind in directions I didn't want it to go. Directions that led to him having a hand in getting that poor bastard killed.

I kept my anger in check. "You seem to know a lot. Your snitches tell you what I had for lunch yesterday? I forgot."

"Crow," Carmichael said. "Same thing you always eat. Sticking your nose where it doesn't belong could get you hurt."

But it got me thinking about something. "I take it those were your boys with the Tommy gun yesterday?"

"Not at all," he said, "but we saw it happen. We see everything, Charlie. And the moment I want you dead, you'll never see it coming."

I watched him take a step closer to me in the mirror. He was a good half a head taller than me, and almost twice as broad. The uniform made him look even bigger. "But I don't want you dead. I want us to be friends. We used to be friends, remember?"

"Sounds great to me. Say, I've got box seats to the Yankee game tomorrow night. You still seeing that Italian broad in Queens? I can get an extra ticket for her if you ask me nicely."

Carmichael let out a heavy breath through his nose. He usually did that before he started swinging. He'd slugged me once. I wouldn't let him do it again.

But instead of throwing a punch at me, he said, "I don't

owe you an explanation for anything I do, but this one time I'll give you one. A lot of people in this town wanted that Fairfax business wrapped up tight and put to bed for good. The mayor. Business leaders. And blue bloods like the crowd Fairfax runs with. Suicide's a nasty business that tends to raise a lot of even nastier questions. They wanted it to go away, so I made it go away. Wrote it off as an accident, even though everyone in their right mind knows different. All was right with the world. Damned thing was all but forgotten."

He bent at the waist and spoke right into my ear. "Next thing I know you come out of your hole and start sniffing around, complicating things. Why is that, Charlie?"

Since he already knew so much, there was no point in denying it. I kept up my routine, straightening out my collar and flattening the lapels of my tuxedo. "I'm not complicating a damned thing. Just trying to help a widow find out why her husband killed himself."

"That's good. Since you're working for her, you can tell her you looked into it and couldn't find a thing. It'll be an eternal mystery, just like it should be."

"I already tried that. It didn't take."

"Why? And if you try to pull that client confidentiality bullshit with me, I'll put you right through that fucking mirror."

I knew he only used that word when he was desperate, and I needed to keep him as calm as possible. "She knows what you did for her, but still doesn't think it was a suicide. She was running all over town, making a fool of herself.

Some of her friends referred her to me and asked me to look into why he did it."

"Friends of hers," Carmichael repeated. "The Van Dorns, from what I hear."

I ignored that. "I explained to Mrs. Fairfax that you did her a big favor at great personal risk, too. But this isn't about you, Andy. It's about her husband and why the poor bastard killed himself in his office on that particular morning."

Carmichael stood up to his full height and folded his arms across his chest. "So that's why you were talking to Dr. Blythe yesterday?"

"He was Fairfax's oldest friend and personal doctor," I said. I left out the part about Mrs. Fairfax's list. Carmichael would have wanted to see it, which would've caused even more trouble. "I thought Fairfax might've had cancer or something and that's why he'd killed himself. Turns out he was pretty healthy." I had no intention of mentioning anything about the countess or the other women in Fairfax's life. Carmichael only would've threatened me to leave them alone. The less he knew, the better off I'd be.

But Carmichael wasn't a fool. "That's all? Nothing else?"

"Quit playing innocent, Andy," I said. "It doesn't look good on you. If you already know I was there, you've already had Hauser and his boys talking to everyone who was working at the club. You know how long I was there, so you know I wasn't there long."

"The good doctor give you the idea to head up to Fairfax's office and shoot the place up?"

"I didn't even have my gun. But whoever shot up the

office were probably the same people who've been following me since yesterday. Probably the same bunch that iced Dr. Blythe, too. You say you had me followed, so you probably already know who did it."

Carmichael's expression changed. Not enough for someone else to notice it, but enough for me to see it.

"I get it. You didn't have someone following me all the time, did you? Your bloodhounds missed that one, didn't they? What happened, Andy? Did I give them the slip? Who was it? That new guy who's working with Hauser? Billy, I think his name was."

I could tell by his expression I was right, but he'd never admit it. "You were the assignment, not Dr. Blythe."

"Then you should be out looking for whoever killed him instead of in here pestering me."

"I can pester anyone I want, especially material witnesses to a murder. Especially if there's a good chance that witness could become a suspect in said murder."

I turned to face him for the first time since he'd walked in. "I had nothing to do with that and you know it."

"Maybe I do." Carmichael shrugged. "Maybe I don't. What I do know is that you found something in a safe in Fairfax's office. That's material evidence and I want it."

"Why? The Fairfax case is closed. You said so yourself."

He uncrossed his arms and flexed his fists. "Tell me what you found."

"Nothing. It was empty."

He punched the wall next to my head. I'd been expecting it, so I didn't flinch. "Don't lie to me."

"Who's to say I'm lying? Who's to say rumors of a suicide note are true?" It was my turn to lean in a little closer this time. "And who's to say Mrs. Fairfax ever has to find out you're sitting on a suicide note left by her dear departed husband. And don't tell me you burned it, because I know you plan on using it against them sometime soon."

Carmichael backed off again and rubbed his sore hand. "You don't make threats unless you want something. So tell me what you want."

"It's not a threat, Andy. Why would I threaten you, especially after all you've done for me over the years? We're friends again. You said so yourself."

The chief's neck reddened. "Tell me what you want or I haul you in for questioning on Dr. Blythe's death right now. They'll love you in Central Booking, especially in that getup."

I figured I'd pushed my luck as far as I could. "I want you to make sure I know everything about Dr. Blythe's death as soon as you know it. Files, pictures, notes, autopsy results, everything. For that, you get my silence about the note and the cover-up about the suicide. I'm not looking to complicate your life, Andy. I just don't want you complicating mine."

Carmichael continued to rub his sore hand as he thought it over. "Okay, Charlie. You'll get Kronauer's report as soon as it's ready. Raw as red meat, too. Nothing taken out." He poked me hard in the chest with his knuckle. "But your silence isn't worth that much, so here's what you're going to do for me. I know you're on to something. People wouldn't be trying to kill you if you weren't. In return for my cooperation, I find out anything you do about whoever killed the doc. Understand?"

I decided to cut my losses and agree. "Done. I don't know anything. Not yet. But I'm working on it."

"Make sure you do." The chief rapped me twice with his knuckle before turning to leave. "Just don't make a fool out of me, Charlie. You know what happens to people who try. Hell, you're the one who used to do it to them."

He laid his hand on the door knob and unlocked it. "And I haven't mellowed any in the years since."

He opened the door and stepped outside. A flood of men in tuxedos rushed in to use the bathroom. I damned near knocked one of them over as I ducked into a stall and threw up.

Chapter 15

I left the bathroom after I'd washed out my mouth as best I could. The lobby had cleared out by then and everyone had gone up to the main ballroom for the party.

The ballroom was a pretty good size, not that I knew much about ballrooms, but it was as packed as a cross-town trolley at rush hour. The only difference was you didn't see too many tuxes or evening gowns on cross-town trolleys.

While looking for the Van Dorns, I spotted Carmichael chatting up Mayor O'Brien and some other clowns who ran the city. O'Brien had been Tammany's pick to become mayor after Jimmy Walker skipped town ahead of an indictment. The boys downtown called him Boo Boo because he always had a knack for saying the right thing at the wrong time. He'd learned about becoming mayor from a bunch of reporters waiting outside his house. When they asked him who'd be his second in command, he said, "I don't know. They haven't told me yet." He was the perfect figurehead for this town.

I headed in the opposite direction of the city elders, threading my way through small packs of revelers until I spotted Mr. and Mrs. Van Dorn talking to some people at the front of the room.

The Van Dorns made a damn good-looking couple. Mrs.

Van Dorn was in her late forties, but had managed to keep a youthful glow about her despite losing her daughter the previous year. Her hair was so blonde it was almost white. She was wearing a black gown and a string of small white pearls. It wasn't the fanciest outfit I'd seen that night, but on her it didn't have to be.

Mr. Harriman Van Dorn was the tall and dignified type, just north of fifty. His full head of dark hair was just beginning to gray at the temples, the way it should on someone like him.

Mr. Van Dorn spotted me, and signaled me to stay where I was as he left his wife to entertain the group they were talking to. When he reached me, we shook hands like old friends; maybe because, after all we'd been through together, we were.

"I got your message about Dr. Blythe," he said. "I was so happy your meeting with Father Mullins went well, but I was devastated about poor Dr. Blythe. The whole room is buzzing about it. They're saying it was a heart attack."

Even though everyone within earshot was busy talking, I kept my voice down. "It was no heart attack, sir. Just made to look like one.'"

"I was afraid you were going to say that. Poor Matthew. I liked him. What do you think was the cause of death?"

"I won't know for sure until the coroner's report comes in, but my money's on murder."

"The timing of his passing was too convenient to be natural," Mr. Van Dorn admitted. "And I'd wager the same people who attacked you and blackmailed Miss Swenson are responsible."

"Agreed. Now all we have to do is find them." That reminded me of something. "Who were those guys you sent over to my place, sir? I've never seen them before."

"We'll get to that later," Mr. Van Dorn said. "Rest assured they're competent men who have experience in this kind of thing. They spent the better part of today looking into the phone number and the mailing address Miss Swenson gave them."

It was the first bit of good news I'd heard all day. "They get anything?"

"We traced the phone number to an office on West 47th Street. It's nothing but an old desk and a phone. Used to be rented by a talent agency that went out of business a few years ago. The landlord said the tenant pays in cash on the first of the month like clockwork. Of course, the contact information the tenant provided is false. Still, we have someone watching the place, just in case they try to use it."

It was something, but it wasn't much. It was the middle of the month, so it would be weeks before we could grab whoever dropped off next month's payment, assuming they sent anyone at all. But my first question remained. "Who's 'we,' sir?"

"In time, Charlie. In time. The mailing address they gave was a post office box in Midtown. Postal Inspectors are watching it to see if anyone uses it. The box is empty now, but I'll be notified if they receive any mail."

I skipped all my questions about how he was able to get the postal police involved. I knew he'd gone to school with

President Roosevelt, so maybe that's how he'd managed it. I had more important questions, anyway. "How's Miss Swenson?"

"She's safe and so is her son," Mr. Van Dorn said, "which may change things."

"What do you mean?"

"Since the people behind this are no longer operating in the shadows, they'll probably change their tactics. They failed to kill you or secure the contents of Fairfax's safe. Chances are they will either get more aggressive, or they may fold up operations and go underground. There's simply no way to tell, which makes talking to Countess Alexandra all the more important since she's our last possible link to whoever is behind this."

"It's looking that way, sir."

"That's what you're going to confirm once and for all. Tonight. Look over my left shoulder."

I looked where Mr. Van Dorn told me to look. I had no trouble spotting her, even in this crowd. I would have spotted her anywhere, even though she had a group of men around her three-deep.

Countess Alexandra von Holstein was an inch or so taller than me, with the longest, straightest, blondest hair I had ever seen. She had sharp features and high cheek bones that would have looked severe on another woman, but on her looked beautiful. Her skin was alabaster white, but just shy of pale. Her green eyes were deep set, piercing yet gentle.

For a guy who usually went for brunettes, I had to admit she was probably the most striking woman I'd ever seen.

Not beautiful like Joan Crawford or Myrna Loy, but she had an attractive quality in the truest sense of the word. Even from across the room, she had a magnetism that literally drew me to her.

It had nothing to do with her being a woman, but who she was. It was an odd feeling I'd had only once before, back in France. A captain I'd served with at Belleau Wood had a way of getting us to follow him into combat like he was asking us to join him for a night on the town. It was a gift some people had, a gift Countess Alexandra obviously had, too.

It had nothing to do with lust or even affection. It was about persuasion. Control.

The same moment I thought it, she looked through the crowd of men around her and directly at me. It was almost as if she could tell what I was thinking. Maybe I'd been staring too long, though I didn't think I had.

She smiled. My mouth went dry.

"Alluring, isn't she?" Mr. Van Dorn sipped his champagne. "I'd like to tell you she's as cold as ice, but she's actually quite charming. Personally, I think it's the accent that puts it over, but that's just me. She manages to make a German accent sound gentle."

"I'm not looking at her accent, sir." I quit looking at her, focusing on Mr. Van Dorn. "What do we do now? She's seen us talking, so she might think we're working together. If she's mixed up in this, that could be dangerous for you, sir."

"Don't worry about me, Charlie. Besides, if she's working with the men who've been hunting you, she already knows that." He nudged me with his elbow. "See how tricky this kind of thing can be? Come, I'll introduce you to her as the man who brought Jack home to us. Let the conversation flow from there. If you get a chance to prod her a little about Fairfax, all the better. If not, don't push it."

I shook off the feeling her look had given me. I felt lit, even though the only thing I'd had to drink since I got there was the water I palmed into my mouth from the bathroom faucet. "I don't think she'll be that easy to crack, sir, especially not in a place like this."

Mr. Van Dorn drained his glass and put it on the silver tray of a passing waiter. "All the more reason we might get lucky and catch her off guard. She's probably not expecting to be asked awkward questions. There's only one way to find out."

"What do I say to her? I'm not big on small talk, especially at parties like this."

"Just be you, Charlie. Blunt and to the point, but subtle when it comes to Fairfax."

"Got it," I said. "Subtlety is my middle name."

Mr. Van Dorn moved toward the countess. "I thought it was Francis."

"You know everything, don't you, sir?"

Mr. Van Dorn kept walking.

***

Mr. Van Dorn had no trouble parting the crowd of men surrounding the countess. I was surprised she recognized him, and even offered her cheek to him.

"Forgive me for interrupting," Mr. Van Dorn said, "but

there's someone here I'd like all of you to meet. A personal hero of mine and also a friend. Something of a local celebrity, though he's too modest to admit it. A man to whom I owe a great debt because he brought my son, Jack, back to me and avenged my daughter's death. Mr. Charles Doherty of the New York City Police Department."

I felt myself blush at the polite applause the small crowd gave me. I blushed even more when Countess Alexandra offered me her gloved hand. She smelled of lilacs and sweet champagne. "What an honor this is. I've heard much about you, Mr. Doherty." The accent was light, just like the voice Miss Swenson had described hearing on the phone. "I'm honored to finally make your acquaintance. It's so rare to meet a genuine hero these days."

Mr. Van Dorn had told me to act normal, so I did. "No reason to be honored, ma'am. Though I've got to admit I've never been around royalty before."

The moneyed crowd laughed that condescending laugh people give when a kitten plays with a ball of string or a dog does a trick.

But Mr. Van Dorn didn't laugh, and neither did the countess. "My title is just a word on a piece of parchment burned during the war," she said. "May I call you Charles?"

"I'd prefer it if you called me Charlie like everyone else, ma'am."

"As long as you agree to call me Alex. Ma'am makes me feel even older than I already do." She gestured to the two men standing to her left. They hadn't laughed, either. "Allow me to introduce you to my associates. Dr. Ottmar Rudat and

175

Herr Gerhard Tessmer, fellow refugees from our troubled homeland."

Both Germans bowed at the waist before shaking my hand. Dr. Rudat was a pinch-faced man of about seventy with thinning white hair and, God help me, a pair of pince-nez glasses perched on the bridge of his nose. He looked as comfortable in a tuxedo as a mechanic in overalls.

I pegged Tessmer to be about fifty, taller than the rest of us by a head or two, and thin as a rail. He looked at me a little harder than he should have, almost like he had seen me before. Or maybe he was afraid I might recognize him.

I played a hunch and gave his arm a good tug as we shook hands. He did a good job of trying not to wince. A sore right shoulder.

Acquired from getting slugged by a guy with a bundle of books in the dark the previous night? That would explain the look he was giving me. Maybe. I made a mental note to keep an eye on him.

The countess went on, "I know Germanic names can be confusing to the American tongue, so just call them Otto and Gerry. Everyone does."

I realized Mr. Van Dorn had skillfully distracted the rest of the group with some banter of his own, giving me a chance to talk to the three Germans alone. I decided to start with Otto. "What kind of doctor are you?"

"Psychiatry," he said. "The study of the mind. Of humanity itself, if I may be so bold."

"Sounds like you've come to the right place," I said. "Plenty of people in this town need a doctor like you. If you ever decide to hang your shingle, you'll have a line of patients around the block in no time flat."

The countess laughed at the confused look on Otto's face, and translated what I'd said into German. I knew enough of the language to get the gist of what she said: The monkey thinks you should open a practice here.

I didn't let on that I'd understood what she said. Like my old man used to tell me, "Sometimes a little ignorance can go a long way."

The doctor remained grim. "Perhaps I will. One never knows."

I looked at Tessmer, who hadn't taken his beady eyes off me since I'd joined the group. "What about you? What line are you in?"

"Industrialist."

I waited for more but that was it, so I pushed a little. "That covers a lot of ground. What kind of industry?"

"Many kinds."

The countess rushed in to fill the gap in the conversation. "You must forgive my friends, Charlie. The nuances of the English language are still difficult for them, so they don't speak much."

"I don't blame them," I said. "I've been speaking it my whole life and still don't know all the words." I stayed with Tessmer. "I couldn't help but notice you winced when I shook your hand. Hope my grip wasn't too strong."

A burst of pride. "Not at all." Then, "I merely injured it in a sparring session this week. Sometimes I forget I'm not as young as I used to be."

An idea popped into my head and I went with it. "You're a boxer? Ever go to the New York Athletic Club? I hear a lot of people go there to box, among other things."

Tessmer's eyes narrowed just enough to show me that the name meant something to him. "So I hear. But I am afraid the expense would be too great, as boxing is merely a hobby for me."

"Pretty dangerous hobby."

A light laugh from Alex quickly changed the mood. "Boxing pales in comparison to the dangers you must have faced as a policeman. Why, I believe you are the first hero we have met since we arrived in New York. So many men like to boast of what they've done, but not you. You're very modest, aren't you, Charlie?"

I ignored her attempt at flattery and stayed focused. "How long have you been in New York?"

"About a year," she allowed. "Maybe less. Time flies quickly in big cities like New York."

"A year's a long time. Guess you've made a lot of friends in your time here."

"No, not that many. I'm afraid some people still hold resentments over the unpleasantness that took place between our two countries."

"I don't know about that." I looked back at the crowd of men Mr. Van Dorn had pulled away. "You seemed pretty popular when I came over here just now."

An eyebrow flicked up. "That's just mere curiosity on their part. The newest flower in the garden always attracts the most bees. They're boys, mostly, not like you."

So we were on to flattery again. I guessed her style had gotten her pretty far with most of the men in her life, so I played along. "Thanks for making me feel ancient."

"Oh, I didn't mean it that way." She touched my arm for the briefest of moments and, despite my wariness, I felt a warm feeling spread through my body. "I meant in terms of wisdom, not years. And in accomplishments, too. Everyone tells us that you're the man who tracked down Jack Van Dorn. The tough cop who went in and got 'im." She actually giggled. "Went in there and got 'im. What a quaint turn of phrase for such a heroic act."

"Don't believe everything you hear or read. It was a hell of a lot more complicated than that."

"I have no doubt of that." Her eyes softened. "Though, I must confess that I find it odd how everyone is happy to talk about how you rescued Jack, but they hardly ever mention a word about poor Jessica's murder. Most Americans I've met are like that. They prefer to focus on the positive as opposed to the negative. Dwell on the light instead of the dark. America is a nation of dreamers in a harsh world."

I could tell she had hoped I'd take it as a compliment, but judging by her tone I knew it wasn't. I decided it was time to quit fencing and do some digging. "I wouldn't say that. Not everyone in America sees the best in everything. Cops and firemen and doctors see bad things every day. Hell, some people even make quite a pretty penny out of misfortune. Take insurance companies, for instance."

Otto and Tessmer either hadn't heard me or hadn't understood what I'd said.

But Alex had heard me just fine. The way she looked at me changed just a little, though I'd be damned if I could explain how. She became less playful and much more focused. "Of course. A successful society needs people who are willing to deal with the unpleasant aspects of living. Those who are willing act, to do that which is necessary, that which others cannot do or refuse to do."

I decided it was a good time to introduce her native language into the conversation. "Wer rastet, der rostet." It meant, "He who rests grows rusty."

The three of them visibly tensed. Suddenly, the monkey comment wasn't so funny.

Otto recovered quicker than the others. "You speak German, then?"

Alex added, "Your accent is excellent, Charlie. Where did you learn it? In school?"

"Not exactly." I grinned. "I picked it up in France. My Uncle Sam paid for a few summers abroad back when I was a kid."

Dr. Otto flinched and looked away.

Tessmer glared at me even harder, if that was possible.

But Alexandra kept playing the part of the charming aristocrat. "The war. Of course. How silly of me. Please forgive me."

Tessmer surprised me by asking, "May I ask where in France you served, or are such things still secret?"

"They put me in a charming little spot by the Marne called Belleau Wood. Would've had a great time if it wasn't for the explosions and gunfire."

Tessmer's eyes flashed. "Teufel Hunden," he swore. Hell hound. The name the Germans gave us after we'd won that hellish battle. "I was there, too."

"I thought you looked familiar." I winked. "Maybe that's why."

Tessmer didn't look like he appreciated my humor. "I highly doubt it."

The countess broke the ice forming between me and Tessmer. "Teufel Hunden? So, you were a Marine?"

"Still am." I smiled. "No such thing as an ex-Marine. I'm Corps to the core, and always will be."

"And what do you do for employment now, Charlie? I mean, now that you're no longer with the police."

It had taken a while, but the countess had finally made her first mistake. Mr. Van Dorn hadn't said I wasn't a cop anymore. And the papers hadn't run any stories about my retirement, either.

She knew more about me than I'd thought.

I kept it simple. "I'm retired."

Tessmer looked me up and down. "You seem too young to be retired. I would imagine a man of your skill and ability could easily find work if he so chose."

I shrugged. "People ask me to look into things for them from time to time. Helps me keep my hand in. Don't want to get rusty."

Dr. Otto piped up. "What kinds of things do you look into?"

"The kind I can't talk about, unless they're clients."

The countess sipped her champagne. "Once a hero,

always a hero, Charlie. Such noble qualities must come naturally to a man, or to a people. They can never be learned or acquired. But it's as much of a curse as it is a blessing. So many people requiring your help, it doesn't leave much time for life's other noble pursuits like marriage or a family. It's nearly impossible for a man and woman to remain together under such circumstances. And when there are children involved, well, the children suffer most of all, don't they? They always do when a marriage dissolves."

That smile again before she quickly added, "But, of course, I don't need to tell you that. I'm sure you must have seen the tragic effects of divorce many times in your career."

But I knew she wasn't talking about divorce in general. She was talking about my divorce from Theresa. She was talking about our daughters.

These bastards already knew all about me.

Her smile changed as she suddenly noticed someone across the room. "How boorish of me to go on and on about such depressing topics. When you were a policeman, did you have the chance to work with Chief Carmichael? I see him over there right now, talking to Mayor O'Brian and some other people."

I figured she was trying to make a graceful exit, and was interested in how she was going to do it. "I've known Andy most of my life. Before, during, and after we were in the department together. I was the best man at his wedding."

She didn't seem to hear that as I watched her eyes move over him. "I've spoken with him several times, enough to think of him as a friend. He's quite a man. Brave, strong, handsome."

"Crooked as a dog's hind leg, too."

She didn't seem to hear that, either.

"You say you were friends," Otto added, "yet I understand he was instrumental in your dismissal from the police, was he not? I find that interesting."

"Not really. It's just politics."

Alex perked up and waved at someone across the room. "Oh, Mrs. Astor is here and I just have to say hello. Otto and Gerry, you should meet her, too. She's been asking all about you." The charm reappeared. "Charlie, it's been wonderful chatting, but Mrs. Astor and I have been trying to meet for ages. It's been lovely to meet you, and I'd love to continue our discussion soon. Enjoy the rest of the evening."

She glided away, with Dr. Otto following in her wake.

Only Tessmer stayed behind and extended his hand. "Yes, it was quite interesting to meet you, Herr Doherty. I hope we have a chance to meet again soon."

I shook his hand. This time, he didn't wince.

I had no intention of letting him go without a parting shot. "Good luck in your industry interests. If you need any help with insurance, give me a call. I know a few people at Fairfax Liability who'd love to have your business."

Tessmer slowly let go of my hand and brought his finger up beneath his chin, as if he was thinking of something. He wasn't nearly as subtle as the countess had been. "I may take you up on that. I've been looking at some properties in upstate New York that have piqued my interest."

Sweat popped up across my back. I didn't like where this

was headed. "That so? Whereabouts?"

"A small town on your Hudson River. Begins with a P, but it's one of those savage words that are so difficult to pronounce."

I felt my face redden again, only this time I wasn't blushing. "Poughkeepsie."

"That's the place. I understand it is an old Indian name. Why Americans insist on using the customs of conquered people, I will never understand."

"Guess that's why we call frankfurters 'hot dogs' now."

Tessmer smiled and raised his finger in the air. "For now, Herr Doherty." He brought that finger to his brow and offered a slight salute. "Until we meet again."

I wanted to grab the son of a bitch by the throat, but knew it wouldn't accomplish anything. The krauts had made their point as subtly as I'd tried to make mine. We all knew who each other were and what we were up to.

Only, they knew more than I did.

So that's why I stood there like a dope, watching Tessmer join Countess Alex and Otto as they chatted up Carmichael. The chief saw me looking at them and moved so his back was facing me.

No, hitting Tessmer wouldn't have accomplished anything, but getting to a phone would.

I darted out of the room, moving as politely as I could without barreling anyone over. Mr. Van Dorn tried to catch my eye, but I didn't have time to talk. I dodged and twisted and excused my way through the crowd until I hit the outer lobby, and bolted for the pay phones near the washrooms.

I damn near pulled the phone off the wall as I had the operator connect me to my ex-wife's number in Poughkeepsie. I fed in enough coins to cover the charge and waited while the phone rang. After the fifth ring, I checked my watch. Almost nine o'clock. Someone should've been there. Where the hell was everyone? It didn't take long for my mind to consider Tessmer might already have them. If he did—

Theresa answered on the seventh ring. I barely let her speak before I said, "It's me. Don't hang up, goddamn it, because this is important."

"Hang up? Why would I hang up? I've been trying to get you on the phone for weeks, you no good, lousy bastard," she said. "All the money you're raking in and you leave your wife and children destitute?"

It was the same argument we'd been having since she took the kids and moved back up to live with her parents in Poughkeepsie. She had left me when Carmichael had put me out to pasture and the graft money dried up. She wouldn't let the girls speak to me while the whole Grand Central Massacre business was in the papers, either.

But once she'd gotten wind that I had a steady job making more than I had on the force, she suddenly wanted to reconcile. Once a working girl, always a working girl.

I sent money for our daughters directly to the girls' school. The nuns made sure the girls had more than they needed. Giving it to Theresa would've been like throwing it in the toilet. She'd buy herself furs and handbags while the kids ate cheese sandwiches on stale white bread for dinner.

"Not now, Theresa. Is your old man home?"

"My father is not an old man," Theresa said. "He's just been named captain of the Poughkeepsie Police Department and—"

I didn't care about his career. All that mattered was that he had guns in the house and knew how to use them. "Is. He. Home?"

"Unlike you, he's working. He's—"

I punched the wall next to the phone. "Goddamn it, Theresa! For once in your life shut up and listen to me. I need you to lock all the doors and windows and turn off every light in the house. Get the girls into one room and barricade yourselves in there with one of Al's guns. You remember how to handle a pistol?"

"Of course, but—"

"I want you to get one and shoot anyone who tries to come in the house who's not him, including anyone wearing a badge. Understand?"

"Charlie?" Her voice got small, like it used to get when she decided she didn't understand something. "What's going on?"

"Everything will be fine if you do what I say. I'll call your father and he'll explain everything when he gets home. Just keep the girls safe."

I hung up the phone before she could argue. Theresa had worked the streets long enough to know how to handle herself. If Tessmer sent people to the house, they'd get more than they bargained for.

I dug into my pocket for more loose change, when I saw

Mr. Van Dorn heading my way. "What happened?"

"They threatened my family."

"Alex?"

"No. The bastard with her. Tessmer."

Mr. Van Dorn looked at the phone. "Have you reached them? Are they safe?"

"Yes, but I was going to call her father to make sure he gets home as quickly as possible. Tessmer knows where they live, sir. He mentioned Poughkeepsie."

Mr. Van Dorn picked up the phone and had the operator connect him with a Washington number on a reverse charge.

I didn't know what he was doing, and I didn't really care. I just had to get Al back home so he could protect my kids. "Sir, I need to…"

Mr. Van Dorn held up one finger to silence me as his call obviously went through. He didn't bother introducing himself to whoever answered the phone. "Contact the New York State Police and have them send a couple of cars to the following address." He gave them Theresa's address.

I'd never given him Theresa's address. "Someone may be watching the house and should be apprehended if they are. The house belongs to one Detective Alfred Proscia of the Poughkeepsie Police Department. Have someone from the state police contact his supervisor and send him home immediately. His family needs him."

Mr. Van Dorn hung up the phone. "Come with me, Charlie. We have much to do."

I hurried after him. "Who were you talking to, sir? And I don't remember telling you anything about where my family lives."

"There's a great deal we've kept from each other, Charlie. But that all ends tonight. The time for secrets is over."

I followed Mr. Van Dorn downstairs to the main lobby and out through the revolving doors, on to Lexington Avenue where he had a car waiting.

As soon I hit the street, I spotted a maroon Cadillac Fleetwood limousine parked three behind Mr. Van Dorn's car. A familiar face was behind the wheel. A blond, square-jawed man who had about as much business being at the Stuyvesant Society Gala as I did. Maybe he was there for the same reasons.

Detective Steve Hauser.

In that single moment, a lot of the things I'd been hearing for the past day or so began to come together. And I didn't like the picture they were making.

Mr. Van Dorn called after me as I walked toward Hauser's car. "Charlie, where are you going? We don't have time to waste."

I squatted at the open passenger window and spoke to Hauser. "Funny, the things you see crawl out of the sewer at night."

Hauser refused to look at me. "If you know what's good for you, you'll keep your goddamned mouth shut and get going."

But despite Mr. Van Dorn's beckoning, I wasn't in a hurry. I wasn't just teasing Hauser, either. I was working. "Good thing for me I've never been that smart. Say, what's a bum like you driving a fancy car like this? It sure as hell isn't

Carmichael's ride. He ditched his Caddy when he found reform. Who are you wheeling for, Steve?"

Hauser punched the wheel. "Goddamn it, Charlie. I told you to get out of here. Now."

That's when I smelled it. A gentle scent that came from the back seat of the limousine. It wasn't fumes from the Caddy's tailpipe or the stale cigarettes on Hauser's breath.

It was the scent of lilacs.

The lead investigator in the Fairfax and Blythe deaths, not to mention Chief Carmichael's Black Hand, was driving Countess Alexandra von Holstein and her friends.

My knees damned near buckled. Sometimes I really hated being right.

"You're in way over your head, Steve."

"And you don't know what the hell you're talking about." Hauser nodded toward Mr. Van Dorn, who was standing by his car looking puzzled. "Run along, now. It's not polite to keep your boss waiting. Your real boss."

I pulled myself up before I fell over, and walked back to Mr. Van Dorn's car. He climbed into the backseat after I did and told the driver to take us somewhere. My mind was racing too fast for me to hear where.

"What the hell was that all about, Charlie?"

It was the first time I had ever heard him swear, even when his children were in danger. But if there was time to trot out a curse, this was it.

"This whole mess just got a whole lot worse, sir."

Chapter 16

I should have been surprised to find Father Mullins waiting for us when we got back to my place, but I wasn't. I had smelled his pipe on the street long before I put the key in the door. Besides, that night was turning out to be a night for surprises.

The aging Jesuit looked up at us from behind my desk through a cloud of thin smoke. "Hope you'll forgive the familiarity of letting myself in, Charles, but I'm afraid we're well beyond the point of conventional politeness."

I'd already had enough surprises and scares for one day to last me a lifetime. This was just one more to add to the list. "When did the Vatican start teaching lock picking?"

"No need, Charles. I've had a key for some time. We have used this apartment as a base of operations for years now."

Mr. Van Dorn had just taken a seat on the couch. "Sit down, Charlie. I promise that everything will be much clearer." He gestured to the empty chair beside the fireplace. "Please."

I shifted the chair so I could see both men in my peripheral vision at the same time. After all the things I'd learned that night, I didn't know who to trust anymore, except for the .38 under my left arm.

Mr. Van Dorn began. "I'm afraid I haven't been entirely honest with you, Charlie, but I promise it's been for a good reason."

"I sure as hell hope so, sir, because my head feels like it's about to explode."

Mr. Van Dorn said, "Before you joined the Marines, you were on the police force at the outset of the Great War. You remember the problems we had with German spies committing acts of sabotage here in the city and elsewhere?"

I'd been a rookie back then, but I'd worked crowd control on some of the bigger crime scenes. German sympathizers had blown up a few buildings, sabotaged shipments to England before America formally got into the war. One of them had even tried to blow up the head of J.P. Morgan one summer. "I didn't work the cases, but I remember reading about them."

"Well, I lived through them," Mr. Van Dorn said. "The bastards managed to smuggle explosives into the cargo holds of several of my ships carrying goods for the war effort. They managed to sink several of my family's ships, and I was determined to find out who was behind it. Not only were they sinking my family's vessels, but they were damaging invaluable goods and munitions the Allies needed for the war. Eventually, I found one of their unexploded devices hidden within the hold of some sugar we were shipping to Europe; a discovery that helped us track down the spy ring behind it."

I was beginning to get annoyed. "Congratulations, sir, but I don't understand what something that happened almost twenty years ago has to do with me now."

Father Mullins cleared his throat. "Because the same people who tried to sabotage this country before are trying to do so again. Only this time, they're trying to do it through far more insidious means."

More pieces began to come together in my head. I asked Mr. Van Dorn, "Is this why you spend so much time in Washington?"

"Part of the reason," he allowed. "I've been affiliated with the federal government since the Great War, in an effort to prevent our enemies from inflicting harm on the homeland. After the war, the German threat was replaced by Communists and other radicals set on spreading their revolution throughout Western democracies. You already know Franklin Roosevelt and I are close. When he became president, he asked me to conduct my activities in a more informal, unofficial manner so as not to tip off any subversive foreign agents who might have a presence within our own government."

"You mean Germany?" I asked. The Treaty of Versailles had ended the war on the condition that the German people pay for the losses the rest of Europe had suffered. The country didn't make a buck without the British or the French getting a piece. "From what I've read, they can hardly feed themselves since Versailles, much less wage war on anyone."

"For now," Father Mullins said, "but one should never underestimate the Hun. He is crafty and unrelenting. You saw him at his deadliest in France. You know how cunning he can be. The Great War may have ended for us, but for the German people it is a continuing affront to their honor that requires reckoning. Harry and I, and a few others, have been monitoring the situation more closely since Hitler's rise to power."

Mr. Van Dorn added, "In addition to monitoring the Communist threat, I've also been part of an effort that tracks German citizens who have emigrated to this country after the armistice was signed. We have watched where they've settled and with whom they've associated since coming to America."

Another piece clicked into place. "That means you must've known about Fairfax and Countess Alexandra. Why didn't you tell me?"

"I didn't know for certain," Mr. Van Dorn said. "I had heard rumors. I suspected. And yes, I knew who she was, but I didn't have proof of the extent of their relationship until you opened that safe. I can't stress enough the importance of the information you gave us that night. It's why they sent those men to stop you."

Father Mullins added, "You uncovered the entire breadth and depth of their relationship. You confirmed Dr. Blythe's suspicions that Alexandra had virtual control over Walter. Now that you have had the pleasure of meeting her, you can see how captivating she can be. Once she converted him into believing in the mystical power of the runes in the notebook you showed me, she was able to convince him to finance several organizations essential to her cause."

I got to my desk and opened the top drawer. I pulled out

the list Mary Pat had given me. "These organizations?"

Father Mullins read the list aloud. "The Teutonia Association, Friends of New Germany, Der Stahlem, Gauleitung-USA." He looked at Mr. Van Dorn, then me. "These are some of the groups in Fairfax's ledger, but you had them before you found it. Where did you get this list?"

"A friend of mine did some research on Walter for me. She said he was in the society pages at events for those groups. It didn't make sense to me then, but after Dr. Blythe told me about the countess, it made a bit more sense. After hearing what you two just told me, it makes complete sense."

Mr. Van Dorn rose and took the list from the Jesuit. He looked uneasy as he read them. "These organizations are run by dedicated German loyalists, but their membership is comprised of amateurs. Most of their members are good people who actually believe they are simple German-American civic groups. I believe the people who followed you and made attempts on your life were amateurs thinking they were serving a greater good."

Mr. Van Dorn placed the list on the desk. "Had I known they were capable of such violence, I would have warned you from the outset. I hope you believe that."

After all Mr. Van Dorn had done for me, I had to believe him. But I still wasn't happy about it. "You could've told me all of this before the gala tonight."

"You met Countess Alexandra this evening," Father Mullins said. "You felt the flutter in your stomach when you saw her, the quickening of your pulse. The magnetism of the woman's very being?" The Jesuit smiled. "Don't look so surprised, Charles. I may be an old priest, but I'm still a man."

Mr. Van Dorn said, "Thanks to what you retrieved from Fairfax's safe, we have been able to find out a great deal about her. Alexandra von Holstein is not really a countess at all, but one of the few women to have studied at the University of Vienna. Psychiatry. She has spent her life learning all aspects of the mind and human consciousness, the very things that make us who and what we are."

"Psychiatry?" I asked. "Dr. Otto said he was a psychiatrist. I even made a crack about it."

"He is," Father Mullins said. "We believe the two of them were working together in the seduction of Walter Fairfax to gain access to his fortune. It was quite a clever operation."

"Had you known who she was and about her abilities," Mr. Van Dorn added, "you may have tipped your hand immediately and she never would've spoken to you. As it stands now you tipped your hand anyway, but at least now you know what we're up against."

I walked away from the desk and ran my hands over my head. I felt like I kept having one wall of information after another dropped right in front of me. I craned my neck until the bones popped. It helped relieve some of the pressure.

It also helped me make sense of the entire mess. "So, Alex, Otto, and Tessmer are working for Hitler."

"Or for people working with him," Mr. Van Dorn said. "Tessmer's background has been tougher for us to uncover, but we believe he may be the organizer of these various groups Fairfax has helped finance. Based on everything

Hitler has said publicly, we believe he's looking to re-arm Germany and strike back at the Allies for the indignity his country suffered at Versailles."

I didn't know much about politics, but I knew something about war. "The French and the British will never let that happen."

"Don't be so sure, Charles," Father Mullins warned. "It's been almost twenty years since the war. An entire generation was too young to remember it. Time heals all wounds, save for vengeance. Some people believe we were too harsh with Germany and that the time has come to let them get back on their feet. They have forgotten the true nature of the enemy we faced then has only worsened with time."

I dropped my head into my hands and tried to rub some circulation into my skull, hoping it might help me understand all of this better. "If you think the three of them are spies, why not arrest them?"

"We've done that in the past," Mr. Van Dorn said. "We got the people we were after, but it forced their network to go further underground. I'm not just interested in Alexandra and Otto and Tessmer. I'm interested in the people they're giving orders to. I've had people from the Bureau of Investigation in Washington and various other police forces around the country following these people. We haven't had any success in finding out where they go or who they support." He pointed at my desk. "But once you opened that safe, now we know plenty."

I was less confused and more interested. "Like what?"

Father Mullins held up the ledger. "Like where Alexandra

196

had Fairfax send his money and how much." He held up the leases. "And what she had Walter purchase for her and where. Real estate throughout New Jersey and Long Island, many of which were donated to some of the organizations on your list."

Now we were talking about something I understood. "The lease for the apartment he bought for Alexandra is in there, isn't it? Because if we have the address, I can—"

"We checked it yesterday," Mr. Van Dorn said. "She moved out the day Walter died. I've already had our associates check the place and they came up empty. It took a little prodding on our part, but the doorman finally admitted that Fairfax was in the apartment with Alexandra that morning. A moving truck was already parked out front when he left. The same truck that moved some of her things out as soon as Fairfax was gone."

I was enough of a detective to know that wasn't a good sign. "Sounds like she knew she'd have to get the hell out of there fast."

Father Mullins agreed. "The question is, how could she have known Walter was going to go into the office and kill himself that morning?"

The answer came to me pretty quickly. "The phone call. Someone called him at his office. A Miss Schmidt, according to what Miss Swenson told me, but she had a German accent. One she'd never heard before, and was surprised Mr. Fairfax took."

"Perhaps Schmidt was Alexandra's code name for an emergency," Mr. Van Dorn said.

"An emergency that would've caused him to kill himself afterwards?" Another piece clicked. "An emergency that made him call his doctor right afterward."

Something Mary Pat had found in the records of Walter Fairfax's past flashed before my eyes. I picked up the phone and dialed the morgue. I got Kronauer on the line; he wasn't happy.

"Damn it, Charlie," the coroner said. "I already told you I'd call when I had something on Blythe, but I won't have anything final until tomorrow."

"I don't care about the final report," I said. "I want to know what your gut tells you. I won't hold you to it, I promise. I need your instincts, Hank, not proof, and I need it right now."

Kronauer hesitated before saying, "It was some kind of sudden event, but not a coronary. The entire body reeked of gin, too much for it to be from normal consumption."

I closed my eyes and damned near prayed before I asked the question I was getting at. "Any other odors?"

"There was a faint scent of almonds when I cut him open, which—"

I'd heard enough and hung up the phone. "We need to get a judge to exhume Walter Fairfax's body as soon as possible."

Mr. Van Dorn said, "That's a drastic move, Charlie. One we should consider carefully before presenting it to Mrs. Fairfax. Any judge will want her permission first."

"And she'll give it," I told him. "Because Walter Fairfax didn't commit suicide. He was already dead."

Chapter 17

Sometimes, I hated being right.

I watched Mr. Van Dorn console Mrs. Fairfax the next morning, holding her hand as she quietly wept into her handkerchief. An anxious maid stood in the doorway, ready in case her mistress needed something.

I sat next to Mr. Van Dorn as we watched the proud widow absorb all the tragedies we had just dropped in her lap. She had not only lost a husband, but her brother, too.

Both of them had been murdered by the same people.

"You're absolutely sure? You know for a fact they were poisoned? Both of them?"

"Cyanide," Mr. Van Dorn told her.

She looked up from her handkerchief, her reddened eyes angry. "But how could the police have missed something so obvious?"

"It wasn't all that obvious," Mr. Van Dorn explained. "The coroner didn't do an autopsy on Walter because the cause of death was clear. The nature of his wounds made a sealed coffin unavoidable, and prevented anyone from detecting the presence of poison until the exhumation."

"And you found the same poison in my brother's system?"

"His death was ruled a coronary at first, but further

analysis showed the presence of cyanide in his system."

"But why would Walter have taken poison? His mother killed herself with arsenic. It took her days to die. He watched her suffer. He knew how horrible a death it would be."

"Which was why we believe the person who poisoned him told him it was arsenic," Mr. Van Dorn explained. "He shot himself to avoid suffering as his mother did. The act made an autopsy moot, and the poisoning went undetected until now."

I was glad he spared her the details. Since she'd ordered Walter's remains to be placed in the family crypt immediately, his body had never been embalmed. I'd been there when they removed the stone covering his crypt earlier that morning. The smell of almonds was overwhelming. A few hours later, Kronauer's tests confirmed it.

Mrs. Fairfax balled up her fists in her lap. "I knew something was wrong. I just knew it. But how he was poisoned?"

Mr. Van Dorn skipped over that point. "Mr. Doherty is trying to determine that as we speak. We don't want to get your hopes up yet, but we have a few promising leads."

I had to fight to keep my face blank. We already knew exactly what had happened.

On the day he died, Walter Fairfax left his house around five in the morning. Instead of going to the office, he went to Alexandra's place across town, probably for a quick romp before work. I didn't know how she introduced the cyanide into his system, but she did. It was a high enough dosage to begin working on him as soon as he got to the office.

Miss Swenson said Walter's stomach was already bothering him, and he was beginning to break out into a cold sweat. Classic symptoms of cyanide poisoning.

A Miss Schmidt called his office and Walter insisted on taking the call immediately. I was pretty sure he knew it was Alexandra. She probably knew how Walter's mother died, and probably told him he'd been poisoned by arsenic, not cyanide. She probably knew he kept a gun in the office and, being a psychiatrist and his lover, knew him well enough to know what he'd do.

Walter called Dr. Blythe in a panic, but when he couldn't reach him, he got desperate. He stuck his gun in his mouth and pulled the trigger. Without an autopsy, the poisoning would go undetected forever.

The scheme was as brutal as it was clever.

But Alex didn't know about the safe or the records he kept. Neither did their spy, Miss Swenson.

I didn't know why Alex had decided to poison Walter. She had the poor bastard jumping through hoops. He had given her everything she asked for and more.

No, I didn't know why she decided to end it, but I intended on asking her that personally, and soon.

Technically, Walter Fairfax really had killed himself, but he hadn't been given much of a choice.

And Mrs. Fairfax was in no state of mind to appreciate the difference.

"And you're sure the same people who killed Walter killed my brother? Was it because I hired Mr. Doherty? Did I cause them to murder him?"

Mr. Van Dorn held her hand tightly. "Don't allow yourself to think like that. These people are murderers. Your husband and your brother were killed by ruthless people whose aims we're still investigating. But don't worry. We're hunting them, and we're very close to finding them. I don't have enough information to share with you now, but we'll know more within a week at the latest, I assure you."

She dabbed her eyes one final time and sat upright. Her moment of weakness had passed and a lifetime of resiliency kicked in. She looked at me. "The only assurances I want are those that only Mr. Doherty can give me."

I could tell what she meant by her tone, but I hoped like hell I was wrong.

Mr. Van Dorn quickly said, "Charles is an excellent detective, Eleanor. We've only found out this much thanks to his hard work having led us this far. We'll catch the people responsible, I promise you."

But the widow never took her eyes off me. "You know what I'm asking, Mr. Doherty. I don't simply want these murderers found. I want them dead."

"Eleanor." Mr. Van Dorn dropped her hand. "You can't mean that."

"I've never meant anything more in my life. I will not abide them being alive while my husband and brother are molding in their graves. I don't care what it takes or what it costs. Double your price. Quadruple it if you must. I will give you a million dollars in cash for each of them if that's what you want. I want them dead and I expect you to kill them."

Mr. Van Dorn went pale. "That's not possible."

But Mrs. Fairfax ignored him. "You killed the men who wronged the Van Dorn family, Mr. Doherty. I expect the same satisfaction. Kill them, or I will burn this city down around me. I will tell the world about Chief Carmichael's perjury in my husband's investigation. I will remind my friends of your own career as a corrupt policeman." She looked at Mr. Van Dorn. "And Jack's willful association with the undesirables who not only kidnapped him, but led to the murder of his own sister."

Mr. Van Dorn pushed his chair away from her as though he'd been slapped.

I'd seen this reaction in grieving people before. They were hurt and cornered, lashing out at anything near them, even the people trying to help them.

A cruel tone was in her voice. "Yes, Harry. The gossip-mongers in our circle don't just talk about my misfortunes, but yours as well. There have been whisperings about Jack's involvement in his own kidnapping. About Mr. Doherty's background, too, and how he's serving as your own personal lapdog now. Perhaps he's sharing everything he finds with you. These are nothing but whispers for the moment, of course. Sparks of information here and there." She leaned forward ever so slightly. "But one puff from me will ignite those sparks into an inferno that will burn this entire city to the ground, and all of you with it."

She stood up so quickly, Mr. Van Dorn and I flinched. "My family deserves justice, gentlemen. Not the kind of justice doled out in a courtroom, but justice in the same manner in which they lost their lives. Earlier, you said you needed a week. Well, you have a week before I begin seeking vengeance on all of those who have failed me, starting with the both of you."

She turned and walked out of the study. The maid followed her out.

The butler appeared with our hats, as if we didn't already know it was time to go.

***

Once we were on the street, it took Mr. Van Dorn a few minutes to speak. "I don't think I've ever seen anyone that angry before, Charlie."

I popped my hat onto my head and pulled the brim low. I kept looking around to see if anyone was following us. Between the krauts and Carmichael's men, there was no telling who might be looking for me. "We've got more to worry about than an old widow's rage, sir. Carmichael's going to be furious when he finds out about the exhumation, if he doesn't know about it already. He'll have my ass in a chair under a lot of hot lights if he finds me."

"Then I suppose we're lucky that we already have a plan."

But I knew luck didn't have anything to do with it. It was called thinking ahead.

Among the papers we had found in Fairfax's safe, three of them were property deeds Fairfax had donated to the Friends of New Germany. One was a ten-acre spread in Suffolk County, out on Long Island. The other two were across the Hudson River, in New Jersey. The plan was for me to check out each one on my own to see what made these parcels so special.

It wasn't much of a plan, but it was all we had.

When we reached his car at the corner, Mr. Van Dorn handed me the keys. I already had everything I needed stashed in the trunk.

"You're sure I can't talk you into taking someone with you, Charlie? Detective Loomis, maybe? Someone?"

"Loomis isn't built for this kind of work, and everyone else I'd trust is still on the force. Carmichael looked pretty cozy with Alexandra last night, and Hauser is driving them around places. Anyone with a badge could lead them right to me, even if they didn't mean to. It's best if I try to handle this alone."

He watched me climb behind the wheel of his car and start it up. He leaned in through the window and said, "I'll expect one call from you in the morning and one call in the evening. I'll be in Washington, far beyond the reach of any phone taps Chief Carmichael might try to use. Father Mullins will be available in an emergency if you can't reach me. Best for you to drive down and meet me there instead of coming back to New York. The chief will be easier to handle if we're beyond his reach."

I was still getting used to the idea that a priest was involved in all of this. Hell, I was still getting used to the idea of how complicated everything was. "After everything calms down, you're going to have to tell me what you're really up to, sir. No more secrets."

Mr. Van Dorn smiled as he stood away from the car. "No more secrets, Charlie. But if things work out the way

I think they will, we will definitely have a more extensive conversation." He patted the door. "Be safe, my friend. We need you."

I put the car in gear and pulled away from the curb. Long Island was a long way away.

Chapter 18

I didn't know why Mr. Van Dorn had a police scanner in his car, and I'd never asked him.

But I'd already reached Nassau County when I heard the dispatcher make the alert over the radio.

"This is an all points bulletin. Be on the lookout for Charles Doherty, retired detective, NYPD. Age forty-five, height five feet seven inches, weight about one hundred and sixty pounds. Hair and eyes are gray. Suspect is wanted in the questioning of a homicide and should be considered armed and dangerous. Approach with extreme caution. Contact chief's office upon apprehension."

Mr. Van Dorn didn't approve of smoking in his car. I lit a cigarette and rolled down the window anyway. I needed the tobacco.

Being hunted by the best police force in the world was bad enough. Having my height and weight broadcast to the world made it even worse. I weighed a buck fifty, thank you very much, and I was five seven and a half. Leave it to Andy Carmichael to find a way to slip a dig into a goddamned APB.

I was already out of his jurisdiction, but that was cold comfort. Carmichael probably already had my phone tapped and men at my place, too. He probably even had someone watching Theresa's house up in Poughkeepsie in case I showed up there. I felt sorry for the poor bastards who'd drawn that assignment. Poughkeepsie wasn't exactly Times Square on New Year's Eve. Goddamned place was quiet enough to hear the deer munching the grass.

He probably already had poor Loomis under the lights, trying to make him spill everything he knew about my work on the Fairfax case. I'd try to find a way to make it up to him.

What I didn't know was why Carmichael had issued the bulletin. Was it because of the Fairfax exhumation, or was it more than that? Did Alexandra have him wrapped around her little finger, too? Was that why Hauser was driving her and her friends to galas? The krauts were bad enough without having to fight my own people in the bargain.

But reasons didn't matter at this point. Actions did. I figured Carmichael would probably give it a day, maybe two at the most, before he issued a statewide alert. I didn't know how thorough Long Island cops were, but it would only take one to ruin my day.

I flicked my cigarette out the window and rolled it back up. I hoped my visit to Suffolk County would answer a lot of questions I needed answers for.

***

It was already past sunset by the time I reached the plot of land Walter Fairfax had donated to the Friends of New Germany. The road was blocked by a metal gate that looked like it hadn't been there too long. Even though the area along the road was thick with sharp overgrowth and shrubs, someone had taken the time to pound stakes into the ground, probably for some kind of fence they were going to put up.

For once, my timing was perfect.

I hid Mr. Van Dorn's car beneath some overgrowth on the other side of the road from the fence line. I used the privacy of the spot to change out of my suit and into a getup more practical for what I'd come there to do. I shrugged into a mechanic's brown coveralls and a brown cap to match. I pulled on some work boots and laced them up tight. I made sure my .38 was still easy to reach under the coveralls. Given the thickness of the brush, I decided not to wear it on the outside and risk getting it caught on branches.

I jogged across the road and pushed my way through a small clearing in the overgrowth. It was the first time I'd been in a wooded area since the war, since my time at Belleau Wood. The memories of combat flooded my mind so fast that I damn near fell over. The sights, the sounds, the feelings of those days all came back to me like they were happening all over again.

I could hear the whistle of the artillery coming in, feel the ground shake beneath me as the shells exploded, the shrapnel peppering the trees around me as I kept my head down. I heard the echoing screams of dying Marines begging for medics who were already dead. I felt the dust in the air that choked every breath just before another shell slammed into the earth and raised hell all over again.

I knew it was all in my head, but it still felt incredibly real to me. I lurched over a fallen log and vomited. Belleau Wood had happened almost twenty years before, but it was closer than that for me. Closer than I knew.

I guessed living in Manhattan helped me keep a lot of things buried, where they belonged. But buried things had a habit of rising from the ground in the woods, especially if they weren't buried deep enough.

I shook off the sickness and wiped my mouth on the back of my sleeve, just as I'd done all those years before in France. And just as I'd done back then, I got up and kept going.

The sky in the west glowed in front of me, and I headed in that direction. I crept along, the wet ground pulling at my boots with each step. The branches of the overgrowth pulling on my coveralls but not tearing them. I moved carefully, trying to keep the noise I made to a minimum.

But the deeper I got, the clearer things became.

I saw the flames from a large bonfire flickering through the branches, and heard something I hadn't heard since I mustered out of the Marines.

Hundreds of male voices sounding at once.

I was still too deep in the woods to hear what they said, but I kept moving.

I stopped when I broke through the tangle and let my eyes adjust. Through the line of trees in front of me I saw about a hundred young men, all wearing the same brown shirt and dark pants, standing in a circle around a large bonfire. Something that resembled a watch tower loomed behind the fire. A man stood in the tower. The dancing flames cast a flickering glow on his face, casting most of him in shadow.

Although I was too far away to hear exactly what he was saying, the men looking up at him seemed taken by every word. I saw him gesturing wildly, and heard the echo of his voice carried on the breeze.

I looked around the area in front of me. There was enough level ground between me and the tree line for me to get a closer look without breaking cover. I belly-crawled over to a tree and looked out at the scene.

I saw banners on tall poles outlined against the bonfire. It was too dark to make out what was on them, but they looked like platoon flags. The men around them weren't men at all, but teenagers in uniforms. The man in the tower was dressed the same way, beneath a gray overcoat.

This wasn't just a bunch of kids camping out in the woods. This was a goddamned military camp.

And the bastard in the tower behind the bonfire was leading it. I still wasn't close enough to hear what he was saying, but I heard the response of the young men loud and clear.

"Sieg, Heil! Sieg, Heil!"

I was trying to work out the translation, when I felt cold gunmetal press against the back of my head. "You never know when to give up, do you, asshole?"

I recognized the voice, but I turned my head enough to make sure I was right. I was.

Steve Hauser was aiming a rifle at the back of my head. And he was wearing the same uniforms as the others.

"Now get up nice and slow, or you're going to make me do something I've been wanting to do for a long time."

Chapter 19

Hauser kept me in front of him, pushing me forward with the barrel of his rifle as he forced me into the clearing.

The man in the tower stopped yelling, and all the kids turned to face me.

"Relax, everyone," Hauser called out to them. "Just a trespasser."

The young men turned and booed me, cursed at me. Those at the back of the group even threw rocks in my general direction. They all missed.

The jeering and cursing didn't bother me. I pretty much got the same treatment from my own cops back when I had been Chief Carmichael's boy. What bothered me most was that these were all American kids. The oldest one I saw was about eighteen or so. The youngest kid was about ten.

They all had a similar look. Thin, athletic, mostly blonds, just like the young man who had run away from me in Times Square a couple of days ago. Maybe he was one of them. Maybe he wasn't even there. I didn't really care. But it told me he'd probably been picked from the same crop of kids I had just witnessed cheering the crazy bastard in the tower above the bonfire.

I noticed something else as Hauser marched me past

them. Two flagpoles at the edge of the parade ground were lit from the ground. One was flying the American flag. The other flag was red with a twisted black cross on a white circle. A swastika.

The sight sent a chill down my back, and it wasn't just from the barrel of Hauser's rifle, either.

"Keep walking, stupid," Hauser said from behind me. "There're some people who want to see you."

I was sick of getting yelled at, and I was sick of being pushed around.

I waited until he jabbed me with the muzzle again and made my move.

My Marine training kicked in, the part about how to disarm the enemy. Hauser might've been a bit bigger and younger than me, but I was still pretty fast.

I yanked the rifle forward as I side-stepped it, dislodging his grip just enough for me to jam the rifle butt into his throat. The unexpected blow knocked him back as he let go of the rifle and grabbed his throat.

I swung the rifle by the barrel, like a bat, and hit Hauser in the side of the head with the stock, knocking him flat. The kids rushed at me in a herd, just as I brought the stock to my shoulder and jammed the rifle barrel against his head.

"One more move and I blow his fucking head off."

The kids didn't back off, but they didn't rush me, either. If they called my bluff I'd be dead, but so would Hauser.

A pistol fired into the air behind me, and a woman's voice called out, "Enough!"

The shot sent the kids scattering further away, clearing

a path for three people who were walking toward us from what looked like a bunkhouse.

A short man in a dark overcoat and a pince-nez perched on the edge of his nose. Dr. Otto.

A tall, gaunt man in a gray overcoat. Tessmer.

And in the middle, a woman in a gray shirt, gray pants, and black Army boots. A black jacket was draped around her slender shoulders like a cape. She might not have been wearing a ball gown, but she was every bit as striking as she'd been at the gala.

Alexandra von Holstein.

When she stopped, the men flanking her stopped as well. That's when I noticed the smoking Luger pistol in her left hand. She had fired the shot.

She said, "Let Mr. Hauser up, Charlie. You've done enough damage for one day."

But I kept the barrel flush against Hauser's head. "No way. We're getting the hell out of here."

She smiled. "Not with an empty rifle. It's not even loaded."

I realized the rifle didn't have a magazine. I checked the chamber. That was empty, too. The goddamned thing was useless. I tossed the rifle at them. It landed in the mud at their feet. I still had the .38 under my coveralls, but I wouldn't get to it in time before she drilled me with that Luger. "Then I guess I'll be on my way."

"Nonsense," Alexandra said. "I told you I hoped we would meet again soon, and here we are. It would be a shame to waste such an opportunity. Besides, you've driven a long way to be here. Join us for a moment."

"Sorry, but I've got places to be."

"Hauser's rifle was unloaded." Alexandra leveled the gun at me. "The Luger isn't. Come with us. Steven will make sure you find your way, won't you, Steven?"

I didn't know Hauser had gotten back on his feet until he punched me in the kidney. I hadn't been expecting the blow, and almost fell over. Almost.

Hauser grabbed me by the collar and steered me ahead of him.

***

The bunkhouse they had built was brand new, but had been meant to look old. I could still smell the paint and plaster on the walls. I felt a thin layer of dust under my boots that felt more like sawdust from new construction than from dirt.

The room they led me into was nothing fancy. Just a desk and some chairs scattered around. A long conference table was in the middle of the room.

I wasn't surprised when the countess took her seat behind the desk, flanked by Dr. Otto and Tessmer. Hauser stayed behind me. I was expecting another kidney punch, but it hadn't come yet.

Alexandra lay the Luger on the desktop as she slowly pulled off her black gloves, one finger at a time. "You are a man of many interests, aren't you, Charlie? I took you for one of those people who never left the comforts of the city unless they had to."

"That's me," I said. "Full of surprises."

"I'm beginning to see that," she said. "Tell me, what

brings you out here to Camp Sigfried?"

I was dying for a cigarette, but it was in my pocket beneath my coveralls. If I reached for them they'd see the gun, and I'd lose the only advantage I had going for me. Since I couldn't smoke, I tried sarcasm instead. "It's the funniest story you're ever going to hear. See, I was out for a drive in the country, taking in the sights, when all of a sudden the sun goes down and I'm lost. At first, I was worried about running out of gas. But then I realized I had an even bigger problem." I whispered as if I was embarrassed. "I had to use the little boy's room. Since I was out here already, I decided to make like a deer and go in the woods. So I pulled over, walked into the woods to start doing my business, when all of a sudden some guy jumps out from behind a tree and propositions me. I was scared at first, but then I realized it was Hauser. You might not know this but he's a little pink in the center, if you get my meaning."

Hauser slammed me twice in the kidneys. This time, I dropped to my knees. And this time, he didn't try to help me up. Neither did anyone else in the room. Alexandra simply looked bored as she pulled off her left glove, one finger at a time.

I got to one knee, then on both feet, though I'd hardly call it standing. I was listing to one side and grateful my bladder hadn't given out. Hauser might not have been big but he was built like a bull.

I bit off the pain. "Sorry you had to hear about it this way, Countess. But I believe an employer has a right to know about the people she has working for her."

I felt Hauser shift again to hit me, but one look from Tessmer made him stop.

Tessmer said, "You're not a very wise man, are you, Detective?"

"Wise enough to find your hideaway in the woods, Fritz."

Now Tessmer looked like he wanted to belt me, but stayed where he was. Alexandra seemed to have her dogs well trained. I wondered what Father Mullins would think about this. I hoped I'd have the chance to ask him, but it didn't seem like I would.

Alexandra said, "Herr Tessmer is wrong about you, Charlie. I think you're a most clever man. Clever enough to find out about this place. Probably clever enough to find out about a lot of things. Care to share?"

"That's the problem with being an only child, your highness. I never learned how to share with the other kids."

From behind me, Hauser said, "Damn it, Doherty. You're already caught. Don't make it worse than it already is."

"How bad could it be?" I laughed. "At worst, you've got me for trespassing. Call the local sheriff and have me picked up. I'll pay the two dollars and be out in time for breakfast." I winked at Alexandra. "Unless you've got more interesting plans for me."

She ran a long, red fingernail down the handle of the Luger. "Breakfast is the furthest thing from my mind right now. I want you to tell me what you found in Walter's safe."

"No."

She persisted. "Some of those things didn't belong to him. They belonged to me. I want them back and I'm prepared to pay handsomely for it."

Normally, talking about money was the best way to get my attention. But this wasn't a normal circumstance and she already had my attention, so she was out of luck. "Wish I could help, but I can't."

"You can't, or you won't?"

I wasn't sure how much she knew about Mr. Van Dorn's operation, or if she knew anything at all. Maybe Hauser had told him we'd left the gala together, and maybe he'd kept his mouth shut. I decided to play it cautious, which wasn't good for me. But I wasn't being paid to be careful. "I guess you could say a little bit of both. I've already been through everything in the safe, so there's no reason to be coy. I know how much you milked Walter for and where the money went. I know what he bought for you and I know how much. To most people, a bunch of leases and a ledger of charitable donations doesn't mean much. A notebook full of gibberish means even less."

Tessmer cursed in German and made a move toward me, but Alexandra grabbed his arm. "Careful, Charlie. You're in no position to bait us."

"Don't be so sure. I'd say I'm in the perfect position to bait you. A minute ago, you were willing to throw some money at me to get back the stuff in Fairfax's safe. That's not going to happen. Now you're going to pay me a lot more to make sure none of that stuff ever sees the light of day."

Dr. Otto cleared his throat. "Or we could simply spend the next several days torturing you until you tell us where the items are."

"With what? That band of Boy Scouts you've got outside by the bonfire? Nah. Let them stick to the weenie roasts and camp songs, at least until their balls descend."

I jerked my thumb over my shoulder. "I hope you're not planning on having Hauser do it. I just caved his skull in without even trying. Poor bastard's probably seeing double right now. He wouldn't know which one of me to grab. Besides, I got the jump on him once and I'll do it again."

I heard Hauser's knuckles crack, but he stayed where he was.

I looked at Tessmer, who still looked like he wanted to tear me apart, but the countess hadn't let him off his choke chain yet. "And I know you don't want him to do it. He'd go too far too fast and probably kill me before I said anything. Not that he'd have the chance." I threw him a wink. "I'm a little tougher than I look, Fritz. Teufel Hunden, remember?"

I snapped my fingers as if something had just come to me. "Or maybe you're thinking of poisoning me like you did Walter and Dr. Blythe." I shook my head. "That wouldn't work, either."

Alexandra actually flinched. Something I'd said finally got to her. "What was that?"

"Cyanide, wasn't it? That might've worked with a love-sick fool and a drunk old man, but in case you haven't noticed, I'm neither. You'd have to hurt me to get me to take it, and then you'd still be left with nothing. That brings us right back to where we started. Paying me off and letting me go is still your best option."

"I'm disappointed in you, Charlie." Alexandra smiled,

but this time it didn't warm me. "Your insults are usually so thorough, yet you have discounted Dr. Otto's talents. He's quite a skilled psychiatrist. Trained in all matters of persuasive tactics, as am I. The carrot and the stick, as I believe you Americans call it."

She was right. I hadn't counted on Otto at all. Served me right for being too smug for my own good.

"I took the time to look over your file," Alexandra continued. "Don't ask me how I obtained it because, like you, I have secrets. It made for some interesting reading. I know you're familiar with the more violent approaches to interrogation. Phone directories and rubber hoses, things like that. I assure you that Dr. Otto takes a more nuanced approach to the matter. His methods leave scars that do not show and never quite heal."

I looked at Alexandra and forced a laugh. "You're some piece of work. I'll bet poor Walter never saw it coming."

"Not until I told him," she admitted. "But he had served his purpose and died quickly, which is more than I can offer you."

I shrugged. "I always got more out of a guy with a carton of Luckies and a bottle of gin. I've put my time in on the other side of the table. Boys like Otto over there tried to get me to talk once back in France. It didn't work then and it won't work now. Either way you play it, I'll dig in deeper just to spite you." I shrugged. "Might as well save yourselves a lot of time and shoot me."

I felt her eyes move across me. Not warmly like they had back at the gala, but different. Like I was a specimen in a jar. She stopped when she looked me in the eyes, probably expecting me to look away. She had an intense gaze for someone who was supposed to have come from money.

I'd been stared down by tough guys before. It was all menace and violence. I'd been given the cold stare from some of my clients, too, especially when they didn't get the news they'd expected. They'd brought all their breeding and money to bear, as if that would change the facts of the bad news I'd just delivered.

But Alexandra had a different look. Cold and analytical that slowly changed to realization and, ultimately, hate. The longer I held her glare, the more her hate grew. She'd expected me to crack or look away. I did neither.

I waited for her to grab the Luger so I could go for the .38 under my arm. I didn't know if I'd clear it before she shot me, but it was worth a try.

The stare held as she said, "You know something, Charlie? I believe you. That's too bad." She broke off the stare and looked behind me at Hauser. "Steven, take care of him."

"With pleasure," Hauser said. "Can I break something, or do you just want him roughed up?"

"I want him dead."

Hauser surprised me by laughing. "Join the club."

Tessmer pounded the desk. "Hauser, Countess Alexandra has given you a direct order. The prisoner is to be executed immediately."

My right hand flicked up toward my belly, but stopped when Hauser said, "You're not serious."

Alexandra looked at him. "Do you see anyone laughing?"

I flinched when Hauser moved next to me. "Look, you want me to kick the shit out of him, that's fine. He's trespassing and has it coming. The fact that I hate his guts makes it even better. But killing him is a whole other thing entirely."

Alexandra bolted out of her chair. "He is a direct threat to our operation. He has refused to cooperate, and he must be dealt with immediately. You know what we're doing here. You've seen what we're trying to build. Do you want all of that threatened by a greasy little man you despise? You've said you're committed to our cause. You've pledged your allegiance to us. Executing this bastard will show the depth of your commitment. Or were they just words?"

"My commitment?" Hauser took another step forward, placing himself between me and the Germans. "Look, I told you I'd drive you around, help you get members. Help you build something that made us proud to admit we're German again. You want me to put Charlie in the hospital? That's fine, but I didn't sign on to kill anyone, much less a cop."

"An ex-cop," Dr. Otto corrected.

"No such thing as far as I'm concerned."

Tessmer reached for the Luger on the desk. Hauser grabbed it before he got there.

I pulled my .38 and aimed it at Alexandra's chest. "Anyone moves, she dies first. Anyone calls out for help, she dies first."

She must've had some kind of buzzer on the floor, because the loud wail of a klaxon sounded throughout the camp. I would've shot her if I didn't admire her bravery.

Hauser took the Luger and aimed it at Tessmer as he took a step back, standing next to me. "What the hell do we do now, Charlie?"

Dr. Otto actually smirked at me. "Fools. You have twelve bullets between the two of you. There are over a hundred young men out there, rushing to our aid as we speak. Every one of them is in top physical condition and completely under our control. Neither of you will make it out of here alive. Wise men would use those guns on themselves."

I changed my aim and shot Otto in the right shoulder. The impact bounced the round little man off the wall and sent him face-first to the floor. Alexandra bolted from the chair and stood behind Tessmer.

Hauser turned and aimed the Luger at the door. "Congratulations, stupid. That shot will bring them crashing in here."

"Not if we do this right." I grabbed Otto by the collar and threw him into Alexandra and Tessmer. "Tessmer, help the doc stay on his feet. Get in front of Hauser and do what he says. If the doc falls down, you get shot."

I grabbed the countess by the arm and put the gun against her side. If she was frightened, she hid it well. "Same goes for you. Tell your boys to back off and we all take a nice quiet drive back to Manhattan. They rush us, you go first." I pushed the gun a little harder into her ribs to make a point. In her native language, I said, "Just don't forget I speak German."

"Don't worry," she said. "I won't forget a thing about you."

I didn't think she would. The klaxon kept wailing as I nudged her forward. "Ladies first."

Chapter 20

The crowd in front of the bunkhouse door was twenty kids deep when we tried to leave.

With Tessmer using both hands to try to keep Otto upright, Hauser aimed the Luger at the kids. "Clear a path. Move!"

The campers backed away. Not as quickly as I would have liked, but enough for us to get out of the building. A gasp went up from the boys when they saw me step out with a gun against Alexandra's side.

I tensed up as she called out to the boys in English. "Do as they say, men. Don't put yourselves in harm's way. That is an order. They will be dealt with soon enough."

I spun her around so Hauser and I were back to back. The crowd moved with us, keeping a constant distance, but keeping pace, too, like a goddamned pack of wolves waiting for the chance to pounce. Teen trepidation and adolescent bravado didn't mix with guns. I knew from experience.

But I wasn't fooling myself. We were moving because they let us move. Hauser and I were still outnumbered fifty to one. If one of these punks decided to be a hero and save a lady in distress, we were in trouble.

Over my shoulder, I asked Hauser, "Anyone else in this

place have guns?"

"Yeah, but no bullets," he answered. "The rifles are just for show. The two men at the gate are cops, but they're my men. They'll back our play. They didn't sign on for this shit any more than I did."

Tessmer said something in German, and Hauser smacked him in the back of the head with his free hand. "Shut your mouth and move."

"You got a car here?"

"Cars are left in town. Parents drop their kids off at the gate. Less attention that way. But we've got a truck we can use."

One of the oldest and biggest kids in the group charged through the line like a running back and came straight for me. I had enough time to shift Alexandra to the side and kick him in the balls. He went down like a sack of flour. Maybe I should've shot him, but I couldn't bring myself to do it.

I pulled Alexandra closer to me as we walked backward, panning the crowd with my pistol. "Anyone else?"

Seeing one of their leaders moaning in the mud killed their courage. The group backed up a little more, but the circle still followed. It faltered a bit as they stopped to help their friend, but they closed ranks pretty quick.

Someone had trained these kids and trained them well.

Someone who probably wasn't with us. Like that crazy bastard who'd been yelling at them from the tower above the bonfire.

I flinched when I heard what could've only been a bullet

whiz through the air between Hauser's head and mine.

Hauser called it before I could think it. "Sniper in the watchtower. Center of the compound."

The kids all hit the deck, leaving the five of us exposed. Alexandra went dead weight, but I grabbed her around the waist and tried to keep her upright. My grip slipped from around her waist up to her neck.

I lowered her slowly, taking a knee as I pressed my face right alongside hers. I tucked the .38 under her chin. "You do anything stupid, you die, and I grab one of the brats, got it? One hostage is as good as another to me."

Hauser moved Tessmer and the doctor in front of him as a shield and crouched behind them. "Damn it, that's Burnitz."

I didn't know who the hell Burnitz was, but I saw the outline of a man atop the tower. The bastard had a clear field of fire and was well out of range of our pistols.

"You people built a regular base here, didn't you?"

"It's supposed to teach the kids discipline," Hauser yelled back at me. "Someone's always on fire watch. Hell, some Boy Scout camps have the same thing."

Another round slammed into the ground about five yards in front of us.

"Except the Boy Scouts don't have snipers. I thought you said this camp didn't have any bullets."

"Guess I was wrong," Hauser admitted. "What are we going to do about it?"

Alexandra struggled to get her wind with my arm around her throat. "You should do the sensible thing and surrender before Burnitz puts a bullet in your eye."

The camp speakers crackled to life as a heavily-accented German voice filled the air. "All unarmed personnel are to remain where they are until further orders. Hauser, you and your friend must throw away your weapons or you will be shot for trespassing. You have three seconds to obey my orders."

I stole a glance over at Hauser. "Is he that good?"

"He's supposed to be ex-German army. Talks big about being a sniper back in the war."

But the war had been a long time ago. I should know. I felt it in my bones every morning I climbed out of bed. I bet Burnitz felt it, too. Probably hadn't shot at anyone in a long time, either. I wasn't worried about his accuracy. I was worried about him getting lucky.

But I'd had snipers shoot at me before and I was still around. I intended on keeping my streak going.

I called out to Hauser, "We crab-walk out of here, back to back, using the krauts here as cover. I'll cover the right side and the tower while you cover the left side of the road. I have a feeling Burnitz isn't the only asshole in here with a gun."

"Imbeciles," Alexandra rasped as I pulled her to her feet. She didn't like it, but the .38 gave her incentive. When she got to full height, I wrapped my arm around her waist again. "Neither of you will make it out of here alive."

"Sure we will." I tucked the .38 under her chin as we started moving sideways. "Just keep moving and everything will be fine. Don't get any ideas about going for my eyes, either, or I squeeze the trigger and you die just like Walter."

"Burnitz will kill you before we get three paces."

"Then my hand will spasm and you die anyway. Ask Otto if you don't believe me."

She must've believed me, because she moved without fighting me. Her hair was soft against my skin. Another time and place, I might've liked that, but I had other things on my mind just then.

I kept her face just in front of mine as the five of us began walking sideways.

We moved sideways as one. Hauser's back to mine as we kept our prisoners as cover. In perfect conditions, a good sniper might still be able to take me down. But in near-dark conditions, with a burning bonfire just below him, Burnitz didn't have much of a shot. And the war had ended a long time ago.

Probably just long enough for a new one to start.

I could see the outline of the man in the tower, the barrel of the rifle tracking us as we moved. But he hadn't fired yet, even though we were well past his three second deadline.

Why?

We were more than halfway to the main gate when I heard someone call out, "Steve! What the hell is going on out there?"

"Shut up and bring the truck out here. We're leaving. Don't ask questions, Donnie. Just do it."

To me, Hauser said, "Donnie and Jack are my guys. We're safe with them, don't worry."

But I didn't have time to worry, even if I had wanted to.

Fire tore through my right side as the countess flew out of my arms. She landed on top of some of the kids who were lying flat on the ground. I saw her as I fell to the ground. I knew by the size of the hole in her side she was already dead.

I turned in time to see another of the camp guards levering another round into a rifle. Hauser and I fired at the same time, hitting the man in the chest and head.

I ignored the burning in my side as I scrambled for Tessmer, leaving the wounded doctor with Hauser. The two sons of bitches were the only trace of cover we had left.

From his perch in the tower, Burnitz rushed another shot that went wide. One of the kids on the ground screamed, probably hit by the bullet.

Donnie, Hauser's man, drew his service pistol and began firing up at the sniper's position. He must have been using a .45 because I heard round after round striking the tin roof of the watch tower.

As I watched the outline of the sniper disappear, I knew this was our chance. Hauser and I practically dragged Tessmer and Otto toward the main gate. Tessmer bellowed for Alexandra, but I pushed him along. The effort took a lot out of me, but I had no choice. If Burnitz or one of his friends shot at us again, we were done for.

We got past Donnie as he slapped a new clip into the .45. "Mike's backing the truck up so we can all get the hell out of here."

A bullet slammed into a tree next to Donnie's head. He returned fire, but didn't stick around long enough to give Burnitz another shot. He fell in behind us, covering our flank.

The kids on the ground looked like they wanted to chase us. They looked like they wanted to rip us apart. But with bullets flying around and a couple of their own injured, their brains overruled their balls.

Mike backed up the truck and Donnie helped Hauser pull Dr. Otto into the flatbed while I kept a good hold on Tessmer's neck. I felt my legs start to go and put more pressure on Tessmer. "Anyone have any cuffs for this one?"

Tessmer saw his chance to get away and took it. He punched me in the right side, exactly where the bullet had gone through me. The shot took my breath away and strength along with it. I crumpled to the ground, fully expecting Tessmer to kick me in the face.

But all I felt was Donnie and Hauser's arms lift me up into the flatbed as the truck.

The pain in my side spiked, and my world snapped into black as the truck sped away.

***

I didn't know how long I was out of it, but when I opened my eyes, I saw Tessmer hogtied next to me in the flatbed. I blinked my eyes clear and saw Hauser tending to Otto's shoulder wound. The doctor was moaning as Hauser applied a makeshift bandage of torn clothing to dress the wound.

Hauser must've noticed my eyes were open. "Look who decided to wake up. Have a nice rest, sweetie?"

I tried to sit up, but the pain in my right side kept me on my back. "How long was I out for?"

"About three hours."

Three hours? It didn't make sense. I felt cold and tried to pull my coveralls over me. But my coverall was gone and so was my shirt. A field dressing had been placed over the bullet hole in my side. "You do this?"

"Wasted all of the first aid supplies on you. Making due with what I've got left so the good doctor here doesn't bleed out on us."

"I didn't know you were a medic."

"I'm not," Hauser admitted. "I've just had plenty of practice piecing guys back together after Carmichael's done with them. Don't thank me too much, though. The bullet went right through you, so I didn't have to dig. You'll be fine when we get to wherever we're going."

That didn't make any sense. I remembered them loading me into the truck and, in the blink of an eye, everything changed. "Where are we going, anyway?"

"About an hour after you passed out, you started babbling about some number you had to call. Kept saying it over and over again."

My chills got worse. It must've told him the number Mr. Van Dorn had told me to call in D.C. His private number, given away in my sleep like some goddamned drunk spilling his guts in a dive somewhere. "You didn't call it, did you?"

The doctor screamed as Hauser pulled the bandage tight over his wound. Hauser backhanded him. "Shut up, Otto. It's better than you deserve." Hauser moved to the other side of the truck to check on Tessmer's bindings.

"Of course I called it." He fished out his cigarettes and

offered me one. I reached for it, but the pain in my side made me stop. Hauser lit one for me and stuck it in my mouth, then lit one for himself. "Couldn't have done us any harm, at least no more harm than the crazy bastards we left at the camp. I didn't know it Mr. Van Dorn at first, but I figured it out soon enough. He was concerned as hell about you. Gave us an address in Delaware where we can go to get you and Otto looked at while we hide out for a while. That Van Dorn guy doesn't seem too bad, considering how rich he is."

I didn't give a damn about this. "Did you tell him about Alexandra? About—"

"I tried to, but he cut me off. Said we'd talk about it in Delaware." He rolled the lit cigarette between his fingers. "So you really have been working for Van Dorn all this time. And here I was thinking you were working for the Fairfax widow. Funny how things aren't always what you think they are, ain't it?"

I took a drag as I looked at his uniform. "Just like I hadn't pegged you for a goddamned Nazi."

"Knock that shit off," Hauser said. "I'm no more a Nazi than I am Chinese." He blew smoke at Otto, which made him cough and paw at his wounded shoulder. "I've grown up my whole life ashamed of my father being German. The poor bastard was already here when the war broke out and they wouldn't even let him enlist. Instead, they had him shoveling shit for cavalry horses in a stable up in the Bronx. So when the Bund started up, I went to a couple of meetings. Suddenly, people weren't hiding the fact they were German anymore. We were having events and picnics and speaking our language again, openly."

"Yeah." I patted my field dressing. "You bastards throw a hell of a picnic."

Hauser flicked his ash at me. "Like I told you back there, it was our version of the Boy Scouts. We didn't want kids growing up the way we did, thinking our people were monsters, that we were less than dirt. We got them out of the city and brought them to places like that camp back there, where they could get fresh air, play sports, and learn the parts of their heritage they weren't getting in the schoolbooks."

The cigarette made me want to cough. Hauser's nonsense made me want to gag. The pain from the hole in my side kept me from doing either. "Nice speech. Now that you've gotten it out of your system, try telling me the real reason."

Hauser finished his cigarette and flicked it out of the back of the truck. "That's a hell of a way to talk to the guy who just saved your life."

I stifled a cough that made the pain in my side spike. "Knock it off. You're Carmichael's hatchet man, just like I used to be. He doesn't give that spot to choirboys or saps gullible enough to fall for that Germanic pride bullshit." As much as the pain fogged my brain, things began to make sense. "You wouldn't be working for them without his permission, either. You two were playing some kind of an angle with these bastards, or else you would've shot me back there. Tell me I'm wrong."

Tessmer grunted and squirmed a little, but his binds held and the gag kept him quiet.

Hauser smiled as he rested his head back against the wall of the truck. "You know, Charlie, you never get credit for having a brain. Everyone says Charlie Doherty is as crooked as the day is long. That he's got file a mile high on everyone in the department. They forget you're a smart cookie, Charlie. Myself included."

I wasn't in the mood for compliments. "Gee, thanks. Now quit stalling and tell me the truth."

"The German pride bit was true," Hauser admitted, "at least at first. But after I went to a few meetings, word got around that I was a cop. They started inviting me to parties and meetings where the rest of the members weren't invited. They asked me to provide security for certain people, drive them around from time to time in my off hours."

"People," I said, "like Alexandra and Dr. Otto and Tessmer. And Fairfax, right?"

Hauser looked at me, and must've read the expression on my face. I'd never been a very good poker player. "Yeah, and all I did was drive."

"And you reported everything you saw and did back to Carmichael, didn't you?" He tried to talk, but I didn't let him. "Don't bother denying it. There's no way you could dedicate that much time to these bastards without him knowing about it. And if you didn't have his permission first, you would've been bounced off the force. How much did you tell him?"

Hauser folded his hands over his knees. "Everything. I told him when they asked me to drive for them, and he let me do it as long as I told him everything, just like you said."

He closed his eyes. "Between my regular job and my night job for this crew and all the reports Carmichael made me right each day, I was run pretty ragged."

"I don't blame you," I said. "Being an accessory to murder is a hell of a weight on the soul."

He pushed himself off the truck wall and snatched me by the collar, his right hand back ready to punch me. I didn't scream out when the pain in my side exploded. I didn't try to defend myself either. I just let him hold me like a rag doll, making sure I kept eye contact with him the whole time.

The rage passed as quickly as it had come. He let me go with a shove, returning to his seat against the truck wall. "I had nothing to do with that and you know it."

"Maybe you didn't kill Fairfax or Blythe," I said, "but you know who did."

Dr. Otto croaked something in German. "Traitor."

Hauser kicked at his leg and the wounded man went quiet again.

Hauser lit another cigarette and looked at me through the smoke. "Carmichael and I suspected, but we didn't know for sure. We knew Fairfax was close to the countess and these two here. When he killed himself, we didn't know why. Carmichael white-washed it as an accident until he could get more facts. When Blythe turned up dead, we wondered if Alex and her friends weren't covering their tracks somehow. No one thought of poison until you brought it up."

He saw the way I was looking at him and blew smoke my way. "That's the God's honest truth, too. You can kiss my ass if you don't believe me."

I believed him.

I tried to flick my cigarette out the back of the truck like Hauser had, but was too weak to make it. The butt fell short of the tailgate and rolled back toward Tessmer's face. The captive squirmed. Hauser left the cigarette where it was.

I coughed as I laughed. "So Carmichael not only planned on blackmailing the Fairfax widow for covering up for her husband's death, but your Nazi playmates for murdering Fairfax and Blythe."

Hauser looked away. "Probably, if we'd gotten evidence that they were homicides. And now that we have it, look what happened. The countess is dead, Otto here is bleeding out." He rubbed Tessmer's head. "And this sorry bastard's in no shape to pay anyone."

"Cheer up," I said. "Maybe your friend with the sniper rifle can pass the hat for you. What did you say his name was again?"

"Burnitz," Hauser said. "And he won't be helping anyone. I found out he's the one who shot at you on the street that day. He had one of the kids from the camp help him. He had the kid trail you afterwards, too."

I remembered. Blondie. "He was with you when you tried to get me at Fairfax's office the night I opened the safe."

"That wasn't me," Hauser said. "That was Tessmer, the kid, and another guy."

"Where's the kid now?"

Hauser shook his head. "Burnitz doesn't like failure. The kid failed him three times in one day. He won't have a chance for a fourth screw up."

Dr. Otto surprised me by laughing. "Burnitz is a patriot, you curs. He is a brilliant man and he is free. Free! He will finish what we have started here. He will avenge us and Alexandra. Your lives are worthless."

Hauser lurched forward and slammed his right hand into Otto's wounded shoulder. The doctor screamed and passed out.

Hauser sat back down. "That hump was always running his mouth with some kind of nonsense."

"Carmichael know about this Burnitz guy?"

"No," Hauser said, "because I don't know much about him. He spent most of his time at the camp. Every week since winter broke, he'd have a small crew working on something. That clearing you saw was all woods when Fairfax donated that land to them. Looks like it's been a field since the flood, doesn't it? He built the tower and bunk house, too. He was at some of the meetings I attended, but not many. He spoke to small crowds instead and helped drum up money from donors. Always said he was a tough guy, but I never saw him in action until today. I wasn't as impressed as I thought I'd be. Maybe he's like the rest of these guys: all talk and no action."

Hauser might not have been impressed by Burnitz, but I was. I'd seen the man hold the attention of over a hundred teenagers. I saw the way he'd gotten them to obey his commands, even when some of them got shot. Maybe he wasn't the sniper he claimed to be, but he wasn't just some lunatic mouthing off in the woods, either.

He was running something bigger than just the countess

and Otto and Tessmer. Something even bigger than the deaths of Fairfax and Dr. Blythe.

This was something new.

And we still had a long ride to Delaware.

Chapter 21

For the second time that day hours turned into seconds, because at some point on the ride to Delaware I passed out. I must've had a fever because my world blurred into a hellish dream of Walter Fairfax and Dr. Blythe wandering through Belleau Wood, begging for my help. Carmichael and Hauser had me on the ground at gunpoint, helpless as Tessmer fired at Fairfax and Blythe from behind sandbags while Dr. Otto laughed. Mrs. Fairfax kept yelling at me to do something, but I couldn't move.

Alexandra and Miss Swenson were nowhere in sight, but I could feel them close by, maybe behind me. But as hard as I struggled, I couldn't find the strength to help them. I couldn't get to my feet and rescue them. I had failed these men for a second time.

They say there's often truth in dreams. Maybe there was some truth in mine.

When I finally woke up, it took me a bit to figure out I wasn't dreaming anymore. There was no sign of the others, and the sound of gunfire had faded as quickly as my nightmare.

The forest was gone, too, as I found myself looking up at a bright, white ceiling. I felt my side and realized the bandages had been changed. They were flatter than the patch job Hauser had done in the truck.

"Welcome back, Charlie," came a familiar voice to my right. I picked up my head and saw Mr. Van Dorn sitting beside my bed. Father Mullins was next to him.

I tried to speak, but my mouth was dry and all I could manage was a raspy gurgle. A nurse raised my head to help me sip some water.

She propped a pillow behind my head so I could comfortably see my visitors, then promptly left the room.

The pain in my side was there, but not as bad as I had remembered. "How bad am I?"

Father Mullins raised his Bible. "Not bad enough for me to read this over you, but bad enough for you to need a hospital."

"Don't know how much good it would do, anyway. Where am I?"

"You're in Delaware and you're safe," Mr. Van Dorn said. "Once upon a time this place served as a foundling hospital, then an infirmary for the indigent."

"Guess you put me in the right place."

I laughed at my own bad joke and paid for it. A sudden, deep pain webbed out from my side and coursed through my body. The pain in the truck had been a paper cut compared to this.

Mr. Van Dorn eased me back down on the pillow. "Careful, Charlie. The bullet went clean through you, but you had a fair amount of internal bleeding that required extensive surgery."

I could damn near feel all of the places where they'd sewn me up. "How long have I been out?"

"Off and on for three days."

Three days? A long time for Mr. Van Dorn to go without hearing about what had happened. I rushed the words as fast as I could say them. "The land Fairfax donated to the Friends of New Germany in Suffolk. It's not just land, sir. It's a camp where they're training kids, sir. It's a goddamn military camp."

"Rest, Charles," Father Mullins said. "Detective Hauser has already told us all about it. About Chief Carmichael's peripheral involvement, too. He's been very cooperative."

Maybe it was the medication, but that didn't sound like the Hauser I knew. "He did?"

Mr. Van Dorn explained, "He knows he's in quite a bit of trouble, so he cut a deal. In exchange for his cooperation, we have promised to protect him from prosecution. And from Chief Carmichael if it comes to that."

Knowing Carmichael as well as I did, I knew it would come to that. "Did you send anyone to the camp?"

"We had people at the site the morning you got here. Except for the house and the tower Hauser told us about, the place was completely abandoned. My people went over every inch of the property with a fine-toothed comb. They didn't even find any spent cartridges, except for your .38 bullet from the wall. No sign of casualties, either. Whoever cleaned up did an incredibly thorough job."

I wondered if the drugs they had given me for the operation were playing with my hearing. No one could've cleaned up the place that fast. "But Alexandra was killed. The same bullet that went through me killed her. And there were kids who'd been shot, too."

"We don't know that she's dead," Mr. Van Dorn said. "Hauser saw her go down, but we don't know that the wound was fatal. He also told us other people were shot, but so far not one doctor in the area admits to treating any gunshot wounds. Given the number of people in the camp, the community may be working to hide something from us, so we're watching them closely."

If Alexandra was still alive, she was probably in worse shape than I was. "There's something else, sir. The camp was run by a guy named Burnitz. We didn't know about him before." Despite my haziness, I remembered how much Mr. Van Dorn and Father Mullins had kept from me. "Or did we?"

"Hauser told us about him, too," Mr. Van Dorn said. "We had heard rumors of a fourth member of Alexandra's group, but we didn't know much about him. Not even Hauser knew the role he played. Alexandra and the others didn't talk about him around Hauser. Burnitz is most likely an alias, but it's the only name we have. We're looking through our files to see if he connects with any of the other operations we're watching in the country."

Then I remembered the car. "Christ, your car is still out there. They probably checked the registration and know you're mixed up in all of this. Your family—"

Mr. Van Dorn eased me back down. "Calm, Charlie, calm. I've got the car, and my people saw only one set of footprints leading away from it. Your footprints." He patted my chest. "You hid it well, my friend. It's highly unlikely they ever found it. They were in such a hurry to clear out the camp, I doubt they had enough time to wonder how you had gotten there."

I was glad Mr. Van Dorn was in the clear, but there were still a lot of things that had gone sideways.

I lay my head back against the pillows. I had driven out to the property to see what it was. I'd thought it might be some kind of farmhouse where Alexandra and the others stashed people or money. I hadn't expected to find a goddamn Nazi army camp in the middle of Long Island. The whole Fairfax incident fractured into a million shards of glass the second I'd gotten out of Mr. Van Dorn's car and crawled through that wood. The camp. Hauser. Burnitz. Carmichael's double cross.

"What about Dr. Otto and Tessmer?"

"We have them," Mr. Van Dorn said.

I looked at him when he didn't say more. "Are they cooperating?"

"Reluctantly."

I noticed a dark smear on Mr. Van Dorn's lapel and another one on his tie. I'd seen smears like that before, usually in a mirror following one of Carmichael's interrogation sessions. "Hope it was worth it, sir. Blood stains more than your clothes and doesn't always wash off."

"It's not supposed to." Mr. Van Dorn didn't look at his clothes. He must've already known the stains were there. "Tessmer is a tough one. He appears to have received significant training in ways to resist questioning, but we'll break him eventually. Fortunately, Otto is in a weaker condition. Our information on him was wrong, by the way. He's not really a doctor. He's actually a chemist who worked for a big company in Germany for years before he joined the Nazi party. He admitted to crafting the cyanide they used to poison Fairfax and Blythe."

One mystery may have been solved, but another one had sprung up. "I know you're looking for Burnitz, sir, but you have to look harder. I saw how he had those kids wrapped around his finger. It was like they were in some kind of trance. A guy like that is worse than Alexandra, sir."

Mr. Van Dorn and Father Mullins looked at each other. The Jesuit asked, "How do you mean, Charles?"

"Meaning she can seduce a wealthy guy to give her money," I said, "or maybe even talk some sap into killing someone for her. But Burnitz can get hundreds to do his dirty work for him, and I'm not just talking about the camp. I'm talking about other places, maybe with people who can hurt us quietly. Like you talked about in the war, sir."

Mr. Van Dorn smiled. "You have a knack for this kind of work, Charlie. There may be a future in it for you."

"I know how crooks work, sir, and Burnitz is a crook. Set aside all the flags and uniforms and speeches, and he's still looking to use people to get what he wants. The sooner we find him, the better off we'll be."

"We're working on a plan to flush him out into the open," Mr. Van Dorn said. "We'll tell you all about it when you're better. The doctor tells me you should be ready to go home in a few days. I'll send a car to take you back to Manhattan."

"Manhattan? But the chief put out a bulletin on me."

"Which has since been rescinded," Mr. Van Dorn said. "I don't think we'll have much interference from Chief Carmichael any further. When he learned Alexandra was a German agent, he turned the color of the ceiling above your bed. I wish you had been there to see it."

Andrew Carmichael brought to his knees? I must still be dreaming. "I would've loved to have been a fly on the wall for that one."

"I'll tell you all about it when you're home. But I wouldn't count him out totally. The chief is an enterprising man." Mr. Van Dorn slapped me on the leg as he stood to leave. "Kind of like someone else I know."

I wasn't as sure. "We still need to be careful, sir."

"And you need to get better so we can find him all that much sooner," Father Mullins said. "We need you now more than ever, Charles. We never would have learned so much so soon without your hard work."

But I didn't care about praise. "What about my family, sir? If these bastards tried to kill me, there's no telling what they might do to them."

"They're safe, I promise you," Mr. Van Dorn said. "Besides, now that we have two of the main players in all of this, they'll be too busy covering up their tracks to indulge in a luxury like revenge."

I hoped he was right, though I wasn't so sure.

Chapter 22

The nurses insisted on getting me up and walking around the hospital grounds the day after Mr. Van Dorn left. I didn't agree, but I didn't get a vote.

The hospital was settled somewhere among the green hills of Delaware. I wasn't sure exactly where I was, but I'd been too focused on getting back on my feet to care.

The hospital was one of those severe Victorian buildings they liked to build back in the last century. Plenty of red bricks, high peaks, and steep roof lines to keep the snow from piling up in winter and the rain from pooling at other times. The round turrets at each corner and steel bars covering the narrow windows made it look more like a castle than a place for sick people.

At some point in the building's history, someone had decided to try to soften the building's appearance by adding intricate gingerbread features here and there. It didn't work.

I didn't know what Mr. Van Dorn or his friends used this place for, but it had a hell of a lot of security to just be a hospital. There was only one road in and out of the campus. No back gates and no other ways in except through the main road, either. A tall iron fence had been built around the place, with barbed wire strung along the top for good measure. Guards with Thompsons slung on their shoulders patrolled the grounds regularly, often waving at me as I limped along with a nurse on my daily walks. I didn't know if the guards and the guns and the gates were meant to keep people out or in. I decided not to find out.

The staff was careful about keeping me away from the others, too. They wouldn't let me see Otto or Tessmer, or talk to whoever was questioning them. I guessed they were afraid I might try to kill one of the sons of bitches. Couldn't say I blamed them for that one.

When I asked to see Hauser, they said he, Danny, and Jack were in another part of the hospital. I couldn't see them, even at meal times. I didn't like it, but there wasn't much I could do about it.

About a week after I'd gotten there, Mr. Van Dorn sent a driver to pick me up and bring me home. I told him I preferred to wait until I was strong enough to do the driving myself, but he insisted. The driver was a tall, lanky kid named Coleman, who showed up in my room while I was sleeping and shook me awake.

"It's a quarter to twelve," Coleman told me as he began to stuff the few things I had with me into a bag. "We need to be on the road by one at the latest."

I'd been there for a week, but now I suddenly had a deadline. "Why the rush, Junior?"

"The name's Coleman, sir. And the rush is due to Mr. Van Dorn's orders. He wants you back in Manhattan as soon as possible." He nodded toward my bathroom door. "I've hung some of your clothing in there. The sooner you get dressed, the sooner we can be on the road."

I went into the bathroom and got dressed. At first, I wondered how he'd been able to get my clothes from my place. Then I remembered Mr. Van Dorn had a key. Father Mullins had one, too. He'd said they had used the apartment as a base of operations for years. Hell, I bet several dozen people had a key. Goddamned place would probably look like Grand Central by the time I got back home.

It reminded me about just how much Mr. Van Dorn had kept from me since I'd begun working for him, especially about the Fairfax case. I hadn't liked it then and I didn't like it now. He may have sent Coleman to bring me back for some kind of a meeting, but I decided we were going to hash out a few things first before our talk. I knew he had his reasons for keeping me in the dark, but he was going to tell me what they were or I'd walk. I'd worry about the fact that I didn't have a place to go later.

I finished dressing and came out of the bathroom, to find Coleman confronting Steve Hauser in the hallway outside my room.

"Get back to your side of the hospital," Coleman told him. "Mr. Doherty will contact you later."

"Up yours," Hauser said. "He's standing right there and I'm going to talk to him now. It's important."

Coleman squared up and filled the doorway. "I said no."

Hauser drew back his hand for a punch, but before he could throw it, Coleman pinned it behind Hauser's head and threw him against the wall. Hauser screamed as Coleman began to twist the wrist. The kid was tougher than he looked. I'd never seen anyone beat Hauser to the punch before.

"Leave him alone," I said. "We've got a few minutes. We'll be on the road by one, I promise."

Coleman released Hauser's wrist and shoved him back against the wall. "You have three minutes, sir, then we have to leave."

Coleman left the room, giving me my first look at Hauser since we'd gotten to the hospital. Although it had only been a week, he looked like a different man. He'd always been a stocky, healthy-looking man. Now his face looked gaunt and he was jittery, like he'd had too much coffee and not enough sleep.

He still had the same defiance in his eyes, though. He glared at Coleman's back as the taller man left the room. "Who's that punk?" His voice was weak, almost raspy.

"Sorry about that. It wasn't my idea." I took a closer look at him. "You look like hell. They treating you okay?"

"Yeah, fine." Hauser rubbed his sore wrist. "Just worn down, is all. They haven't even let us go outside. Say it's for my own good. Yesterday, I tried to go for a walk around the grounds, and the second I stepped outside, three guys with Thompsons damn near shot me."

I'd seen the gunmen myself. "I guess it's a more secure building than we thought. They're just doing their job. They still leaning on you about your German friends?"

"Nah. They finished questioning us about that stuff a couple of days ago. Guess they liked what I told them because they offered me a job, if you can believe that. Here I was worried they were going slap the cuffs on me, and they say they're going to put me on the payroll."

It was the first I'd heard of it. "What kind of job?"

"They say they're still trying to figure that out. Had a goddamn head shrinker in with me yesterday asking me all these stupid questions. I would've thrown the bastard out the window if they didn't have bars on them."

I smiled. Hauser was still Hauser. "Just do whatever they want. Like you said, you're lucky you're not in jail."

"Yeah, lucky me." He looked at my bag on the bed. "You leaving?"

"Your sparring partner out there came to bring me home. What about you? They say when you're getting out of here?"

"To be determined is all they say, which is fine for now. They treat us pretty good now that we've told them everything we know. They keep pumping me for information about Burnitz, though. Guy seems to have them spooked. They think he'll try to find us if they let us loose."

Burnitz again. "What do you think?"

"I know everyone in the group was afraid of him," Hauser admitted. "The countess. Dr. Otto. Hell, even Tessmer didn't like to be around him. I figured he was just a creep until he started building up the camp. That's when I saw how nuts he really was. The fence line? The tower? The bonfires and the flags? All his idea. He even had the kids broken up into groups and close-order drilled them. I heard he took some of the older kids into the woods for overnight marches, but I never saw that myself. He's a nut, but I don't know if I should be afraid of him. I'm more worried about the people running around here. Or those who aren't here."

I didn't know what he meant, and it bothered me. "Quit talking in riddles. You're making my head hurt."

"When we first got here, your buddy Van Dorn was here all the time. That priest friend of his, too. Now he's gone and so is the collar. Now you're leaving. It doesn't feel right, Charlie. Something's off. I know it."

I put my .38 on top of my stuff, closed my case, and pulled it off the bed. My right side complained a little, but not enough to make me stop. "That's just your cabin fever talking. Take my advice and do what they say. I don't know what's going on around here, either, but I know Mr. Van Dorn. He always has a reason for doing what he does. Just don't lie or hold anything back. Mr. Van Dorn doesn't like it when people lie."

"Tell that to Tessmer. You should see what they're doing to that guy. Won't let him sleep. Won't let him eat. Hell, I thought you and I did some bad things for Carmichael. These guys make us look like milkmaids."

"Then I guess we're lucky we're on their side, aren't we?"

That was the first time I'd thought of myself as part of anything bigger than just me and Mr. Van Dorn. Once you started using terms like "we" and "us," it was only a matter of time before you found yourself part of an organization. That's how it had happened with me and Chief Carmichael and the Tammany boys. It felt like it was happening again, even though I still didn't know who the hell "us" was.

Coleman appeared in the doorway behind Hauser and

pointed at his watch. "Time to go, sir. Now."

To Hauser, I said, "Take care of yourself, Steve. I'll call tomorrow to see how you're doing. I'll pull some strings to get them to let me talk to you."

I started to leave, when Hauser grabbed my arm. He'd always been a powerful man for his size, with a hell of a grip. But his time at the facility had definitely taken something out of him. Not just out of his body, but his soul. I could see it in his eyes when he said, "Watch yourself out there, Charlie. I mean it. Something's wrong."

Coleman pushed Hauser out of the way and took my bag from me. "We need to go, sir." He placed his hand on my back and moved me into the hall. I didn't see any reason to stop him.

I didn't look back at Hauser, either. I didn't dare. I didn't want to see that look in his eyes again.

***

Coleman put me and my bag in the backseat, got behind the wheel, and drove down the road at a good speed. The motion of the car made me a little sick to my stomach, and I rolled down the window in case I got sick. The smell of cow shit hit me in the face and I damn near lost my breakfast.

The rebuke from Coleman came fast. "Roll up your window, sir. It's tempered glass in case someone takes a shot at us. We believe you still might be a target."

"Who the hell's going to shoot me out here? A cow?"

Coleman didn't laugh. "Roll up your window, sir."

The nausea had passed anyway, so I did what he wanted. It was a long drive back to New York and I didn't want to argue.

Besides, some of the things Hauser had said were beginning to gnaw at me. I decided to make with some small talk. "Tell me your story, Coleman. Where are you from?"

Coleman kept his eyes on the road. "I work for Mr. Van Dorn. He doesn't like us to talk about it much, not even among ourselves."

"Us?" I repeated. "Ourselves? Sounds like a lot of people." I remembered what I'd been thinking about back in my room at the hospital. About "us," so I decided to try it on for size. "How many of us are there, anyway?"

"Mr. Van Dorn will tell you everything you need to know when he feels the time is right. All I was assigned to do was get you out of there safely before—"

He stopped talking and kept looking at the road.

If he'd hoped I'd missed it, he was wrong. "Before what?"

"Before one o'clock, sir. He wanted us to be back in New York for dinner." He tried a smile. "We're a few minutes ahead of schedule. Mr. Van Dorn will be pleased."

But the smile didn't wash. I was going to press the issue when I saw two cars barreling up the road toward us. Coleman hit the gas and drove onto the grass to avoid them.

I looked at the people in the cars as they passed us. Both cars had five men jammed into them.

One of the men looked damn familiar. More familiar than I wanted to believe.

"Who the hell are they?"

Coleman glanced at me in the rearview mirror as he kept driving. "They're replacements, sir. The interrogations of the Germans are taking a new phase. Don't worry. Like I said, we're ahead of schedule."

More things Hauser had told me began to come together. Neither Van Dorn nor Father Mullins were around. The goon who showed up without warning to pull me out of there. The guards who wouldn't let Hauser walk around a guarded, fenced-in area.

Hauser was right. Something was up, but I was pretty sure it had nothing to do with a relief team.

I pulled my bag closer to me and popped it open as I said, "I think I forgot to pack something, Coleman. I need to go back."

"I'm afraid that's not possible, sir. The transition needs to be seamless. Your presence would only muck things up. Don't worry about your stuff. Just tell Mr. Van Dorn what you missed and we'll have it sent to you in the morning."

I noticed he took a double take in the rearview mirror, but not at me. He checked his side mirror, too, before looking at the road.

I looked behind me and saw a thin wisp of dark smoke snaking up from behind a hill. From where I judged the hospital was located.

Something was wrong.

I pulled the .38 from my bag and stuck it behind Coleman's right ear. "Turn around, asshole. We're going back."

Coleman didn't even flinch. He just hit the gas. "That's not going to happen, sir. Everything is in hand and happening according to plan. It's none of your concern. Mr. Van Dorn will explain everything when we get back to New York."

"Maybe your ears are clogged, Junior." I thumbed back the hammer on the .38. "I can help with that. Last chance. Turn the car around."

Coleman grinned in the mirror. "We're already going over fifty miles an hour. You shoot me at this speed, you'll kill us both."

"You, yes. Me, maybe. I'm in the backseat, remember?" I jammed the barrel against his head as hard as I could. "You want to take that chance?"

I braced for Coleman to slam on the brakes. He surprised me by bringing the car to a gradual stop and putting it in park. "Shoot me if you want to, but going back there is a bad idea."

I pulled the gun away so he couldn't grab it, but kept it aimed at his head. "Why?"

Coleman kept looking at me in the mirror. "Because we weren't having any luck finding Burnitz or his crew, so we decided to flush them out. Those two cars that almost ran us off the road are proof that it worked. Those sorry sons of bitches are driving into a trap."

Any effects of the medication they'd been feeding me burned right off. "You told them where we were holding Tessmer and Otto, didn't you?"

"We leaked word of where they were being held, and waited to see if anyone was listening. Our spies told us that Burnitz got a group of his thugs together to storm the hospital today to rescue them. It was set for one o'clock, which they believed was right in the middle of a shift change." Coleman grinned. "We've got twenty soldiers in that place right now, regular army, with automatic weapons. Burnitz and his goons won't know what hit them. Hell, they're probably already dead."

"Bullshit. There's no way Mr. Van Dorn would allow something like that to happen."

Coleman turned all the way around and looked at me. "Who do you think came up with the idea?"

I suddenly didn't have the strength to lift the gun. Mr. Van Dorn couldn't be that careless.

Coleman and I flinched as thunder rolled across the hills, rocking our car as the shockwave reached us. We both looked out the back window, and saw a thick plume of black and brown smoke billowing up from the hospital site.

Coleman suddenly didn't look so confident anymore.

I asked a question I already knew the answer to. "None of our people had any artillery, did they?"

"No. Not even grenades."

Son of a bitch. Sometimes, I hated being right. "Guess Burnitz brought his own. You got any guns in this heap?"

Coleman was already getting out of the car. "A Thompson, a shotgun, and several boxes of ammo in the trunk."

I got out of the car, too. "Looks like we're going to need them."

Chapter 23

I had the Thompson on my lap and my .38 in its holster under my arm as we sped back to the hospital. Coleman had his .45 and the shotgun next to him up front.

"You sure this car's bulletproof?"

Coleman kept his eyes on the road. "Built the same way Al Capone's car was, so they tell me. Let's hope they weren't lying about that."

I had a feeling we were going to find out soon enough. "You ever been in combat before?"

"I've had some training, but no, I was never in the army."

I didn't know what kind of training he had, but as long as he knew one end of a gun from the other, we'd have a chance. "When we get there, turn the car so the passenger side is facing the action. We come out the left side and use the car as cover. If there's shooting, take your time and don't rush the shot. Aim for the chest and shoot."

A brown mist drifted across the road as we reached the main gate. The fence was smashed in and three men were dead next to the guard shack. They'd practically been cut in half by a burst from a Thompson.

The smoke cleared a bit as we reached the main building. A man backed into the road, firing up into the hospital. He bounced off the hood of our car and over the windshield as Coleman swerved to the left. The passenger side of the car faced the hospital, just like I'd told him to do.

Bullets raked that side of the car as we spilled out the driver's side. Pistol and automatic gunfire filled the air. Coleman shut his door and took cover while I angled a bit further out to see who we'd hit.

The man was on his side, in a crumpled heap. He was wearing a coarse gray overcoat and didn't look like any of the men I'd seen at the hospital. He reached for his Thompson and began to swing it in our direction.

I pulled my .38 and put two into his chest. I hoped to God he wasn't one of ours.

Coleman cupped his hands over his mouth and tried to shout over the gunfire. "It's Coleman and Doherty. Don't shoot!"

Some of the gunfire stopped for a moment, but some still came our way. I belly- crawled to the trunk of the car and tried to see what we were up against.

I saw the back fence of the compound was a gnarled mess, charred as if it had been blown apart to make way for a truck that not only rammed the back of the hospital, but exploded on impact. That must have been the large explosion Coleman and I felt on the road.

The first several floors of the building had crumbled, with large chunks of smoldering steel and concrete littering the once-immaculate lawn. The two cars that had sped past us were across the green space, firing up into the wreckage of the hospital. Rounds struck exposed steel and broken masonry in the gaping hole of the hospital. Rounds fired from the ruin by soldiers who had survived the explosion slammed down into the cars. Some of Coleman's men were still putting up a fight.

Not just Coleman's men, I thought. My men, too.

Realizing the pistol was useless, I tucked it back in the shoulder holster and grabbed Coleman. "Edge around the front of the car. Stay low and focus your fire on the cars. Don't shoot until you have something to hit. We need to conserve ammo."

Coleman snaked around the hood of the car, staying low. With the Thompson, I dropped to a firing position behind the rear wheel of our car. Another Tommy gun opened up on Coleman the moment he appeared over the hood. The kid was forced to duck for cover again. He didn't look or act like he'd been hit.

I saw that the shooter wasn't hiding behind the two cars. He was firing from a side door to the hospital. That meant Burnitz and his people had already gotten into the building, and these bastards was covering them.

We had to get inside before Burnitz got away.

Coleman popped up again and fired blind in the direction of the hospital. The shotgun blast peppered the door, throwing the gunman back.

I aimed the Thompson at the door. I waited.

Coleman racked in another round as the gunman kicked the door open and stepped into the doorway to get a clearer shot.

He'd let his temper get the better of him.

I didn't.

I fired two shots that caught him high in the chest, sending him back into the hospital for good. The ruined door swung limply on its hinges.

More gunfire rained down on the cars from the hospital. I heard a pop and a hiss from the invaders' tires as our men in the hospital fired another volley into the cars.

One of the Germans rose just high enough for me to see the outline of his head and shoulders. I fired but missed.

But I'd seen why he stood up. A grenade was sailing through the air into the gaping ruin of the hospital.

"Grenade!" I bellowed, but it was too late. The damned thing exploded and I saw a Thompson clatter out of the broken concrete and wood, falling into the burning heap of the bomb truck.

Coleman didn't wait for me to tell him what to do next. He pumped round after round into the cars, shattering glass and rubber and steel.

While he kept them pinned down, I scrambled to my feet and broke cover, running until I got enough of an angle on the men behind the car. I dropped and rolled behind a concrete bench on the edge of the green, and got back into a firing position.

Five Germans.

One on the ground, a pool of blood forming around his leg.

The other four scattered between both cars. All of them holding Thompsons. All of them waiting until the shotgun stopped firing.

The man with the leg wound was fiddling with a bag next to him. I saw him pull something from it. A grenade.

This time, I didn't wait.

I squeezed the trigger and raked them with the Thompson. A bullet either went low or the clown dropped the grenade back in the bag because the bag exploded. I stopped firing and waited a few seconds for the smoke to clear. When it had, all five Germans were dead.

"Coleman!" I called out. "See anyone else out there?"

"No. You?"

I stayed prone and looked around. I didn't see anything moving except the flowers and grass from a lazy wind. I listened as best I could, but all I heard was the burning and crackling of the exploded truck under the rubble.

I was going to tell Coleman I'd cover him as we went into the hospital. But I didn't have to tell him. He was already running toward the side door.

I kept the Thompson trained on the door as he ran. When he got to the side of the door, he leveled the shotgun at the entrance and beckoned me to follow. Now he was covering me.

I was starting to like this kid.

I got up and ran toward him.

***

We stepped over the man I'd killed and moved further into the hospital. The entire center of the building was gone, but the east wing was mostly intact. We made our way up the stairs to the second floor, where my room had been and the Germans had been held.

Bullet holes pockmarked the walls and stairs. Smears of blood lined the way, but no bodies.

Half of the door to the second floor had been shredded, only jagged portions of the bottom remained. Coleman took the left side and I took the right. I pulled the door open and Coleman pinned it behind him. He checked my side of the doorway.

Clear.

I checked his side of the doorway.

Also clear.

Since one of us had to go first, I decided it would be me.

I stepped into the hallway and saw the remains of a pitched battle. The firefight that had started in the stairway had moved up here. Three men in coarse gray overcoats lay dead across from two soldiers. I kicked the guns away from the Germans just to be safe.

Coleman and I crept past the dead, down to the end of the hallway, and checked both ends. To the left, a shattered ruin of rubble. To the right, walls blackened with smoke and blood.

I thought I heard something, and motioned for Coleman to be quiet for a moment. Then I heard it again, a metallic clack and a curse.

I'd heard that curse before. "Hauser?"

"Charlie?"

"Anyone else here?"

"No. Come ahead."

I met Hauser in the hallway as he stepped out of my old room, his Thompson raised above his head with both hands. "Don't shoot. It's empty."

I lowered my weapon. So did Coleman. "What the hell happened?"

Hauser set the empty Thompson against the wall. "They drove a truck into the center of the hospital. It exploded and wiped out most of the staff. I hid when the shooting started, but managed to get one off of them and hold them back. Burnitz was with them, Charlie. He was with them!"

I didn't care about that. "Where are they now?"

"They went straight for Tessmer and Otto. I don't know how they knew where they were, but they did. They got them, too, and killed a lot of guys doing it. I tried to stop them, but they had too many guns. I picked off a couple, but they went down the back stairs.

Coleman asked, "How long ago?"

"Right before I heard you out here."

They were still close.

I ran to the stairwell with the other two close behind me. I leapt over a man Hauser had killed and missed a few steps, skidding on the blood on the treads before catching my balance. I practically tumbled down the rest of the stairs, but stopped when I heard another burst of gunfire from outside. It didn't sound close, but I didn't want to take any chances.

When I got to the bottom, I pulled the door open and stepped aside, waiting for someone to shoot at me. No one did. I looked outside in time to see a car speeding away from the hospital. The car rocked heavy on its axels, like it was overloaded. One man with a rifle was standing on the running board, holding on for dear life.

I caught a glimpse of a wounded man on the ground between us and the car, just as bullets began peppering the left side of the doorway. I ducked back inside just in time.

"Looks like we've got a live one. Left side, ten o'clock."

Coleman stepped forward with the shotgun. "I've got him."

I stepped aside as Coleman took a knee, stuck the shotgun out the door, and fired.

No one shot back.

"Clear."

Although I saw the car was picking up speed, I ran after it. "Coleman, get the car. Hauser, you go with him. We can still catch up!"

I ran after the fleeing car as hard as I could, ignoring the pain that spiked in my side with every step. I stopped to bring up the Thompson when the car hitched as the driver shifted into higher gear. Despite the growing distance, I raked the car with bullets, my rounds punching holes in the back of the sedan and webbing the rear window as the car lurched into a higher gear.

One man dropped off the left running board, followed by the man on the right. The rear window was cracked, but hadn't shattered. Bulletproof.

Damn it.

I kept running, even though my empty Thompson had locked open. I kept running, even when I heard Coleman tell me our tires had been shot out.

I threw the empty machine gun aside when I reached

the spot where the men on the running boards had fallen and picked up his Thompson. I kept running, even though the car was getting further away with ever stride I took.

I reached the first man who'd fallen. His head was mostly gone, but I hardly noticed. I barely stopped as I grabbed his Thompson and kept running. I watched the car disappear over the gentle hill along the hospital road and willed myself to run even faster. When I got to the hill myself, the car had to slow down to take the harsh curve of the road.

I leveled the Thompson at the car and fired, full blast. I squeezed the trigger until the drum went dry and the car was long gone from sight.

Burnitz and Tessmer and Otto had gotten away.

I threw the empty rifle at the road and screamed for as long and as loud as I could. I screamed because of all the people who had died because of a stupid plan. I screamed because Burnitz had won and I had lost.

I screamed because screaming was about the only thing I could do.

A gentle wind carried my rage along the hillside. And the cows barely noticed.

Chapter 24

Neither Mr. Van Dorn nor Father Mullins would look at me.

The two of them just sat there in the Van Dorn study lined with oak shelves and handsome books, snifters of Cognac at their elbows and grim looks on their faces.

I had decided to stand.

Coleman, Hauser, and I hadn't made it back to Manhattan until well after dinner, which was just fine by me. I didn't have much of an appetite anyway.

Mr. Van Dorn looked at his polished shoes while Father Mullins puffed away at his pipe. If I hadn't known these two were responsible for the deaths of over a dozen people, I would've thought it was just another Tuesday night in old New York.

But it wasn't a regular Tuesday night. Not for me. Not for the dead left behind down in Delaware, either.

Mr. Van Dorn cleared his throat. "Are you going to say something, or just stand there and glower at us all night?"

"I should shoot both of you right now."

Neither man reacted. Not even a flinch. Neither of them looked at me, either.

Mr. Van Dorn kept studying his shoes. "I won't deny you your rage, Charlie. God knows you're entitled to it after all that's happened. I'm sorry."

"About what? The part where a bunch of Nazis blew up a hospital, or the part where our only links to the Germans got away?"

"All of it, actually. The entire episode was a mix-up from the start."

"You call twenty-four dead people a mix-up? Jesus. I'd hate to see your idea of a slaughter. What the hell were you thinking?"

"We took a calculated risk," Mr. Van Dorn explained, "because we were desperate. None of our usual sources in the German community had the slightest idea of where Burnitz was. Or, if they did, they were too afraid to admit it. They didn't even talk about him amongst themselves when they thought no one was listening. We didn't even know if he was still in the country. That's when we decided to try to flush him out by letting word of their location slip to some key people we suspected of knowing Burnitz. If he came for them, we planned on surprising him, and either catching him or killing him. It turns out our suspicions of their association were correct. It's cold comfort, I know, but—"

"It's pretty cold comfort to the men who died today," I said, "including Donnie and Jack, who helped me escape the camp in the first place. I owed those men my lives. They deserved better than to die in some half-baked setup like this."

Father Mullins took the pipe from his mouth. "It wasn't as though we took out an advertisement in the New York Times, Charles. We only spread the information to sources we suspected of being in contact with Burnitz. The strategy was sound and, ultimately, correct. We took every precaution to lay as strong a trap as possible. We hardened the installation with troops and guns and fences. We lured him to a remote location, far away from the city. We even evacuated the hospital staff so the danger to innocent lives was minimal. We believed that once Burnitz and his thugs found themselves up against experienced troops, he would lose. As it turns out, we appear to have underestimated his abilities." He slid the pipe stem back into his mouth.

"Underestimated his abilities?" I repeated. "You knew Burnitz tried to gun me down on the street just for talking to Mrs. Fairfax. You knew he had a goddamn military camp set up in Long Island. What made you think telling that maniac about the hospital was a good idea?"

"None of the prisoners said Burnitz had that level of capability," Mr. Van Dorn said. "Not even your friend Hauser knew he was capable of such an attack." He pointed at a table across the room. "It's all documented right there in the file I planned on showing you at dinner tonight. Tessmer and Otto's interrogation reports. Hauser and his colleagues, too. The War Department even performed a full assessment of the hospital and gave us detailed instructions we should follow to set the trap. We followed everything they said right down to the smallest detail. I'd hoped to be able to tell you the attack had failed and Burnitz was either captured or dead. I'd hoped tonight would be a celebration instead of this. It's all right there. Look at it for yourself, and you'll see this wasn't some half-baked scheme we hatched one night over sherry."

"We lost a great deal today," Father Mullins added, "but look at what we have learned. I mourn the dead as much as you do, perhaps more since I had a hand in the plan that led to their deaths. But we learned the true nature of the enemy. Of the kind of man we are dealing with, and a great deal about what he is willing to do to accomplish his goals. This will help us convince those in Washington to take this threat seriously and give us the resources we need to fight them. I promise you, Charles, their deaths shall not be in vain."

I didn't bother looking over at the table, much less the file. And the more they talked, the more my stomach turned. Not because of the pain in my side, but because of what they were saying. They were too busy justifying their failure to realize they had already lost.

I felt my anger begin to rise as I said, "Today wasn't about Nazis, or German agents in the country, or funding from the government. This isn't even about Burnitz. He did what he was trained to do. He did what I would've expected him to do, because I understand how men like him think. He didn't go after Tessmer and Otto because they were important. He didn't go after them to keep them from talking, because he knew you'd already broken them."

When the two men looked at each other, I knew they hadn't thought of that.

I went on. "Burnitz came for them because we took them away from him, and you don't take something away from a man like that without consequences. You two were playing chess while this guy was playing smash-mouth football."

I looked at Mr. Van Dorn. "This isn't 1917 anymore. You're not dealing with spies or saboteurs. You're dealing with committed lunatics who think they have God on their side." I looked at the Jesuit. "Or did you forget that? Hell, you're the one who explained it to me. They don't think like us and they don't act like us."

I pointed at the file on the table across the room. "I won't read that goddamned thing because there's not one word in the whole pile that's worth the paper it's printed on. You think it justifies what you did today, don't you? Well, I've got news for you. It doesn't, because you don't understand the kind of man you're fighting. Men like you never can. Oh, maybe after today you'll get some rough idea, but even then it's too late. It shouldn't have taken twenty-four bodies for you two to get the goddamned point."

I wanted them to be offended by my language. I wanted them to give me just one disapproving glance, anything that would give me an excuse to go at them. But they didn't.

The Jesuit looked up at me through his pipe smoke. "We didn't misjudge their intent or their resolve, Charles, only their capacity to do the unthinkable. I promise you, we won't make the same mistake again."

"I sure as hell hope so. Not for your sake, but for the sakes of whoever else you throw into this meat grinder. Because I'm not part of this University Club or whatever you two have going on here, and I'm not going to be. You boys are on your own. I'm out."

Mr. Van Dorn slowly rose from his chair. "You can't possibly mean that."

"Goddamn right I can. I can take being lied to by perps and by other cops, and even my ex-wife. Hell, I can even take being lied to by clients. But the one thing I won't take is being lied to by the people I thought I could trust. People I admire, or at least used to."

Mr. Van Dorn's lips moved, but he didn't say anything. I guessed because I had said it all for him.

"You've been good to me, Mr. Van Dorn, but I don't let anyone use me as bait. I'll be out of the apartment by tomorrow night. I'll leave the keys with your maid when I'm done."

"Where will you go?" Mr. Van Dorn asked. "What will you do?"

"Don't worry about me. You'll hook another fish. The force is full of them. Hauser said you offered him a job, so give him a shot."

I turned to leave, when Mr. Van Dorn said, "I never took you for a coward."

The words stopped me cold. I slowly turned around, feeling the rage that had been brewing inside me all day begin to rise to a boil. If he'd been any other man, I would've already lunged at him. But some remnant of respect kept me where I was. A remnant that was crumbling awfully damned fast.

But Mr. Van Dorn didn't look afraid. "Can you really

walk away from all of this, Charlie? Especially now, after everything you've learned about what's going on in this country? Can you throw up your hands with the knowledge that a foreign government is trying to build an army within our borders? To subvert our very way of life? To subvert the very things you fought for in France? The very things your friends died for?" He pointed toward the window. "You saw how easily Steve Hauser and other men like him were sucked in by their vitriol about being good Germans, about being proud Germans."

"Hauser was in it because Carmichael ordered him to get enough dirt to blackmail them."

"Is that so?" Mr. Van Dorn asked. "Do you know how many meetings he attended before he reported back to Carmichael? I do. Over twenty. He only reported to Carmichael when he realized he might be getting in over his head, but until then he was no different than any other recruit."

"He saved my life."

"Only when they ordered him to kill you." Mr. Van Dorn paused for a moment to let that sink in. "He would have beaten you, though. Breaking your legs, fracturing your skull, putting you in the hospital would've been perfectly fine by him. There are worse things than killing a man, Charlie. He would have crippled you if Alexandra let him." He pointed at me now. "You know I'm right. You said as much yourself. He even admitted it to us. Think about that for a moment. Murder is a bridge too far, but maiming for the cause is acceptable. So was covering up the murder of Dr.

Blythe. Now think about how many other men like Hauser are out there. Relatively decent men who won't go as far as murder, at least not intentionally, but will hurt people and companies for the sake of the German people. Now think of all of those entirely willing to cross that line, men just looking for validation to kill those they hate. Think about what happens then."

Mr. Van Dorn lowered his hand. "Now think about what would happen if such men were in this country. Men who were organized and well-funded, willing to protect their beliefs by any means necessary. What happens when there is no line to cross, Charlie? You've seen how easily loyalty can blur that line. Do you really want to give Burnitz and the others like him the chance to turn good men against their own country? Today it's just picnics and beer and boy's camps. All of it appears to be quite innocent enough on the surface. Tomorrow it's violence in the streets when people speak out against their beliefs. As resistance hardens, so will the Bund's resolve. We've learned that after today, haven't we, Charlie? What then? Protesters getting shot on the street or organizers murdered in their homes? Police unable to restore order? Newspapers firebombed by those who don't like what they publish? Think about what happened in Delaware today and tell me I'm wrong."

He took a few steps toward me. "You're a free man, Charlie. I owe you the life of my son, which means I owe you everything, more than I could ever repay you. What's more, your country owes you a debt for how you uncovered the extensive German activities in the country. It owes you for what you endured today. But there's still much more to do, and you're the ideal man to do it."

It was quite a speech. Good enough to keep me from leaving. Good enough to remind me of why I admired Mr. Van Dorn so much. "Me? I'm just a cop, sir, and not a very good one, either. You need people who know what they're talking about to handle this kind of thing."

"Experts, you mean? People who know what they're doing?"

"I suppose so."

Mr. Van Dorn pointed back to the file on the table. "The trap we laid out for Burnitz today was coordinated by some of the finest minds on the subject. Intelligence professionals. Military experts. We even had psychiatrists who claimed they could predict how a man like Burnitz would attempt to rescue his men. You saw how well that turned out with your own two eyes."

Mr. Van Dorn smiled. "No, Charlie, you're not an expert because there are no experts in fighting people like this. Politicians, geniuses, and doctors all fall short because of what you said earlier. None of us knows the kind of man we're dealing with. But you do. If we have any hope of rooting them out of wherever they are in this country or elsewhere, we're going to need you with us. I fear if you turn your back on us now, what happened at the hospital will happen again and worse."

I almost flinched when he held out his hand to me. "I ask for the honor of shaking your hand. If you decide to leave, then it's goodbye. But I hope you'll shake my hand in agreement to stay and join our cause to stomp out this evil before it spreads."

I looked at his hand, and felt the anger that had been building in me all day since Delaware melt away. I'd come to his house angry and spoiling for a fight. I'd wanted to spit in his face and storm out the door. What a difference a speech made.

I shook his hand. "You can count on me, sir."

Mr. Van Dorn beamed. "I always have, Charlie. Thank you."

A stupid thought flew into my head. "Did you really offer Hauser a job?"

"We did, but only if you think he can be useful. Even if you don't think he can be trusted, he can still be useful in a way."

Mr. Van Dorn had a point there. He went on. "You'll be working with one of the most important organizations in the country today. One that has the blessing of the president and, soon, will have the authority of Congress thanks to the efforts of Congressman Samuel Dickstein of the House Committee on Immigration. Father Mullins is our resident expert on Germany, and will fill you in on the operational details as we go along. But I strongly I suggest you start by reading that file first. It explains our entire operation, and what we know about the Nazi menace within our borders. It's an active file that grows larger every day. Reading it may answer a lot of questions before you ask them."

There was one thing I wanted to get clear before I made anything official. "I want to make the same demands as

Mrs. Fairfax, sir. I want to kill Burnitz. That's not up for discussion."

"You'll have no objection from me." He took my hand in both hands. "It's good to have you with us, Charlie."

"I second that," Father Mullins said, bringing a new match to the bowl of his pipe.

The butler appeared in the doorway and cleared his throat. "Forgive me for interrupting, sir, but that man is on the phone again. He keeps asking for 'the dean,' and despite my telling him that there is no dean here, he insists this is the right number. Shall I tell him to stop calling?"

"No, John. That's for me. I'll take it."

Mr. Van Dorn guided me over to the table, where the bulging leather file sat tied with black ribbon. "We'll talk more about this after my call. Until then, Father Mullins will handle any questions you might have."

I looked at the folder but didn't untie it. I saw gold letters embossed in the leather.

Operational Manual of Nazi Intelligence

O.M.N.I.

As Mr. Van Dorn walked away, I said, "Why is someone calling you 'dean,' sir?"

He stopped just outside the sliding doors. "Because I'm head of the University Club. Happy reading, Charlie. I'll be back soon."

He slid the doors closed, leaving Father Mullins and me alone in the study.

The Jesuit puffed on his pipe. "Get yourself some Cognac and a cigar, my boy. You've got a lot to learn about our Nazi enemy."

I pulled apart the knot on the file. "I think we all do."

About the Author

Terrence McCauley is the award-winning author of three James Hicks thrillers: *SYMPATHY FOR THE DEVIL, A MURDER OF CROWS,* and *A CONSPIRACY OF RAVENS,* as well as the historical crime thrillers *PROHIBITION* and *SLOW BURN* (all available from Polis Books. He is also the author of the World War I novella *THE DEVIL DOGS OF BELLEAU WOOD,* the proceeds of which go directly to benefit the Semper Fi Fund. His story *El Cambalache* was nominated for the Thriller Award by International Thriller Writers.

Terrence has had short stories featured in T*huglit, Spintetingler Magazine, Shotgun Honey, Big Pulp* and other publications. He is a member of the New York City chapter of the Mystery Writers of America, the International Thriller Writers and the International Crime Writers Association.

A proud native of The Bronx, NY, he is currently writing his next work of fiction. Please visit his website at terrencemccauley.com or follow him at @terrencepmccauley.

CPSIA information can be obtained
at www.ICGtesting.com
Printed in the USA
LVHW04s2020200418
574348LV00001B/1/P